CLOSE ENOUGH TO HURT

CLOSE ENOUGH TO HURT

A NOVEL

KATHERINE A. OLSON

CROOKED
LANE

NEW YORK

Copyright © 2023 by Katherine A. Olson

Published in the United States by Crooked Lane Books, an imprint of The Quick Brown Fox & Company LLC.

Crooked Lane Books and its logo are trademarks of The Quick Brown Fox & Company LLC.

Library of Congress Catalog-in-Publication data available upon request.

ISBN (hardcover): 978-1-63910-501-4
ISBN (ebook): 978-1-63910-502-1

Cover design by Heather VenHuizen

Printed in the United States.

www.crookedlanebooks.com

Crooked Lane Books
34 West 27th St., 10th Floor
New York, NY 10001

First Edition: October 2023

10 9 8 7 6 5 4 3 2 1

For my mama and papa bear.
Thank you for reading to me.

CHAPTER

1

I'M NOT ONE to kink-shame, but consent is a key part of any sexual endeavor—and the professor of anthropology onstage did *not* inform his partner he'd opened their marriage.

Did I mention his wife, the mother of his three children, has stage three breast cancer?

That's my cue to enter the Herbst Theatre in San Francisco and interrupt his TEDx Talk.

I make my way down the aisle and settle into an empty seat at the beautiful Beaux arts building, enjoying the dimmed lights and pleasant anonymity among the audience, my dark hair hidden beneath a wavy blonde wig. If I had popcorn, I'd be crunching.

Most of my cases are not so cut-and-dried. Navigating the messiness of people and their relationships takes special skill. And patience. My clients pay well for my due diligence—as well as my catered punishments.

Nadine, however, presented such a clear and visceral wrong. She'd given up her tenure-track professorship at Berkeley to raise their children, suffocated under the weight of motherhood, and days before her fiftieth birthday, found a sinister lump in her left breast. Three months later, she discovered salacious photos on his phone. One of his graduate students, apparently. A few years older than their eldest daughter.

If ever the universe was asking for balance, tipping the scales back in a wronged person's favor, I'd never seen a clearer sign.

Nadine heard of me from other clientele and kept her discovery quiet. The person with the knowledge holds the power.

We've waited for months, Nadine and I. My business requires a strange intimacy—to do my job well, my clients must crack open their hearts and expunge their greatest hurts. When I know the scope of others' betrayals, I know what shape justice might take.

Like capturing photographs of her self-important philandering husband and the graduate student.

Like waiting for the TEDx conference in San Francisco to strike. Under his biography, he's listed as an "Anthropologist/Philosopher/Provocateur," and I could've told you then he was a narcissist with an overly inflated opinion of himself, but hey, no harm in gathering evidence. After all, he'd left so much. The unsolicited dick pics alone (Are they ever solicited? Inquiring minds want to know) could've filled a whole photo album. The world's worst.

"Our historical record shows humans were not destined to live in strictly monogamist relationships. Rather, monogamy is but a mere *cultural* construct . . ."

The provocateur/wanker on stage is doing well so far, making eye contact with the audience, me included. Once. Twice. A third time. It's far from accidental. Even now, he searches to replace his wife. Perhaps he wonders whether I'll gush to him later about his performance. Perhaps he hopes.

Soon, though, his presentation will take a turn. Little does he know I swapped his PowerPoint for my own before he began his screed and left him with an identical remote with no batteries. All the while, I've been watching him carefully, mirroring his changes with my own remote. Giving him the illusion of control.

I wonder how long it'll take the audience to realize the naked man with a blurred face is the same one before them, with his avuncular elbow patches and trim goatee, and the dark bedroom eyes he turned on another while his wife pumped poison into her body in a desperate crusade to save herself so they might grow old together, as they'd promised each other in better days.

With each case, I grow to hate the wrongdoers just as much as my clients do. Dark Horse Consulting wouldn't be successful unless I took my clients' hurt inside myself and burned for justice too. I never see the happy couples, the unicorns living in la-la land. I'll never find the promised land for myself. As my clients' trust has been broken, so has my ability to give anyone the benefit of the doubt. I've seen too much, full stop.

The spy cam freeze frame fills the screen. A man and woman having sex atop a luxurious hotel bed. The graduate student and the good professor. I blurred her body and his face, of course, but added some important footnotes for audience edification:

1) *NOT his wife.*
2) *Monogamy may be a cultural construct, but this is still cliché.*

A gasp punctures the hushed audience. The first person to notice. Several technicians rush up the aisle. Oblivious, Provocateur keeps talking, provoking, though no longer for the reasons he imagines.

My blood pumps fast and hot. It's a rush, watching a bastard's life implode in real time. Watching a whole-ass man being kicked to the curb and thrown away. Knowing I was the catalyst orchestrating his fall from grace, piece by meticulous piece.

"I was the last to know," Nadine told me. "Like a fool." Her voice was hard, her head was bare. I'd wanted to cover it, to protect her bronze skin. But she didn't need protection; she needed retribution. Her skin was as fine as any armor, smooth and impenetrable.

A few scattered, uncomfortable laughs escape in the theater. Provocateur pauses, wondering if he's made an unintentional joke. He still hasn't looked at the frozen frame on his presentation, spliced in without warning, as unwelcome as a roving hand.

Or maybe he knows, but he's clinging to the last moments of his life as he knows it. He tries to pick up the thread of his presentation, but people are standing, shaking their heads, pointing. Smartphones lift to capture his plight.

Only then does he turn and see himself, twenty feet tall, in flagrante delicto.

The last one to know.

He makes a frantic push at the remote.

I'm ready for this too. I advance to the next slide with the real remote. On to the video we go! If I had to watch, everyone else must too.

Moans and raunch.

Thankfully for the luckless TEDx goers, the technician cuts the video, and the screen goes dark.

Nadine isn't in the audience. Some clients like to watch their revenge; others just want it done. Later, after a time of plausible deniability, she'll present him with divorce papers. I hope like hell she lives, if only to feel the sun on her skin each day and know in her bones she deserved better than him.

The day's main character exits stage left, scurrying away from the intense spotlights. I doubt if he'll be giving another of these presentations anytime soon. The rest of the theater has erupted into pandemonium. It takes time for the dust to settle after the scales have been rebalanced, but my work is done. I stand.

My name is Dylan Truman, aka Lady Justice, with sword and scale in hand. Rather than a blindfold, however—I prefer a pre-sixteenth-century Justitia, thank you very much—I keep my eyes open and put on my shades. The blonde wig goes into my bag, and I shake out my long brown hair. Then I walk into the oblique sunlight of autumn, the wind from the bay blowing in my face. A Friday afternoon full of possibility.

Cross my heart, I wouldn't trade this job for Tim Cook's bank account.

Thank you for coming to my TED Talk.

* * *

Most Friday afternoons, I take off. My work requires hours logged on the weekend, so I make sure to get out of the city—back to my houseboat in Sausalito—and spend my free time on the water.

There's no reason for melancholy, but that blue haze crept into my soul while I drove across the Golden Gate, and it's settled in to stay. When I started this business, the high of taking down an asshole (male, female, nonbinary—jack-hole behavior doesn't discriminate) lasted for days. Weeks. Lately, it hasn't held the same appeal. I keep feeling like there should be . . . more. More than this hollow sense of triumph.

It'd be better if I celebrated with someone, maybe, but I guard my anonymity with nondisclosure agreements Harvey Weinstein would envy. The one ironclad promise I made when I ventured down this road was that I wouldn't involve anyone else unless they explicitly agreed to the risk. It's perilous, and if I were to pursue justice through . . . alternative means, it had to be me getting in the shit. No one else.

Maybe I should move on.

Or! Maybe I need to fry a bigger fish. God knows there are enough of them—the bastards with enough lawyer armament to guarantee immunity. Laws for thee, not obscenely wealthy me. I've dreamed about it for years. A white whale on the horizon, waiting for my abilities to mature. Waiting for me to reach my full potential.

From my back deck, I glide my kayak into the water, straddle it, and plop my butt in the cockpit. The Pacific is a cold mistress—fifty-two degrees—and yet I love her so. If ever there was a heaven on earth, this slice of California counts. Especially on days like today, cobalt sky and water, fog a distant memory. Same for wildfire smoke. No one can forget when the sky turned scarlet, as if we all lived in some Dantean hellscape.

On the water, the muscles in my core and arms and shoulders warm and loosen. The comedown after the high of battle fades away and I drift into hypnotic reverie between the sun and sea. My peace is here.

Only, it's a lonely sort of peace. I fight the wind on my way home.

At my houseboat, there's a text message waiting.

I smile ear to ear. It's from Daniel Haas, my part-time collaborator, the Bay Area's best digital PI. He's also the only person who knows where I reside—ergo, possibly my only true friend. The fact he has cheekbones I could cut my hands on is just a bonus for me.

Congratulations, Lady Justice! Another day, another scumbag in the bag! Soju on me? I may have another client for you. And something else to discuss.

My smile stretches to both sides of the houseboat. Daniel knows what presents I like best: the ones that lead to another day, another scumbag in the bag. Besides, soju and Korean barbecue with my bestie sounds like the perfect antidote to the post-takedown blues.

Hell, yes. What time?

😉 *I'll pick you up at eight.*

Galvanized, I stow my paddle, strip out of my sweaty kayaking clothes, and rush to the shower.

2

DANIEL WAITS AT the parking lot for the marina, lean-ing on an ancient black Prius he insists on driving despite having more money than God, wearing black slacks and a white button-up, looking broody under a streetlight. Why is he absolute catnip?

He glances up when he hears my footsteps, a smile in his eyes. "She emerges."

"When the need arises." I try not to sound too breath-less. Wouldn't do for him to know I've showered and dressed in record time, fast enough to catch the last light of the day setting over the bay, painting the broad plates of his cheek-bones and jaw in pink and gold. "You had me at soju."

"Don't I always?"

"Touché, Haas."

He opens the door for me, a throwback chivalrous ges-ture I shouldn't like or read too much into. Daniel is polite to everyone, even that blonde wench who sideswiped his poor Prius in Marin years ago. She came out hissing and cursing though she was at fault, and I was ready to shank her, but all he did was snap a photo and say, "Ma'am, I hope you have a good firewall."

It's why we make a good team. Where I go full rabid honey badger, he goes cold. Fire and ice, yeah? There are always two ways to solve a problem.

I never did ask him what became of her, after his car was repaired. I hope he doxed her. I hope she lost her job. Then I hope hackers emptied her accounts, and I hope Daniel got a cut for his efforts. Savage, maybe, but I always have been when it comes to him.

"Daeho?" I ask when he gets in. "They'll probably be packed on a Friday, though."

"You know this face opens doors." He smirks.

"Ugh, don't." I roll my eyes, even though he's right. Being conversational in a few languages—Korean (Mom), German (Dad), Mandarin, English—doesn't hurt either. He can go anywhere and talk to anyone.

He appraises me from the corner of his eye. "You look nice."

And chilly. It's not really sundress weather in San Francisco, ever, but dammit, I felt like celebrating. Getting gussied up, just a little. Hence the strappy emerald dress, leaving most of my shoulders and back bare. "I do, don't I?" I give him an angelic smile.

He shakes his head, though I think he was about to smile. "So humble too."

"Said the guy bragging about his beautiful face."

"Just reminding you we'll always have a table."

Always is a long time, I want to say. In all the years I've known him, Daniel has remained close-lipped and inscrutable, until he says something like that. Something sweet and suspiciously forward-looking. It's hard not to spin into tail-chasing circles trying to puzzle him out. Puzzle *us* out.

Not that there ever has been an us, in that sense. We're just friends and occasional colleagues who see the world the same way—how bullies get away with it for-goddamn-ever—and itch to smash the status quo.

Somehow, a parking spot near the restaurant opens, and Daniel parallel parks on the steep slope without a word.

"Parking karma," I say. "I should've known."

And somehow, a table for two materializes, despite the restaurant being packed to the gills. We're tucked away in a corner, a perfect, secluded spot, with dim lighting and cushy seats.

"A toast to my formidable friend." After pouring soju for me—though that's supposed to be my job as the younger person here—then himself, Daniel raises his glass, dark eyes twinkling. "And to scum being scraped off the face of the earth, one tampered PowerPoint presentation at a time."

I beam and clink my glass against his. "I'll drink to that." The sweet rice spirit races down my throat and pools in my stomach with pleasant warmth, enough for my goose bumps to disappear. "So, tell me about this prospective client. What's the deal?"

"On to business, mm?" He sips and leans back, looking mildly affronted.

"Well, yeah," I say. "I thought that's why you wanted to meet up."

We're interrupted by our server coming by to take our order. I'd never let anyone else speak for me, but every time we've come here, I've let Daniel choose, and I've yet to be disappointed.

After the server has left, Daniel says, "I've got something else I need to talk to you about too, but since you asked about the potential client, it's a friend of my cousin," he says. "Dr. Evelyn Chang. Stanford grad, pharmacologist at a pharmaceutical company."

"All righty. And her complaint?"

"She says she was fired for speaking up about some of the company's, er . . . shady practices," Daniel says. "But now, because the CEO has wide reach, she can't get another job. She's essentially been blacklisted from every other lab."

"Because she had a spine, in other words." The soju burns a hole in my stomach, and I pivot from chilled to overheated in a matter of seconds. "What a prick. I wonder why she didn't go to the press."

"She said she had to sign an intimidating NDA in order to get her severance package. So far as she knows, she was the only one to share her concerns with the CEO."

"A lonely place to be." But my kind of woman exactly. "I bet there are others too, though. If it's that bad."

"Maybe." Daniel's face is a blank mask, cool and anodyne. You'd only know he was angry by the set of his jaw. I don't feel half as calm, neck and cheeks flushing with heat. I lift the hair away from my nape, trying to cool down. Daniel looks away.

"Did you already say what company?" I ask.

"Prometheus Pharmaceuticals."

"Little on the nose, but okay." I smirk.

He snickers, and a thrill sizzles up the back of my neck. Daniel's a tough nut to crack, but I do my best.

Something about the company's name tickles the back of my brain. I must've seen it in the news. Frowning, I toss back the rest of my soju. "And who's the guy generously bestowing pharmaceutical gifts on humanity for a no doubt exorbitant price?"

"The CEO? One Brent Wilder."

I lower my shot glass slowly. The walls of the restaurant close in, warping. "Brent . . ." My brain can't finish the thought, inundated by a tsunami of memories. "Wilder."

No. I kick against the idea. It *can't* be the same man.

Of course, he wasn't a man then. At least, that's what everyone said, despite the fact that he was eighteen, a college freshman at Cal, like my sister. *But he's just a boy!* How could we talk about holding him accountable? Jail time would ruin his entire life. As if my sister's life hadn't been ruined the second he had her in his sights. The second he pinned her down and raped her at knifepoint, because garden-variety cruelty wasn't enough for him.

"Dylan?" Daniel's concerned voice punctures my haze. His voice and his hand, stretched across the table, palm up. A link, an anchor. "Are you okay?"

I may have touched him before, but I can't remember anything before this moment. Carefully, I reach out. Welcome heat presses into my palm and wrist. Even the smooth band of his watch is a comfort, warm metal gliding past my skin.

"I've never seen that look on your face before," he said. "Like you've been kicked."

"I'm sorry, I . . ." I inhale deeply. "I really want to help, but if it ends up being the same guy, I don't know if—"

"What do mean, the same guy?" Confusion wrinkles his face. "What are you talking about?"

I shake my head. "My older sister. If it's the same guy, he . . . hurt her. Badly. Sixteen years ago, when they were both freshmen at Cal. I was sixteen, still in high school." I choke the explanation out.

Daniel sighs, a small puff of understanding leaving him. It's a reprieve I can't share. I *wish* the pain were mine to carry, rather than Gabrielle's. Anything would've been better than watching the joy seep out of her in slow motion. Staring at a face too much like my own—the beaming smile she used to never be without marred by a wicked scar running up her neck and cheek.

I haven't cried in years. I promised myself—and my sister, though she doesn't know—that I'd be the one making other people cry. It's even on my favorite coffee mug: *Tears of My Enemies*. The urge to weep is strange and unfamiliar, like a vestigial reflex I can't shake no matter how much I try to harden myself. An annoying, humiliating prickle in my sinuses, making my eyes sting.

Then water leaks, racing down my cheeks, splotching my dress. I wish the floor would open and plunge me to the center of the earth. Better that than letting the person I most admire witness my meltdown in a busy restaurant.

Daniel says something to our server, and before I really know what's happening, he's whisked me outside, dinner tucked under his arm. Rather than hurrying, however, he seems content to wait and let me gather my wits.

The night is cold, a true taste of fall, the scent of dry trees and ocean and woodsmoke carried on the wind.

"I'm sorry." I hate saying those words, the ones every girl learns so she can smooth over any situation. I shiver when the wind picks up, annoyed with myself for dressing impractically. Like I wanted to turn Daniel's head my way.

"Why?" He sets our food on the hood, unlocks the car, and grabs his suit jacket from the back seat. "Want it?"

I nod and slide my arms into the smooth silk lining. The outer shell is fine wool and blocks the wind well. The fabric smells like him too—which is to say, delicious. Bright and citrusy, underpinned by deeper cedar notes.

"Thanks. And I don't know why I'm apologizing. I'm sorry if I made things weird. I know I haven't really talked about my family much. So." I cut myself off and kick at a few fallen leaves on the sidewalk with my bootie. The more I try to dig myself out of this awkward hole, the worse I make it.

"So, what?" Daniel asks. "It's not like I don't want to hear about it."

I arch a brow.

He folds his arms. "I want to hear anything you have to say. I'm sorry I brought up something painful. I wish I'd known, so I wouldn't have ruined your night."

"You didn't. I simply . . . wasn't expecting it." Though I should've been. For God's sake, it's not as if Brent fell off the face of the earth. In a just world, he'd be behind bars for the rest of his life, but our society practically guaranteed it wouldn't happen.

The wind dies, and Daniel glances over his shoulder, then at me, a tentative expression on his face. "Would you like to eat our dinner at my place? Talk some more? It's not far from here."

Funny that he knows where I live, but I haven't seen his home. I guess I'm not the only one who values their privacy. "I'd love that." I try to dilute my sincerity by lifting the food. "It'd be a shame not to share this."

A smile curls the corner of his mouth and pops a dimple. God help me. "Let's go, then."

He so rarely smiles, each one is a present, wrapped in black Burberry gabardine. Dangerous, but I get in his car anyway.

* * *

I still don't know what specifically Daniel does during his day job. He's told me a few times, and the words "senior engineering manager at Apple" have stuck in my brain, but I'm still pretty sure he contributes to the growth of AI that will take over the world, despite his assurances to the contrary.

Regardless, the wealth funding his home is a little astounding. His apartment is minimalist—immaculate white walls, white marble, contrasting light fixtures and furniture in matte black. There's probably a metaphor in there somewhere, but I'm too buzzed on soju and excitement at being in the inner sanctum to tease it out.

He lights a fire in the gas fireplace, casting gold light across the walls and windows, and the high-ceilinged space slowly warms.

By contrast, my boho houseboat with incense and mac-
rame and too many houseplants seems quaint. Can't leave
my crunchy beginnings behind, I guess, though I haven't set
foot in Eureka for years.

"Have a seat anywhere." Daniel grabs a rubber band
and pulls his hair into a half-up knot. He's grown it out over
the summer, his one nod to free-spiritedness, and true to
form, it looks great even pulled away from his face. "Chopsticks? Fork?"

"Fork, please." I curl up on the high-pile rug in front of
the fireplace, admiring the view—thousands of twinkling
lights glowing along the hills in the indigo dark. "I'm lucky
I haven't spilled anything on this dress already."

Daniel nods, looking amused, and offers a heavy fork,
saving stainless chopsticks for himself. For a few minutes
we're silent, enjoying the meal together. Devouring the
savory beef bulgogi and vegetables and sipping more soju.

"Well, look at us live wires." I wipe my mouth and
laugh, trying to ease the tension. It's too quiet for me. Too
intimate. "Sorry I ruined our night out."

"You didn't," he says with enough force to make me
pause. "This is more my speed anyway."

"Spoken like a true introvert." I wink.

"Guilty." He plinks his soju down on the glass coffee
table with a rare, broad smile. "You know me well."

It's a good thing my mouth is full of food; otherwise I'd
do something dumb and tell him how stunning he is. Saved
by kimchi fried rice! There's a first for everything.

"Your home is beautiful." That much I can say. I wrap
my arms around my knees. "Thanks for having me over."

"Thank you," he says. "I should've invited you sooner."

The fire pops and hisses, light flickering across his fine
gold skin, emphasizing the curve of his cheekbone, the hollow beneath his full lower lip. When did I start noticing

him like this? As if his face is something I need to memorize in case I don't get to see it again?

His gaze is steady. "Will you tell me what happened with your sister?"

I shake my head and curl inward. An immediate, knee-jerk refusal, like I've touched a fire coral. "It's not a pretty story."

"Of course it isn't." Exasperation truncates his words. "Of course it's ugly. It's always ugly." He downs his soju, head tossed back, long neck exposed.

I eye him. "It's not personal, Haas. I just . . . it's what set me on this path."

Not content to wait for the grief to pass of its own accord—like everyone else in my family, it seemed—I fled right after her court case was done, as soon as I graduated from high school. For seven years, I traveled wherever the current took me, learning the lay of the land in each new country, learning how to wield a knife and size people up and blend in and approach absolutely everything from new angles, working just long enough to save for a plane ticket to the next corner of the world. Making fair-weather friends who never knew the contents of my scarred and misshapen heart. Whenever someone asked where home was, I lied, determined to shun my family's corner of California and its wooded, oppressive gloom.

At least until I saw Brent's Ken doll face on the cover of a glossy magazine in the Singapore airport.

He'd been rewarded for being a Brilliant Jerk™, a necessary quality in the consecrated pursuit of wealth. Despite all the hurt and trauma he left in his wake, he'd ascended to the top of the food chain.

The urge to rip all the magazines off the wall and set them on fire in the nearest garbage can was overpowering. And shared by me alone.

Somehow, I made it onto my flight without getting myself arrested. Only I didn't sleep on the fifteen-hour red-eye back to California. I drank coffee and plotted from my peon's seat in steerage on the last of my one-way flights.

After seven years on the roam, I wouldn't run any longer. I'd stay and find my own way to right the scales. Put my odd skills to use and fight small battles—and sometimes large battles—in service to anyone who needed it.

"But I still don't like to think about it." I clear my throat. "In fact, I try to forget. All the time."

After several long beats, Daniel sighs, looking resigned. "All right."

"You said you had something to tell me?" I redirect the conversation, relieved to have the intense searchlight of his focus away from me. His eyes are those of a thinking man; seeing much, revealing little. If he doesn't play poker, he ought to.

He clears his throat, looking uncomfortable all of a sudden. "Yeah, I do. I know this is bad timing, but with Nadine's case done, I wanted to let you know that, ah . . . I'm not sure how much I'll be able to help you with cases going forward."

I stop chewing. "What?" The word is garbled, my mouth still full.

"My parents want me to get married. And I can't keep doing this job with a wife and family—it's too risky."

"Oh." I feel punctured, like a paper lantern with a giant tear.

In response to my silence, Daniel rambles. "They're older, you know? And they want grandchildren, and my mom is . . . pretty sick. And I turned thirty-seven last month, and they're apoplectic I haven't already found a wife and started a family. It's . . ." He shakes his head. "I'm their only child, and they're not getting any younger, or healthier, is what I'm trying to say. So I promised them I would settle down." His voice lowers. "Really, it's the least I can do for her."

For a few stunned seconds, I can't respond. Maybe because I've never heard him say so much in one stretch about his family, much less that his mother is ill, perhaps terminally. A lie of omission so large it craters my chest with self-absorbed hurt.

Never mind the fact that it stings, thinking of him with anyone else.

That's silly, though. It's never been like that with Daniel in all the years I've known him. I have no reason to be crushed, aside from losing a top-notch investigator.

"Your mom is sick?" I ask. "Is it very serious?"

He nods, slowly, like it's an effort to even move. "Multiple sclerosis. Hers was the aggressive variety anyway, but it's progressing fast. And I just . . ." He swallows. "I want her to know I'll be okay, you know? That she doesn't have to worry about me. And I want to celebrate while she's still able to."

"Oh," I say again. Rendered dumb, it seems.

The fire crackles, and I focus on the sparks, blinking back tears. Fuck, I hate this feeling of powerlessness. I never was good at sitting with it. How do I fight something invisible? How do I wipe this terrible expression off his face, erase the grief swimming in his eyes?

"Some bestie I am." My smile is chagrined. "I had no fucking clue. Didn't know you just celebrated your birthday either."

"How could you have known, Dylan?" His voice is soft. A low, tickling purr. "I never told you, on either count."

"Why not?" I sound petulant. Hurt.

"You know me." His tongue presses into his cheek. "Why open up when I could not?" His smile is bitter, the first sip of Shiraz when you're not ready for it. "Same goes for birthdays. A *Don't perceive me* sort of thing. Besides, I was afraid you'd alert the waitstaff and make everyone serenade me." He shudders.

"You were right to worry." I cackle into my drink. "I for sure would've done that just to watch you squirm."

"She-devil." His smile is all sharp corners, but there's no heat in his voice.

I hide my smile by taking another sip. "When is your birthday, though?"

"September fifth."

"Virgo, huh? I might have known." I bump him with my elbow. "I'll add it to my dossier. And now I have to get you a gift."

"Please don't." He looks horrified.

"Why not? You get me presents."

"But you *like* presents."

"And you don't?" I laugh. "Don't be a birthday martyr! Let me have some small joy, Daniel."

He sighs. "Fine."

"Is there anything I can do?" I ask after a minute, crossing the Rubicon, his self-protective armor be damned. "I mean, with your mom?" My shoulders aren't as broad as his, but he could cry on them if he wants. I would take his hurt onto my frame and let it settle like a second skin, if he'd let me.

"There isn't, not really, but thank you for asking. Oma has a good team behind her. We're far luckier than most."

"Okay," I relent. "But if you need a shoulder to cry on, or anything at all, you know I'm your woman."

He cuts me a curious look, so I hurry on. "Unless I'm not? Is there a future Mrs. Haas in the picture already?" I don't really want an answer to that question, but morbid curiosity won't allow me to leave well enough alone.

"Not at the moment. But there will be soon, I think."

I hide my interest with another blithe pour of soju. "I gotcha. As for the cases"—I throw back my drink—"that's totally fine. I'm always glad when I get to work with you, but times change. And your family comes first." Even if it means I won't see him again.

"You're not disappointed?"

"Why would I be? If you're going to stop moonlighting and move on, isn't that a good thing?"

He sprawls his long legs out on the thick rug. If I didn't know better, I'd say he's sulking. "It's not really my idea."

"No, but you're going to do it anyway. Because you love your parents. Love your mom." That much is clear. It was in the way his voice softened when he brought them up, especially her. I wish I had the same closeness with my own parents, but my years away have taken their toll. Gabrielle still lives close by to them in Eureka, but I can't even remember the last time I went home. We text sporadically at best, small tidbits of our lives. Checking in over holidays and birthdays. A pale fraction of what we had, and why? Because I left and the guilt is corrosive, eating away at me. I don't know how to mend the bond I tore with every mile I put between us.

Still, a part of me is curious to know whether he's ever spoken about me with his family. "Do your folks know anything about me? How we've worked together?"

He actually laughs. Then he catches himself and clears his throat. "Uh, no. I wouldn't know where to begin, to explain what you do. I don't think they'd understand, even if I tried."

"I get it." I laugh too, but the sting burns through another layer of my dragon-scale skin. How dumb. I gave up on finding a partner a long time ago, and I've never wanted the marriage-and-kids kind of life anyway—it would be impossible with my odd career.

It's just . . . sometimes I think it *would* be nice to have someone to share my days with. My nights too. I've leaned on Daniel more than I knew. Scary, how easy it happens.

"I can't imagine many people would want a professional revenge artist among their family," I say, as much to myself as to him.

Daniel shrugs. "Their loss."

There he goes again, with another sweet, laconic turn of phrase. I glance at him, bemused. The soju must be talking, because I can't look away. My gaze roves over the firelight dancing in his eyes, his thick brows and messy, pushed-back hair, raven black and just as iridescent. This man can't possibly be thirty-seven. He's too pretty.

Our shoulders are touching. I hadn't noticed; then I can't *un*notice. Warmth from his oxford shirt seeps into my chilled arm. He has a runner's build, lean and spare, but there's strength too. And something else, a low, vibrating frequency. Something contained, checked.

"Dylan?"

"Yeah?" I snap to it, breaking the spell I didn't know he was casting.

"Will you hunt him, if I convince Dr. Chang to step forward?" he asks. "This Brent Wilder? Even if it's the same man that . . . that hurt your sister?"

I take a deep breath, but I already know my answer. "Have I ever said no?"

Daniel shakes his head.

Never have I turned away a client after vetting them. Fire streams through my veins, priming me for battle. Little fucks like eighteen-year-old Brent grow into men who learn *no one* will hold them accountable. God knows Gabrielle tried, and all she had to show for her belief in justice was a settlement, an NDA, and a well-funded smear campaign—against *her*.

In short: I owe it to Gabrielle to fight. Fight every one of these bastards who walk through the world maiming others without consequence, throwing rocks on their way to the top.

I empty my glass of soju. The alcohol burns all the way down. "Besides, I don't have much choice when you put it like that, do I?"

Daniel gives me a wary glance, like he senses my shift in mood, sees my chain mail sliding into place. "Why do I feel like I've poked a tiger?"

"Yeah?" I turn to him with a tipsy smile, hoping I look endearing and not just sweaty and frightening per my usual. "The tiger would like to make a request, then."

For the briefest moment, his smile fills my whole field of vision. "Anything for you, Dylan." Ah, but there it is.

"Would you help me, just once more? Then find a lovely wife and gift your beautiful children with your dimples? I'll kidproof my houseboat and be their eccentric aunt if you need a babysitter."

Lord, I have had too much to drink. The thought of him moving on from this, my strange calling, is making me unbearably sappy. If I'm not careful, I may cry on him again.

Daniel leans close, a downright predatory gleam in his eyes. "One more for old times' sake, hmm?"

He can play it cool all he wants. That look tells me all I need to know: he loves the hunt as much as I do.

"You've got a deal," he says.

3

SUNDAY DAWNS AND I still haven't heard from Daniel.

I try not to fret about him or his mom as I pour more coffee and sit on my back deck, covered in the wool wrap I bought when I was backpacking in Tibet, listening to the gentle lapping on the hull. I should eat something, but my nerves have kept hunger at bay.

My jitters aren't helped by the research I did, always the first step in a pro case like this. I spent Saturday compiling information; first for Dr. Evelyn Chang, then for Brent, scouring the internet and his social media and business profiles. It hurts my pride to admit it, but the "self-made" wunderkind CEO won't be an easy target. A recent headshot from a downright worshipful media feature is fixed in my brain. Still "boyishly handsome," whatever the fuck that means, with a round face and blond, curly hair and large blue eyes. Vacant looking, really. As if the camera caught him between personalities before he could decide which one would better press his advantage.

More importantly, however, good ol' Brent's got more than enough wealth nowadays to insulate himself from recrimination. Clearly, as there wasn't the slightest whiff of fraud, not in any of the newspapers or magazines I scoured. I'm dying to get Evelyn's side of the story and learn what she envisions for justice.

Frustrated and overcaffeinated, I hop in my kayak to get the blood moving. Burn my restless energy, immerse myself in blessed solitude on Richardson Bay.

Except . . . another kayaker encroaches on my space. A novice, maybe? I drop a blade, make a sweep stroke, and survey.

Rented gear, maybe from the local tour company. Too wide a grip on the paddle, muscling his way through the water like he can tame the ocean itself. No wonder he's struggling to straighten himself against the prevailing wind blowing down the Sausalito hills into the bay, getting pushed away from the marina and into the boat channel.

Something about him is vaguely familiar. The hapless recipient of Lady Justice's punishment? It must be. After enough time, faces are bound to blur together and trigger my déjà vu. He has some height, long legs extended on his kayak. Gauging by the width of his shoulders, though, he ought to have the upper-body strength to figure his life out and get out of the way of oncoming yachts.

Convinced of his relative safety—never let it be said I'm heartless, just appropriately ruthless, Khaleesi scorching the earth when need arises—I sweep stroke again and continue my merry way north.

"Hey!"

The man's voice reaches me in the wind. Distant but clear.

"Wait up! Please!"

I grit my molars shut and sweep stroke once more to face him. "Are you lost?" I raise my voice. "The shore is that way." I indicate with my paddle in case the message is lost in translation.

If he hears my gratis advice, he ignores it. Maybe he can't hear over the fuss he's making struggling to get to me, stroking and thrashing. It's painful to watch. Finally, he's within yards, close enough we don't have to shout.

Shaggy red hair. My age, maybe younger. A smile like he's never been happier to see someone in his entire life. The overall impression is that of a manic, handsome golden retriever.

"Hi!" he says. "I know this is weird, but you looked like someone I knew when I was young, so I had to—"

Oh, great. A pickup artist. That's a sure way to ruin whatever was left of my victory high from Friday. "Do I know you?"

He seems jarred by my abrupt manner, but I enjoy my time alone. He turns hazel eyes on me like lasers. "Are you Dylan?" he asks carefully. "Dylan Truman?"

I blink several times, glad for the mirrored shades covering my eyes. Few in San Francisco know my real name. I left it behind like I left Eureka behind. Like I left Gabrielle behind when I couldn't be around her anymore. Couldn't see that scar on her face and not want to cut Brent the way he did her.

"Who wants to know?" My voice is hard.

"I do," he says with such sincerity, I have to laugh.

"You've got the wrong person. Sorry." I turn again—so many about-faces today; how annoyingly wishy-washy— and make to leave. My precious time on the water is being eaten away by this hyper hot mess of a man who knows my name.

"You stood up for me. In second grade. Well, I guess you would've been older, fifth grade maybe?" He laughs, a little awkward, but dogged. I'll grant him that. "Freshwater Elementary School, in Eureka? Home of the Dolphins?"

I pause.

He knows me. The real me. Somehow.

Then I remember, and it's as if all the water beneath me has drained away.

"We were on the playground after lunch," he says, "and I was getting beat up by some older kids. You stepped in like you were Wonder Woman and told them all to go to hell. I couldn't believe you cussed like that. My seven-year-old head almost exploded."

I side sweep a last time, slowly, and face him. "Rhys? Rhys . . . Morgan, right?"

He gives a small wave, hand close to his chest.

The wind roars over my ears and years fall away and I see him, so much smaller than he is right now. Smaller than I was, and I wasn't much. I'm still not much, sitting pretty at five foot two, but years of Krav Maga and kayaking have given me the dense build of a gymnast.

He's gained at least a foot on me since then, and yet many things are the same. The panting eagerness, like a puppy. His righteous, do-gooder seven-year-old heart. No wonder he got picked on. Anyone could tell he cared about things, even then. How very uncool.

"I can't believe it's you," Rhys says.

There's something potent in his voice, but the emotion is gone before I can wrap my brain around it. If it's awe, I can't blame him. This is bizarre, finding someone from elementary school out on the water, without the aid of social media. How you like me now, Zuckerberg?

"Sorry to chase you like some stalker," he says. "I just had to know."

"Well, you were right after all." Rhys must be a bloodhound, not retriever.

"Do you live here?" he asks. "In the city?"

I nod. "You?"

"I moved a few months ago."

"For work?" I'll keep asking questions, let him do the talking. It's so easy to do, and it's not until afterward people realize they know nothing of importance about me.

"Yeah. I was in LA for a while, writing for the *Times*, but I couldn't stand the commute. The *Chronicle* will let me work from home, so that's where I'm at now."

A journalist. Ah, yes.

Whatever warmth I might've felt at seeing an old class-mate disappears like fog. My hackles lift, suspicion crack-ling under my skin. This wouldn't be the first time I've been approached by someone trying to identify the person behind my alias, Lady Justice. My clients come to me from word of mouth, but the chain of anonymity is bound to have weak links. And if someone from my past knew who I was before, they could've recognized me at the scene of ret-ribution, even with my myriad disguises. Damn everyone's camera in their pocket and the internet's long memory.

And that's to say nothing of human error. It's impossible to keep your guard up at all moments, though I do my best. Did I slip up? I don't know, but I *do* know this meeting is not serendipitous, no matter the guileless expression on his face.

I give a noncommittal nod. "That's great."

He waits for me to offer information about myself, but I meet him with silence.

Around us, the sun rises, and the water is colored by the sky in shades of teal and deep navy blue. The wind has died down, just a gentle breeze ruffling our hair and cloth-ing. When we were young, Gabrielle loved being out on the ocean on calm days like this. She always brought her camera with her, no matter where she went, until she stopped going anywhere at all. Normally, a day like today would thrill me to no end, but all possibility of enjoyment is gone with my spidey sense tingling.

"I won't keep you, but it's nice to see a familiar face," Rhys says, still searching mine. "I haven't . . . well, I guess I haven't really found my footing here yet. It's hard making friends as an adult, right?"

I already know where he's heading with this, and I already know what my answer will be. Must be.

"Would you like to meet for coffee or something? Catch up?" he ventures.

Absolutely fucking not. "No. I don't think so."

"Oh! Okay." He nods, too vigorously. "Sure, I understand."

He has the worst poker face in the world, his entire being deflating. Maybe that's his trick for investigative journalism—guilt. I won't fall for it. I've seen every dirty trick in the book.

"Nice to see you again, Rhys. Take care."

Before he can respond, I paddle away in determined strokes, carving into the water. If I let my feelings lead the way, I'd be in jail rather than enjoying vigilante life and the taste of reckoning and real power, strong as the tides. The kind most people only dream about.

At home, I shower, jump into a green wrap dress, and head to my office in Bay Front Park right by the water. Seeing a journalist and knowing I'll have to put him off the scent has ruined my morning, but if nothing else, I can get some admin work done while I wait to hear from Daniel regarding Dr. Chang. Anything's better than sitting around, waiting for the starter pistol to fire.

In the office, I flop down in the vintage leather armchair and admire the view through succulents and cacti in the window. Dark Horse Consulting has come a long way from the days when I shared an apartment in the Tenderloin with three other roommates. It's been seven years since I returned to California and officially started my business, but the details are still clear as soju. Petty revenge for hire held me over for almost two years until I reeled in my first big client. Ruth. The woman who told me how she'd been fucked over on a crucial performance review after refusing her superior's advances and reporting him to HR. When she finished the three very dry martinis I'd whipped up behind the bar at the St. Regis—the perfect haunt for hearing the stories of misogyny and maliciousness, over and over—I slid her my business card, heart in my throat, sure I'd never hear from her again.

She called me the next morning, her voice crisp and bitter as vermouth. *How do we fuck him right back?*

Leave it to me, I said.

I spent weeks following her boss (married, two children at home). Photographing him with Gabrielle's camera, which felt more than a little apropos, and still does. Much of my research happens via the internet—if pervs and stalkers can do it, why not me?—but people leave so much of themselves online, they forget there are eyes in real life too.

Within a month, I had photos of him picking up a string of women and various sex workers, including my friend Nadya. She helped me score the money shots, lingering outside the hotel with him, blonde hair like a sheet of platinum in the encroaching dusk. The compendium of evidence was sent to his wife, then leaked online. When the floodgates opened, years of pent-up fury from others he'd groped, demeaned, and threatened swept him away. He lost his job and wife within a week, and my new best friend Ruth took his job and sent the promotion pay my way, balancing the cosmic scales at last.

After Ruth, things took off. She referred me to a friend of hers, a Black start-up founder being harassed by a VC who proposed funding in exchange for sex. After her, the guy who ran off with his sidepiece and used his fiancée's money to finance their escapade. Then the guy posting his ex-girlfriend's nudes online. The whisper network brought me a never-ending torrent of douchebags, long overdue for a taste of their own poisonous medicine.

I jump when my phone buzzes, excavating my tote bag until I find it.

Dr. Chang wants to speak to you. Can you meet her at noon? Daniel's text lights up the screen.

I type my reply. *Yes, today would be perfect. Your timing is impeccable—I'm already at my office. Thank you for convincing her to see me,* I add. *I wasn't sure if she'd come.*

She's still spooked, Daniel says. *Hellfire may not be the best approach. So go easy, tiger.*

I will.

Of course she's still shaken, if she was threatened on her way out the door. I would've put that together anyway when I met her, but I appreciate his heads-up. It'll help me tailor my approach.

When she arrives, Dr. Evelyn Chang is taller than I expected. My nose barely comes to her collarbone when we hug.

"Volleyball," she says, when I ask her if she participated in any sports for Stanford.

"I might've guessed."

She sits across from me in the large hanging wicker chair, lighting up at the mention of her sport. The chair might be an odd choice, but my clients enjoy it—something about the gentle swaying helps people open up. That and the essential oil diffuser, filling the room with my favorite cedar and sage scent, mellow and relaxing.

As far as the Division I sports goes, it doesn't surprise me. She has the upright posture of an athlete. A woman who knows the strength of her own body as well as her mind.

"Can I get you something to drink? Water, coffee? Tea?" I ask. "I have rooibos, sencha, chamomile?"

"Tea would be great. Chamomile, please."

"You got it. I'll have chamomile too. I hit my caffeine quota at zero dark thirty, and I think I hear colors."

She looks tired. Deep-purple circles darken her eyes, making her seem older than my own thirty-two. Still, she musters a smile for me and my silly joke as I heat our water and pour it into two earthenware mugs. I can't help it—my liking for her is intense and immediate. She's a fighter, too, in her own quiet way. She wouldn't be here otherwise.

As our tea steeps, I have her talk. We must know each other and trust each other to embark on this project. "So, tell me about your job for Prometheus."

I read about the company already, but listening to her story in her own words helps me learn what's important to her. The things she pays attention to, the details she highlights. All the while, I build a portfolio in my mind, gauging the scope of her ambition. The nature of the revenge she'll seek.

"It started years ago. Brent was obsessed with the idea of finding an antidepressant that 'cured' major depression and pitched the idea to investors before we even had a viable product. At the time, I swallowed the Kool-Aid and was flattered he'd tapped my department to make it happen, though what he was asking for was extremely difficult."

She sips her tea, and her face hardens, tightening around her eyes. "When I couldn't deliver, I and my entire team were replaced with students straight out of grad school."

"Yes men, in other words." I jot it down in my notepad with the heavy, fancy-pants fountain pen Daniel gifted me with a few years ago.

She nods. "Yeah, but in all honesty, I probably would've said yes too, if I were in their shoes, if I had less seniority.

And less sense of responsibility. Who wants to blow a huge opportunity working for a unicorn pharmaceutical start-up straight out of college? Of course they're going to sign off on the science.

"Against all odds, the new team managed to get the antidepressant to phase-three clinical trials. But"—she pauses—"they didn't, not really, because Brent falsified the safety data from the clinical trials. Risederon has significant toxicity and numerous side effects." She ticks them off with both hands. "Headaches, high blood pressure, hallucinations. For some, intense muscle spasms, paresthesia—pins and needles. And worse, a huge percentage of people in the early clinical trials attempted, and sometimes succeeded in, suicide."

Goose bumps break out on my skin, small hairs lifting over my entire body. This is much bigger than I imagined.

"And you found out," I say.

Her smile could freeze the Mojave. "But I don't have physical proof—I just saw the papers on his desk. Which is where you come in, or so I've been told."

It's quiet in my office. Just our breathing and the gentle hum of the air conditioning as it kicks on, adding to the purr from my sound machine, masking our voices.

"And now he's defrauding his investors," she says. "Pushing to promote the drug, despite the toxicity, despite knowing at some point or another the general public will catch on."

"Have you considered going to federal agencies about this?" I ask. "Reporting the falsified data—the existence of it, anyway? The SEC, maybe? There has to be a way to do this and stay anonymous."

She shakes her head vigorously. The first fear I've seen from her. "Not unless I had the proof. Officially, I was fired for not delivering on Risederon, but I think he knows what

I saw. I think . . ." She looks out the window. "He has some-one following me. There's been this car parked outside our apartment for several weeks now. I'm taking a huge risk being here."

It's no surprise he has someone tailing her. With billions of dollars at stake, a sociopath like Brent would do anything to protect his image and wealth. Anyone who gets in the way will be collateral damage.

"I'll put you in touch with a private security special-ist," I say. "They'll bill me, so don't be shy about asking for what you need. And in the meantime, don't talk to anyone else. Don't answer your door, don't answer phone calls from numbers you don't recognize, don't answer any new emails. You should assume anyone trying to contact you is working for him."

Her eyes widen. "You don't think I'm just being paranoid?"

"I listen to women when they feel threatened. They're rarely wrong."

Evelyn's face crumples. Tears leak when she blinks.

It hurts to watch. I remember every one of my cases. The details stay with me years down the road. This job is like holding a double-edged sword in my palms, hoping I don't get sliced along the way, but even when I do, it makes me want to hold on harder.

"I don't know what to do," she says. "Part of me wants to raise hell and see this man finally get what's coming to him. The other part of me is so scared. Confronting him was the right thing to do." She sniffs hard. "But it came with such a price. You can imagine how well he took it. He smiled, told me how I was mistaken, I didn't have all the correct data . . . he said all the right things, voiced the rationalizations I myself had come up with. Made me ques-tion my sanity, my perception of reality. In the end, though,

I knew I wasn't losing my grip, because all the while he was speaking, he looked at me like he wanted to . . . I don't know . . . kill me or something." She shudders, shoulders quaking.

"Without that job, that income, I don't know how I'll provide for my family. We can't get by on only my husband's salary. I've applied to a dozen different jobs, and everything has turned up empty." She holds her head in her hands and cries.

"You've been blacklisted." I blink hard and rise to meet her.

She inhales, quick, like she's fallen. "You think so?"

"I know so."

"What more does he want from me? I left already!"

"It's exactly as you thought when you confronted him," I say, matter-of-fact. "He wants you dead."

She looks up, eyes wide with surprise. Women learn to ignore their instincts, the ones warning them of disaster. They learn to be polite at all costs. To never be angry, nor anger others. It takes time to unlearn, to tease out the inner voice. To learn how to roar.

"Dr. Chang, you did the right thing. The person threatening you, falsifying data, and defrauding investors is at fault. Don't forget it for a second." I offer her the box of tissues and place my hand on her shoulder. Grounding her into the earth. "You graduated magna cum laude from one of the world's best universities and, by God, we will find another job for you somewhere. Someplace deserving of your ability and your integrity."

She wipes her face with the back of her hands. "Okay. But *someone* has to find the real data. If I had to guess, I'd say he's keeping it at his home now—he wouldn't risk keeping it at the Prometheus offices." She bites her lip.

I let my hand slip away. We're quiet again and I clench and relax, letting my frustration and anger seep out one breath at a time. So much of my work is patience. As much as I'd like to press a knife to Brent's neck and watch blood trickle—for Gabrielle, for Dr. Chang, for everyone he's ever hurt along the way—I'd also like to not go to jail. Ergo, patience. Waiting for her to verbalize the nebulous goal she might have, then plotting to make it happen.

"What do you envision, Dr. Chang?" I ask. "If I find the data, if you had your heart's desire? We can go as big as you want. Or as limited and specific and incisive. Regardless of what you choose, I'm here to make it happen."

She looks up from her lap. There's fire in her eyes, and damn, I already know she's chosen the nuclear route. My heart beats faster and faster, waiting on her words.

"I want Brent to be so radioactive, he'll never do business again. He'll never again be able to do what he's done to me. Threatening me, my family." She inhales, shaky. "This bastard's career ends with me. That's what I want."

I lean forward on my elbows. "Some men can't handle their polonium, hmm?" I smile wide.

"Maybe not so literal," she says, a little alarmed.

"I know." I try to reassure her. "So, what I hear you saying is you'd like to make sure he's never in a position of power again. He'll lose his job, his standing, his wealth, his freedom. He'll lose everything he values, with no chance of ever being redeemed."

"Is that . . ." She looks skeptical, one brow scrunched. "I mean, that sounds like a lot. Can you actually do all of that?"

"Yes," I say. "Consider it done." My three favorite words, and why shouldn't they be? So few outcomes in life arrive with a guarantee, but that's what I promise my clientele, and I'm not about to stop now.

"As far as pricing," she says, sounding nervous. "My friend, she said your asking fee is expensive. I know I asked for a Mars landing with Brent, but is it possible to pay on a sliding scale? Or some other payment plan?"

"I'm glad you asked." I smile. "I offer a thirty percent discount for minorities and LGBTQIA-plus." I tap out a few lines into my iPad, a basic agreement, and hold it out to her. "However, your case will be pro bono."

"What?" She gapes. "Free?"

"One hundred percent."

"Why?" She views me with suspicion for the first time, eyes narrowed.

"My sister," I say, throat tight. "It so happens Brent hurt her too, when they were freshmen at Cal."

As she hears my subtext, comprehension lights her face, slowly, then all at once. "The worst kind of small world. I'm so sorry." She signs her name on the dotted line and returns the iPad.

I roll my shoulders and unclench my fists. "So, I have a personal interest in taking this bastard down too." I offer her my hand, to press some conviction to her palm. "Everything is going to be all right, Dr. Chang. I promise."

After a second, Evelyn takes it, her grip firm and determined.

"The arc of the moral universe may well be long," I tell her. "But before the year is through, Brent Wilder's life as he knows it will be over."

4

DESPITE MY ASSURANCES to Evelyn, I don't know how I'll ruin Brent's whole life. Ordinarily, my subjects are more pedestrian and easier to target. Not so for the CEO. The hunt for ideas consumes me after our meeting, consumes my commute home, and substitutes for my dinner, at least until Daniel texts me.

Be sure to eat something, he says. *You can't take him down if you're hangry.*

I smile at my phone, then catch sight of my expression in the long hallway mirror. I look like a dog lover who's received surprise puppies. This isn't good.

I shouldn't think about him like that, but I haven't gotten Friday out of my head either. Specifically, the moment when our shoulders brushed and something passed from his body into mine, amperage flowing. Disorienting and . . . amazing, but so quick I might've imagined it. I must have.

With a hard mental slap—*he's dating someone or will be soon enough!*—I don't reply. Immature, maybe, but I can't imagine any future where Daniel and I could be together. Not when I do what I do, not when he does what he does, with family expecting him to settle down. Better to disentwine. Maybe it won't hurt as much, then, when I inevitably see him with a wife and children.

"Well, that's fucking depressing."

I sulk to the kitchen, uncork a bottle of Chardonnay, and rummage through my fridge for anything edible, but all my leftover bulgogi is gone, damn it all. I settle on cheese and crackers and grapes and chew, feeling sorry for myself. Gross. I switch to research mode, reading every article I can find about Brent. Trying to imagine the best way to insert myself into his world.

When it's late and I'm blinking tired tears at my computer, I crawl into bed and hope my subconscious will keep working.

My sister visits me when I dream. Gabrielle's hair is long, like mine, only with more wave to it, and redder, especially under sun. We kayak on the ocean back in Eureka, next to each other at first. She's so fast, though, slicing through the water. It's what makes her an unbelievable swimmer too—our dad's height, and her effortless upper body strength. I hurry and hurry, but I can't catch up.

"Hold on," I tell her, shouting over the roaring wind. "Wait for me!" Like I always said when we were young and her long legs carried her everywhere she wanted, while I grew tired and whined and no doubt drove her crazy. To her credit, she always slowed down for me.

Not this time. Either she doesn't hear me or she chooses not to, disappearing around a cliff jutting into the ocean.

Too tired to fight, crying like a little kid, I let the waves roll me, one after another. Let them carry me toward the shore, toward the place where ocean and rock meet, a ceaseless boxing ring.

A breaker flips my kayak, plunging me into frigid water. It's a cold, alternate universe with different physics, different organisms, different rules. I don't try to flip myself upright with a sweep roll but hold my breath and stay under, observing the mysterious and dangerous upside-down world. If I had gills and cold blood, I could stay. Shapeshift into a creature at home in the dark, whirling chaos.

I could meet Brent where he's at.

I wake with a gasp.

Eureka indeed!

I have found it. A plan so good and insane it makes my hands shake and my heart beat fast. A plan so good, I won't need to create alternatives for Evelyn.

If I want to see the apex predators—the human ones—I need to go where they live. Not out into the Red Triangle with the great white sharks, but Pacific Heights. The wealthiest neighborhood in the United States.

I'll be Dylan next door. Only, not Dylan. I'll need a throwaway identity, but those are easily fabricated. I close my eyes, imagining. Sugar, spice, and everything nice. Little will Brent know I'm a rat, crawling through the walls of his house, devouring everything in my path. Finding the clinical trial's data and shouting it from his rooftop.

My phone says three AM, but I launch out of bed, wrap myself in my silk robe, and plop my butt at my laptop desk, searching for an article I read earlier, a feature in an architecture magazine about Brent's new home in Pac Heights—*the* place for the nouveau riche. He's been throwing his money around with extensive renovations at the top of the Lyon Street Steps, infuriating his neighbors.

Feverish, hands shaking, I search the real estate listings surrounding his home. I bite my fist and squeal at my unbelievable luck when I scroll in and see a property for rent right next to his. The perfect entre to preneur. Four bedrooms, furnished, ungodly beautiful, and on the market for far longer than property in Pac Heights ever stays. The noise and construction next door must've discouraged prospective buyers from moving into the townhome.

As predicted, the monthly rent is enough to make me choke on my tongue. I calculate the amount I'd need to pay and figure I could swing it for three months, max. And that's with wiping out my savings. Anything more and I'll be out of business.

My stomach hollows out with dread as my rational brain pooh-poohs this dicey, all-or-nothing plan. As a rule, I don't get close to my victims—or anyone, really, but that's beside the point. Too messy. Too much room for mistakes.

I stand, walk out on my deck, and look south.

Across the water, a reflected glow on the clouds from the city lights, San Francisco rises on the hills, so much power and money in such a condensed space that its GDP surpasses that of small countries.

How else would I enter his world? Get close enough to hurt? Cold mist envelops me, and I wish I could float on it, wraithlike, and slip into his home, slither into his ear like a parasitic worm.

Does he ever see Gabrielle when he dreams? Or has narcissism granted him a spotless conscience, wiped clean of every sin? It's worse, in all probability. In his inverse world, he's recast as the victim of a witch hunt.

I close my eyes. Hatred spews from my pores, burning around me like a scarlet cloud. *You've never seen a witch, Brent, but you will.*

I'll make myself conspicuous, so even a self-absorbed turd like him will notice. Piece by piece by piece, I'll strip Brent of everything he has, until there's nothing left. He'll fight a war on all fronts, starting with his ostentatious, Edwardian home—the place he thinks of as safe—and extending ever outward. Much the way violence travels beyond the intended recipient, waves of hurt rippling over and under and straight through, stealing breath.

Love comes with such a high price sometimes.

I hold on to the rail of my deck, feeling the smooth, damp wood beneath my palms, and let the tears run down my face.

"I love you, Gabrielle," I say to the dark.

It's a long way to Eureka, but I hope she'll hear me picking up a sword anyway.

*   *   *

I brew coffee that could strip the paint from the hull of my home and send Dr. Chang an email from my VPN letting her know I've arrived at a plan and offering to set up a time to call to discuss. I have no sense of whether she'll be cool with my hand-to-hand-combat plan for revenge—and I suppose I can't blame her if she's not on board. Truthfully, even I have my doubts I can pull off this bird-brained scheme. I don't normally get so close to my targets, preferring to keep several degrees of separation, but Brent's case is unique: he already has too many layers of protective privilege around him. Still, I hope I can convince her—and myself.

A knock on my door around sunrise makes me jump out of my skin. Who's here at this hour? If Rhys has gotten his nosy, grubby paws on my address, I'll have him disappeared, free press or no.

I wrap my robe tighter around my waist. Daniel is always trying to set me up with a home camera system. There are good reasons for my being a Luddite—leave no incriminating digital trail that'll wind up in a hearing, am I right? That's how they get you. But times like this, it'd be nice to know who's darkening my door.

Through the peephole, I spy a black waistcoat and a familiar lean torso.

I throw open the door. "Haas? What are you doing here?"

"Breakfast?" He holds out two boxes of pastries. "If you brew coffee?"

He's so . . . shiny, in the morning sun. His crisp white button-up is blinding. As is his wide smile. He could wear shorts and flip-flops pretty much anywhere in the Bay Area, but I love the fact he doesn't. Lingerie is to men what suits are to women, is it not?

For a few dumb seconds, I can't wrap my brain around him, standing on my front step. He's been to my home before, but usually I know when he's stopping by. It's also never so early—my night owl and his occasional insomnia commune in the wee hours, not when the sun is shining.

He seems to realize he's made a miscalculation. What a morning-person move. He ought to know I don't get up before eight AM. Not unless I'm struck by creative brilliance and up to no good.

"This little place opened around the corner from me, so I stopped in. You didn't answer last night, and I wondered if you were all right." He clears his throat. "But if this isn't a good time . . ." He looks everywhere except at my bare calves or sleep-mussed hair. I'm sure I paint a medusan picture.

I can't help my smile. "If you wanted to play hooky from work, all you had to do was say so." I step aside and gesture for him to come in.

"Wish I could." He returns my smile. "But I'm just here for more java. Do you still have the stuff from Costa Rica?" He settles in at my breakfast bar and rolls his sleeves back. I look away before I can make too close an inspection of the muscle and veins.

"I do, lucky dog." I pour him a mug from my still-warm stainless carafe. "But you sure didn't have to come all the way here to feed my sugar dragon. Especially if you're heading to Apple Park?" I nod to his sharp getup.

He shrugs and doesn't say one way or the other, which means he's due to show his face in person. "Like I said, you didn't answer last night. Just wanted to make sure you were doing okay after talking to Dr. Chang."

I investigate my mug, coffee swirled with heavy cream, buying myself time to be chill about his offhand concern.

"It was hard—like you said, she's pretty demoralized and frightened—but I'm used to it." I turn and face him. "How's your mom, by the way?"

"Doing okay. She has physical therapy today, so I'm going to drop by later and check on her."

"Well, give her a hug for me." *Even though she doesn't know me.*

Embarrassed, I open the box, grab a blueberry muffin, and devour it. Lavender, lemon, and juicy berries burst over my tongue. Daniel has an uncanny knack for finding the best places, little holes-in-the-wall others overlook. The introvert's superpower: keen observation. "Gosh, you're right. This revenge stuff does make me hungry. Also, this muffin is crazy good."

"Yeah? Good to know." He sips his coffee, closing his eyes with a small groan of appreciation.

That *sound*. Christ. How I'd love to hear it in a different context.

"Aren't you going to have something to eat too?" I do my darnedest to rally and stop being a lecher.

"It's all yours." He shakes his head. "I already brushed my teeth."

"I don't see how that factors in."

"Fair point." He laughs and noses in the box, grabs a cinnamon roll, and takes a careful bite. "It sounds like you've arrived at a plan for Brent?" he asks casually, but his alert gaze belies his interest.

"I have." I lean on the counter across from him and smile. "I'm going to be the girl next door. Literally."

Daniel pauses midbite, then swallows hard. "You're going to move in next to him?"

"And from there, worm my way into his home in Pac Heights and get proof of his wrongdoing. If I damage his stupid house along the way, ten bonus points." I sip my coffee, pleased with myself.

I expected Daniel's version of excitement—tempered enthusiasm by way of a small smile and bright eyes—but his stone-cold expression slows my roll. "You're going to move in next door?" he asks again. "Next to the same man who hurt your sister?"

"I know exactly who I'm dealing with." I ply him with my best Cheshire cat grin. "Sadly for him, he won't have a clue who I am. Or why the universe has conspired against him."

Daniel hasn't eaten anything else. "I don't like it." He finally looks up. "Besides the obvious risk to your safety, what if he figures out who you are and what's going on? And it won't be inexpensive, trying to get a home in that neighborhood. How will you afford it?"

"Let me worry about the risk. And finances."

"Is it possible you're letting your sister's history overrule your common sense?" His voice is tentative, halting. Stepping from one rock to another, trying to meet me on the other side of a growing divide.

"Fuck yes, it's personal, Haas." I clank my mug down hard, surprising us both. The anger scorches up out of nowhere, lava breaking through a cooled crust. "When else will I have an opportunity to avenge my sister and Dr. Chang? Take this guy out for good?" I smack my hands together. "Now's the time to strike and make sure he can't hurt anyone ever again. And half measures aren't going to cut it."

Daniel just looks at me, steady and imperturbable.

"I don't expect you to understand." I march away and plop down at my laptop. I need to apply for the townhouse rental. "If someone else snags this place, I'm back to square fucking one," I mutter. "Trying to hurt someone nigh untouchable."

Daniel's soft footsteps near me. "There are other ways, Dylan." He places a hand on the back of my chair. If I were to lean back, his hand would touch my shoulder. I feel the warmth even at a distance. "You don't always have to be the tip of the spear."

I turn and look at him over my shoulder.

He meets my gaze. "Do you want me to hack him?"

His offer is genuine. He wouldn't have said it otherwise.

While it's tempting to outsource, I'd never ask Daniel to risk himself in such a major way. If he were caught, he'd lose everything—his job, his family. His entire future. "No."

He pushes away from my chair, irritated. "Of course not."

"It has to be me." I'm not about to apologize for being a one-woman army. "You know that's the way I work."

"There's also this thing called asking others for help. Aren't you afraid?" His eyes are dark pools of concern. Treacherous.

There's no need for him to elaborate. "Of course I'm afraid. It's always been a matter of when, not if this catches up to me and I go to jail. But if I didn't take risks, you'd find me living on the sidewalk. So."

He turns away with a deep grunt, exasperated.

"Aren't you moving on from this anyway?" I follow him onto my deck as he wends his way through the maze of potted plants, including the claw-foot tub I planted full of cacti. There's *my* metaphor—cute but spiky! "Since when did you care this much about the methods behind my madness?" I demand.

He grips the railing and shoots me a dirty look from the corner of his eye.

Really, he's adorable when he pouts. I can't help riling him more. And conveniently deflecting attention away from me. "How's the dating going, by the way? Have you found Mrs. Haas?"

"Not yet." His tone tells me to back off.

"Ticktock, sir." What is wrong with me? I don't know why I keep trying to antagonize him, especially when he brings me things with powdered sugar on them, but I can't stop myself either. At least he's not asking more impossible questions. "I could sign you up on Tinder, you know. Vet everyone for you. I'd be an excellent filter."

"No need." He cuts me another dark look. "Our moms have already set us up."

Us. There's a pronoun I don't much like the sound of. "Oh?" Somehow, I force words out. "Anyone I'd know?"

"My friend Yoon So Ah, chaebol heiress. Her father is the chairman of Yoon Motor Group."

Holy shit. I knew his family ran in wealthy circles—for God's sake, his relatives own Levi's Plaza—but a daughter poised to inherit a large South Korean conglomerate?

"I don't know if I ever talked about her, but she and I dated off and on when we were at Stanford for grad school," he continues, oblivious to my shock. "So, yeah. I'll pass on the dating apps, thank you." His voice drips with condescension.

My stomach hollows out, filling with dread. The wind whips past my face, blunting my hearing. It's either that or the blood booming over my ears.

"My, my. A second-chance romance with the heiress?" I try to smile. "That sounds . . . serious."

"You don't know half of it." He sighs, a huge rise and fall of broad shoulders. "But if it has to be someone, I guess . . ." He trails off.

"Seems fast." *And fait accompli.* Will he move to South Korea, then, if he marries her? Will I ever see him again if he does? "I thought you said you hadn't started dating."

"I haven't met up with her yet."

But I will soon, he doesn't say.

With his back to me, I watch him, the way the wind sifts through his glossy, black hair. What would it feel like in my hands? It looks like it'd be soft, strands fine as heavy silk. I should probably, uh, stop admiring his hair and examine why I take such perverse enjoyment in his disquiet, but I have neither the time nor the inclination for that kind of self-reflection.

"Well"—I aim for glib—"let me know where you guys are gonna register so I can buy you another stand mixer or something."

He does turn around then, and his wounded expression stops me in my tracks, ices my blood. "Why are you being like this?"

Why indeed. Can I blame the wind for my suddenly watering eyes too? My throat swells and I wish I could rewind, say something kind instead of snide and above it all. Daniel only ever sees the best or worst of me, nothing in between. "I . . . I don't . . ."

"You make me so mad sometimes." He shakes his head, a decision reached, and brushes past me. "I have to go to work. I'm sorry I bothered you."

"Are you leaving? Like right now?" I scurry after him, back inside to the kitchen.

"Yes."

I wilt but try to make amends. "Do you want another muffin for the road? I really can't eat all of these."

"No."

He closes the door after him with quiet restraint.

I stare at the door for a long time. When I'm sure I won't give in to the absurd urge to cry—Daniel has never once raised his voice to me; what kind of ass must I be to have earned his animosity?—I look around. Try to gather my thoughts, the plan I laid in place this morning before Daniel swept in and filled my brain.

On the counter, his coffee still steams, ribbons curling in a beam of morning light. Of course he has to linger about like a benevolent ghost. Come to think of it, little traces of him are everywhere.

A signed paperback from my favorite romance author on my coffee table.

The huge framed photograph on my wall: Volcán Arenal in Costa Rica, erupting at night, dramatically backlit by lightning. *A gift for Ms. Fire and Blood on her 30th*.

His coffee.

Without thinking too hard about it, I grab the heavy earthenware mug and press my lips to the rim, wondering if I'll taste anything other than coffee. Cinnamon, maybe. Like the mints he always carries.

No trace.

I lower the mug. Serves me right, I guess.

5

I'M SO ANNOYED with myself and Daniel's abrupt exit, I hop into my kayak immediately after, ready to paddle to Hawaii and back and be home in time for dinner.

Unfortunately, I find Rhys on the water again.

"Gaia, what have I done to displease you?" I ask the heavens.

"Dylan!" Rhys waves, wearing a wide smile. "Fancy seeing you again."

Could I flip him and make my escape while he's overboard? A tempting prospect, but he looks too heavy to tip with an oar. Besides, he clearly wants something.

Or knows something.

I fix a bright smile on my face. "How's work?"

"The article I'm writing is coming along. Still have someone I need to interview, though."

"Anyone I'd know?"

His smile is indecipherable. "Better than you'd think."

I don't like the sound of that. Not one bit. A former client of mine? A former target? *Me?* No end to the trouble Rhys could ruck up, nosing around in things that are none of his damn business.

"What's your angle?" I feign polite interest.

He pauses. Considering. "Who's orchestrating instant karma?"

The wake from a sailboat rolls our kayaks. That must be why I feel sick.

"You know who I am."

There's no sense being coy now. I have to figure out where the gap occurred, which is the weak link. Figure out how to stop him from exposing me and blowing up my life and livelihood.

He nods, balancing his paddle across his knees and leaning forward. "Imagine my surprise when I discovered— after years of research—it was none other than one of my childhood classmates. It felt destined, to be honest."

I sweep closer to him. "Who told you? Was it one of my clients? A mark?"

He shakes his head, a wry smile on his face. "None of your clients squealed, though they had every chance to. No, I had to go about it the hard way. Searching through video footage from the public takedowns to find my Carmen Sandiego."

As if that makes me feel any better. My entire life is in this person's hands. All he has to do is publish an article, or hell, even a goddamn tweet, and my career—and the chance to hurt Brent—goes up in smoke.

"Name your price, Rhys."

"What?" He actually has the gall to look offended.

My patience thins. "Everyone has one. Tell me what you want in exchange for your silence."

"I'm not trying to blackmail you; I'm trying to get your side of the story!"

"I have no side in this story; that's the entire fucking point. You publish *anything* about me, and it's all over. I go to jail or get sued or go on the run."

Finally, he seems to understand the stakes, searching my face. "I just wanted to talk to you, Dylan. I . . ." He chews his lip. "I admire you."

I blink. He seems so . . . earnest. But then, many people do. A public mask and a private sneer.

"If that's true, then . . . will you give me two weeks? Before you publish?" Enough time to ruin Brent's life, I hope. After which point, it looks like I'll be hanging up my Lady Justice hat for good, unless I convince Rhys otherwise.

"I can do two weeks." He sighs. "But I still want to talk."

I'm already paddling away, furiously carving into the water. I have no time to lose.

At home, I rinse off and dress in a navy-blue, flowy, tie-waist jumpsuit and collarless blazer with nude pumps. In Silicon Valley, the land where smart sartorial choices go to die, my clothing marks me as an intriguing oddity, especially among the Y chromosome set. Look at me totter in fuck-me stilettos! Do I look commanding, ready to bring a boardroom to heel, or do I look vulnerable, unable to outrun predation? All part of the Lady Justice mystique.

Dressed to kill, I head straight to the salon on Divisadero, ready to enact my plan.

Inside the relative safety of my car, I blast the air conditioning. Sweat collects around my hairline and in the small of my back as I drive across the Golden Gate. One conversation with a nosy journalist was all it took to remind me the foundations of my life are made of sand.

"One crisis at a time." I pull up in front of the salon. Thankfully, it's not busy on a Monday morning. Another perk of my job: flexible hours that suit my random soul.

Noah Rodrigo, the salon owner, assesses me when I step into the brightly lit space with its potted plants, distressed hardwood floors, and funky vintage furniture. Bougie, but what can I say? I make enough money to be vain about my hair, my one outstanding feature, and spend accordingly.

"Girl, what have you been doing with yourself?" He *tsk*s. "Your outfit is fire, but you look like a washed-up pelican this morning. Rough weekend?"

I embrace him. His unflinching honesty is one of the many reasons I've gone to Noah for years and years. Not only is he a hugely talented stylist, but he'll also let me know when a style is beyond my hair's reach and a wig would be the better option.

"For real, what's going on with you, Dilly?" He gestures at my sweaty face, concern filling his. "Are you on the run?" He folds his wiry, tatted arms and sighs at my hair, which I've thrown up in a messy topknot.

"I woke up super early," I say. "And yeah, it's been a weird morning." Weird couple of days, to be honest. I still feel unsteady after parting on bad terms with Daniel this morning. And discovering Rhys already knows about Lady Justice and her exploits. Fuck.

"Tea?" he offers, heavy brows crinkling in sympathy. Noah's a prickly sort until trust is established, but he has the biggest heart of anyone I know. He ushers me to the side and puts a mug of my favorite peppermint tea in my hands.

"Thank you much." I take a grateful sip, the Daniel + Rhys headache dissipating. "But I actually have a big question for you: Can you turn me into the 'girl next door'? And would you have time today? I'm in a bit of a crunch."

Noah claps his hands together, glee lighting his warm hazel eyes. "Honey, I thought you'd never ask. I've been trying to get you to go lighter for years! With those big brown doe eyes? C'mon!"

I nod, amused. "That's the plan. I need to look sickeningly, do-no-wrong, maple-syrup sweet." He knows me well enough to know I won't tell him why, but he may have guessed my profession anyway, as several of his clients have been referred my way. I'm sure he's heard it all. Having someone's fingers in one's hair helps a person open up, you know?

"Say no more." He's already pushing me toward an empty chair and removing my scrunchie, sifting through my hair and evaluating.

"Maybe some bangs," he says, more to himself than me. "Sideswept, softening your jaw line. We could do a honey shade or even lighter, and it'd still work with your skin." He meets my gaze in the tall mirror. "You ready to be a little blonde monster?"

"I guess so!" I laugh. "I put myself in your capable hands, sir."

The bleaching and dyeing take a long time, but I don't mind chatting with Noah while the magic happens.

"So, tell me about dating app life," he says. "Now that I'm a smug married, I have to get my entertainment from you." I was so honored to attend his and Zach's wedding last year.

"Sorry to disappoint, but all's quiet on the Western Front," I say. "I have gone on terrible dates with one tech bro too many and sworn them all off."

"Wait, let me guess. You were lectured about not going keto? Or intermittent fasting?"

"Yup!" I laugh. "That was a couple guys ago. He could not for the life of him understand why I wouldn't forgo breakfast, meanwhile ignoring the fact that no one wants to see me hangry. Let me have small joys in life, you know? Who doesn't like breakfast food?" I sigh into my mug. "Before him, I had to listen to this guy's puerile anarcho-capitalism sensibilities. 'Ancap' this, 'ancap' that. For fuck's sake, call yourself a libertarian and be done with it! Don't try to make it fancy."

Noah laughs and sips more tea, gesturing for me to continue.

"Before *that*, I pretended like I didn't know what Bitcoin was, just for the hell of it. That was a colossal mistake—I swear, he would not shut up about it. Like, my dude, I'm not here to learn about cryptocurrency!" I set my mug down. "That was before he called me nubile, out loud. After that, I lost my shit and left the restaurant. Didn't even eat dessert." I sigh. "What a waste."

"Wow." Noah's face has turned red, and tears leak from his eyes. "Wow. So glad I'm missing out on these experiences."

"It's pretty grim out there." I smile at him in our shared reflection in the mirror. "Count yourself lucky to have found Zach. He's a good one."

"He is." His expression softens. "Never thought I'd find someone who puts up with me and all my crap, but here we are."

What I wouldn't give for someone to put up with my hot mess express too.

"What about that guy you were talking about a few months back?" he asks. "A PI or something, right? Haas?" He purses his lips. "He sounded chill. Like he wouldn't have too many self-validating opinions to foist onto you."

"Oh, Haas?" I aim for casual. "He works in tech too, but I have to say, he knows the value of silence."

"How did you guys meet, anyway? You've never told me."

I smile before catching myself. "Well, he helped me with some work stuff a long time ago." It's as specific as I can get with Noah, but in truth, Daniel slipped clutch details on several targets right into my in-box, the sly devil. Didn't ask for anything in return, didn't try to hinder me in any way. It made me nervous at first, but after the sixth time it happened, I figured *DH* might be worthy sidekick material. "And he didn't even try to take credit for my ideas! So of course I had to meet this guy in real life. I asked him to meet up for drinks, and turned out we had lots in common with traveling and martial arts and stuff, and . . . I guess the rest is history, as they say." Though whereas I stayed in hostels, Daniel's experiences abroad were conducted from boutique hotels. Still, the differences in our upbringings never seemed to matter. Inveterate kindness and the fact that he wore his money like an itchy coat he couldn't wait to shed made me like him all the more.

Noah watches me with an intense expression, like I've said something particularly revealing.

I clear my throat and shift in my seat. "Anyway, it's just a friendly thing with him. We've known each other so long, it'd be weird if the dynamic changed now."

Noah's eyes narrow as though he wants to press, but he squeezes my shoulder instead. "Keep panning for gold," he says. "Someone might surprise you. And sometimes"—he leans down—"you'll find a nugget's been in your back pocket the whole time."

Without further ado, he whisks me back to the sink to rinse the lightener out of my hair.

A good cut and dry later, I barely recognize myself when Noah spins me around to face the mirror.

"Whoa." I smile, light-headed. Read: scared shitless. Still, he's done magic, and he ought to know. "Noah, you're a wizard!"

He pretends to do a spell with a magic wand. "Your fairy godfather, at your service."

I laugh and inspect my beachy waves, admiring the shades of vanilla and caramel. I look unrecognizable. Younger. And a few shades more innocent. It's perfect.

Noah leans over my shoulder and grins. "Smile, angel. Pretty sure you could rob a bank and get away with it. Just don't name me as an accomplice." He kisses me on the cheek. "Be back in four weeks for your roots!"

* * *

Pockets considerably lighter, I leave the salon and check my email on the way to my car.

Congratulations!

I stop in the middle of the sidewalk, annoying everyone walking past me.

My application for the townhouse in Pacific Heights has been approved. It's time to pony up a deposit—three months' worth of rent. I blink when I see the total and try to fight the surge of panic.

"Jesus Christ, that was quick." I wipe a sweaty palm on my skirt. The landlord must be desperate to fill the vacant property. Still, the sooner I can move in, the better. The jig is up in two weeks unless I manage to convince Rhys to keep his discovery to himself.

The idea of cutting a check for several, several grand, however, makes me queasy. I still haven't gotten a reply from Dr. Chang, either. At this point, my vengeance process has been one hundred percent selfishly motivated and unilateral. Before I get too far ahead of myself, I need to get her on board.

In my car, I dial her number and wait.

"Dr. Chang."

She sounds tired. I wonder how she's holding up at home, whether someone is still following her.

"Hi, Dr. Chang, it's Dylan. Have you had a chance to check your email?"

"Sorry, no." She sighs. "I had an interview this morning."

"Yeah? Good vibes?"

I hear her frown. "They cut it short when they found out about my previous place of employment. It's like I'm wearing a scarlet *P* or something. Ridiculous."

"I'm so sorry," I say. "But the good news is, I have a plan." I give her the brief and wait for her reaction.

"This sounds . . ." She trails off.

"Awesome?"

"Risky," she finishes. "Please don't take this the wrong way, but getting so close to him might leave too much room for error." She pauses. "You don't know him as well as I do. He likes to play Mr. Affable, but he's a shark. He gets off on it, the mind games, trying to control everyone."

I sit in my car, sweating in the greenhouse it's created but still cold.

"All you'd have to do is not respond one time to whatever alias you've chosen, and he'd put two and two together." Evelyn hums, a small, anxious noise. "I really can't have my name getting back to Brent on this. I have to think of my family's well-being."

"I understand your concerns," I say, "but I don't do sloppy work. Your name will *never* get back to him. You have my word."

There's a long pause. "Is there another way to do this?"

"None so viscerally satisfying."

Another long pause. "Then I leave it in your hands. Do what you think is best."

"He's already set himself up for a fall," I say. "Hubris is the oldest story in the book, and the most predictable. All I have to do is see him through to the natural consequences of his choices."

Evelyn snickers. "You think he'd appreciate that, with the Greek mythology namesake."

"I have a feeling the irony will be lost on him." I smile at my newly angelic reflection in the rearview mirror. "I'll check in with you when I've set up shop in my lair."

"Good luck, Lady Justice." This time, her voice sounds less strained. "Give that bastard hell."

I laugh, startled, and nod, even though she can't see me. "I'll do my best."

6

Noah was right about one thing: the next part of my transformation must be my clothing. If I'm going to look the part of vacuous tart, the flowy thrift shop tie-dye duds I live in most days when I'm not on the clock will have to go.

I turn toward my favorite boutique out of habit, then pause. I have a good rotation of work wear, but high-powered professional won't be Brent's taste. Too much equal footing for his liking. Better to pretend I'm living on someone else's money.

Rather, I'll be a . . . newly minted heiress myself, with socialite aspirations. Not too far up in the one percent club, such that Brent could double-check my background, but high enough for me to afford to live next to him. Potential arm candy if he plays his cards right. The skewed power dynamic will grate on me, but I can't imagine a better carrot to dangle in his stupid, punch-me face.

Hours later, wearing my new armor—a slinky black camisole, skintight jeans I can barely squeeze into, stilettos, oversized shades, outrageously expensive handbag—I drive to the property manager's office to sign the lease and put down my deposit. Then I head home with the rest of my lavish loot. My credit card statement is going to put gray in my hair when it grows in, but maybe some of this can be a tax write-off. The interest I get from men, however, tells me I'm on the right track. Brent's not going to know what hit him.

Even so, I feel gross and fake, dressing for attention. I frown into the sunset, winding my way back to Sausalito for one last night in my real home. One more night of a lowered guard before I jump into the lowest rung of hell.

An old song comes on, one I haven't heard in years. One heartbeat later I'm awash in memories, driving with Gabrielle in our parents' beat-up Mazda. Singing at the top of our lungs on a fine midsummer's day before she headed south for school. I didn't want to tell her how much I'd miss her when she moved. I kept the secret close to my chest like a losing hand of cards, determined to bluff my way through her departure.

I should've told her.

But I didn't. So now I'll die on this godforsaken vengeance hill.

I wipe my cheeks with my palm.

Then, on a whim—or really, giving in to the impulse that's dogged me all goddamn day—I turn and head back to Daniel's apartment. It's the later side of evening, and he should be home from work and visiting his mom. Hope flares in my chest as I park in front of the building, the last day's light reflecting off the glossy, geometric windowpanes. LEED construction, no doubt, complete with the gorgeous rooftop garden overhanging the edge of the building.

My heels click across the smooth black marble in the lobby. I smile at the doorman I saw the other night, but it's clear he doesn't recognize me. "Hi," I say. "I'm here to see Daniel Haas, apartment 408."

The elderly doorman gives me a skeptical look—to be fair, I do look like an escort—but reaches to call the man in question anyway.

As the doorman dials, Daniel appears in the lobby, filling the stairwell's doorframe.

"Good timing," I say.

He stops midstride, eyes widening, blinking when he recognizes me. "Dylan?" His brows knit together in concern. "Your hair . . . ?"

I grin and make a small circle, careful not to lose my balance in the ankle-breaking heels. "What do you think?"

"Well, you definitely look different." Which is Daniel-speak for *Woman, what have you done?*

Not the reaction I was hoping for, to put it mildly. Then it strikes me, how hurried he looked coming downstairs. Like he had somewhere to be.

"Sorry for not giving you a heads-up I was headed your way." I fidget with the ends of my sandy hair. I was really hoping to have this conversation in private, but here will have to do. "I wanted to stop by and, um, apologize for being a jackass this morning. I don't know what's wrong with me, but you have so much going on and I'm so sorry for being a jerk." I force myself to be brave. "I know we left things on a crappy note. It's been weighing on me all day."

"I forgave you before I left your boat," he says, looking amused. "But you do a good grovel."

"Well, I do try to own up when I've fucked up." I laugh, relieved. "Which happens a lot more than I'd like. But hey, you got a haircut too!" It's alarmingly attractive on him, shorter up the sides and longer on top. Approximately three men have the bone structure to pull it off, and the others are Cillian Murphy and Manny Jacinto.

But he's not even paying attention, fussing with his polished cuff links. He looks sharp in another tailored three-piece suit in charcoal, with cognac wing tips on his feet. Between that and the haircut, he's all angles, like the facets of diamond. For real, how dare he? Why must he always look like he stepped out of another dimension full of beautiful things?

"Anyway, no need to apologize," he says to his shoes.

"Why won't you look at me, then?" I sound more petulant than I'd like.

He looks up and his expression softens, releasing the tautness around his eyes and mouth. "Really, you don't need to be sorry, Dylan. You're doing what you think is right." He leads me to the artsy velvet chairs in front of a fireplace and folds his long body into one, indicating I should do the same.

I sit opposite and cross my legs and arms, a little peeved with him, then annoyed because I'm peeved. I was working so hard to be magnanimous.

He studies me in earnest, taking in the hair and clothing. My new costume. His glance slips from my face to the line of my cleavage, more visible than usual with my new, low-cut silk cami.

Like any self-respecting she-devil, I lean forward on the pretense of listening.

His gaze snaps away, a frown marring his face. He speaks to the gas fireplace. "Like I said, it's none of my business how you run your operation. I shouldn't have butted in where I wasn't wanted."

"Sure, but you know I respect your opinion." I wave to him. "If you have doubts about my harebrained plan, feel free to spit them out." I give him a cautious smile. "But do it now, or forever hold your peace."

He chews his bottom lip, thinking, then finally shakes his head. A rueful grin curls the corner of his mouth. "Objectively, any guy would have a hard time keeping his mind on the straight and narrow when you look like this. You won't have trouble catching his eye—"

"I thank you, good sir."

His smile fades. "Mostly, I just worry, which isn't helpful to either of us. So"—he leans forward on his knees—"instead, what will you need from me?"

I glow several shades of happy pink under my sticky spray tan. "I won't know until I see the inside of his house, but if he has a home security setup, and I'm sure he will"—I lower my voice—"I'll need help disabling it so I can move freely." I peer into the fire, as if the flames could outline the shape of my future, living a bizarre double life.

Daniel nods, sanguine. "Should be simple enough. I'll just need to know the brand. Anything else?"

"That's it for now, but I'll let you know. Aside from bypassing home security, there's the issue of payment." I pop my knuckles, a nervous habit I still haven't managed to drop. "Of course, normally I'd cut you in for your work, but I told Dr. Chang her case would be pro bono. I can still pay you the usual twenty percent, though—"

He shakes his head, looking amused. "I've been donating my cut to the homeless shelter for a few years now, if it makes you feel any better."

"Rascal." I smile at him. "Being so self-deprecating about it too. I'd never have known."

Daniel returns the smile, popping a dimple. He's handsome in any light, from any angle, but there's something about him in the soft glow of firelight that does me in, every time.

Dylan, you've got it bad. So bad.

The thought hits me with the force of a tsunami.

How long? For how long have I been leaning into the impossible? Months? Years? My heart beats a brisk cadence against my ribs, my brain spins, but no matter how I try, I can't track the path from tentative friendship to him becoming the most important person in my life. Like water, he was quiet and inexorable, seeping into all my cracks and filling them up.

"Dylan?"

"Yeah what?" I blink back to awareness. "What's up?"

"I do have to get going." Guilt softens his words. "You just happened to catch me on my way out."

I hope my smile doesn't look as fake as my blonde waves. "Oh yeah?" I gesture to his fancy suit. "Big date?"

"I'm picking her up from the airport." He looks at his lap, seeming so nervous, I almost empathize. Almost. "Yoon So Ah. The heiress."

"Got it." I stand, leaking joy like a crappy air mattress, but keep my smile firmly in place. I'll have to get used to Plasticine facial expressions if I mean to wield them against Brent anyway. "Well, I won't keep you. Traffic will be a beast."

He stands and takes a step my way, close enough I have to crane my neck to see his face again.

"Good luck," he says, so soft it's hard to hear him.

"Thank you. I hope your date goes well." I try to at least sound sincere, if I can't feel it in my heart. Being an adult is the worst sometimes. "Bye, Haas."

I walk away, unsteady, like a helium balloon with my ties cut. Drifting.

He catches my wrist with a warm hand and tugs. "Wait."

I turn and find myself nose to his chest.

He wraps arms around me, pulling me close. The smell of wool and his bright, lemony shampoo fills my nose.

"Be careful, Dylan," he says. "Be careful."

It's a plea.

Finally overcoming my surprise, I wrap my arms around him too, marveling at the gift of his touch. He's never given it away lightly. Then, because he won't see me, I close my eyes. Even through layers of clothing, he's solid, lean and dense. For the shortest moment, I want to tell him about Rhys, but quell the urge. He has enough to worry about already, and it's not fair for me to drag him into yet another of my problems.

"I will be," I say, throat tight.

"And don't do anything I wouldn't do."

"Does that include feeding him lead paint?" I ask his smooth, pale-blue dress shirt. "Leaving a few rusty nails for him to step on?"

Daniel's laughter quakes against me, tensing the muscles beneath my cheek. "Remind me to never get on your bad side."

I scoff. "Like you even could. You get a pass for pretty much everything." I roll my eyes, though he can't see me. With anyone else, it's knives out, but not him. "It's ridiculous, actually."

We've held on for far longer than friends could get away with, but neither of us moves away. Could I freeze us in amber, hold on to the fleeting?

"I don't know." He snickers, breath a cool wash over the crown of my head. "Something tells me I'm about to cross the tiger again, traveling this road that's been laid for me."

So he senses it too. The precipice. I'm not the introspective sort, but maybe it's natural to question what the hell you're doing with your life when a friend is poised to reach a major milestone.

That must be why I feel like an annoying younger sibling he's outgrown.

I stiffen and pull away. There's probably a Taylor Swift song for my predicament, but I don't have the heart to sing it, not even to embarrass him with my tone-deaf vocals.

"Can I be melodramatic and ask for something really selfish?" If I had any decency, I wouldn't voice the question, but I have the emotional maturity of a goldfish, and am not a decent sort besides.

He nods, eyes crinkling.

"Don't forget me?"

I sound small and push my shoulders back reflexively, trying to take up more space than my height allows.

His face shifts, myriad emotions altering his expression until he settles on grim resignation. "I should be asking you. In five years, I'll probably be a chronically sleep-deprived zombie, driving a minivan with a bumper sticker that says *I used to be cool.*"

I snort a laugh. "Hey, don't hate on a swagger wagon. And if you do have to trade in, I'll get you one of those stickers that says *Adults on board. We want to live too.*"

Finally, he smiles in earnest. It's like seeing the sun again after the gloom of winter rain, rendering the world in color again.

"Haas . . . you're going to be such a great husband; you don't even know." I try to be clinical. Matter-of-fact. "And a great dad, if that's what you and the missus choose. It's who you are." Patient, kind, smartest person I know—there's no doubt in my mind he'll be an amazing partner and father.

His eyes widen as I speak, and he looks ready to answer, so I rush to vomit out the rest of my words before I chicken out. "As for me, I'll be your friend no matter what." I shrug, trying to offer up my undying loyalty casual-like. "Do what you need to do, and don't worry about me. Okay?"

I turn and leave before he can say anything else, walking into the dusk of a crisp fall night. There's smoke on the wind, some part of California on fire like always. I've lived all over the world, wandered paths that took me thousands of miles from home, trying to escape Brent's radioactive fallout, but I never could drag myself away from this state for good, toxic particulate matter be damned. My roots run too wide and wild, interlocked like those of the redwoods around my family's old home.

It's not until I reach my car that the tears come, streaking my face, ruining my spray tan, lending tiger stripes to my skin.

7

I WAKE UP HUNGOVER, having downed the rest of my soju the night prior, trying and failing to put a certain heiress and Daniel out of my mind.

"Dumb." I look at my streaky orange reflection in the mirror over the sink with disdain. I should've been doing more research on Brent, collecting as much information on him as possible before moving in. At the very least, I should've smoothed out my spray tan so I don't have garish stripes. Even a nonobservant person can tell my glow didn't come from St. Barths. For fuck's sake.

Instead, I let my maudlin tendencies take over, getting stupid drunk and howling at the moon—literally—about the unfairness of it all. I pinch the bridge of my nose. My neighbors must love me. I guess I'll be gone for a while, so maybe that'll give them enough time to forget my drunken serenade.

At least I still have breakfast, courtesy of friend-zone-forever Daniel. I inhale another stupendously good muffin and drink my coffee on the deck, trying to clear out the cobwebs. I need to get my head on straight before I crash-land next to Brent. Not the viper's nest—that would be an insult to snakes, really—but close enough.

Still hungover, I pack my trunk with my costumes and tricks of the trade, then lock up and drive across the Gate again, the last time for the foreseeable future.

The floor plan for my townhouse is ridiculous for one person—not that that's ever stopped the überwealthy before—but I do my best to sprawl my things everywhere, setting something in each room (four in total, with three bathrooms). I'll have to get used to taking up more space, after all. Walking through the world with my Louboutins and White Girl Privilege card at the ready.

Through the windows, I scope out where I'll have the best view of Brent's comings and goings. My master bedroom overlooks his spacious courtyard, a clear shot even with the scaffolding and construction clutter around his home. He'll have a nice view of my shaded patio as well; his property is situated on higher ground.

I smile at my reflection in the glossy windowpane. How fortuitous. I know where I'll set up camp, then. A few props will be all I need.

When I've settled in to my satisfaction, I check my phone. Dinnertime. Shit. I hurry to put together a giant antipasti plate with the groceries I picked up on the way and pour myself some vino. Then I check my reflection in the wall-to-wall mirror in the dining room. Yep, I'm still the perfect amount of skanky: jeans ripped to the point of absurdity, a white tank top just sheer enough, barefoot with red toenails, and loose waves thanks to Noah.

"It's showtime, Lady Justice." I purse my carmine lips. "Tits up. Knives out." Knife strapped to my calf, in fact, but I digress.

I grab my glass of wine and food and saunter out onto the patio, methodically arranging myself like an orb weaver creating her nightly web. The heat of the day is gone, the sky turning a lovely shade of lavender. A cool breeze floats from the ocean, leaving goose bumps on my skin. It's either that, or the thrill of knowing I might come face-to-face with Brent this very evening. Minutes separate me from the man who ruined Gabrielle's life. My family's life. *My* life.

I sip my burgundy and wait, drumming my heels, trying to focus on the cascades of bougainvillea draping over my wall, enclosing me with reds and fuchsia.

The wind shifts, and I catch a whiff of star jasmine from the trellis on my patio. The scent of my sister.

My mind spins, a tide of memories engulfing me. Gabrielle's water-soft voice, murmuring to my ten-year-old self when I woke after a nightmare. I was too old to need comforting, but she climbed into bed and lay next to me to help me fall asleep again anyway. Of course she did.

A door opens from a neighbor's house.

I tense and ignore the stinging in my eyes. Hardening myself. It's tempting to stand and see if it's Brent, but I restrain myself at the last second. Like any controlling fuckwad, he'll live for the charm campaign. The manipulation. Turning my own mind against me.

My grip tightens on the fragile stem of the wineglass, but I take a deep breath and let go. Let him think he can. I'm going to be a splinter and wedge myself so far under his skin he'll never be rid of me.

"I told you I wanted those tiles by the weekend!" A nasal voice that could only be Brent's reaches me over the hedges. "The shipment has already been delayed four fucking times!"

A mumbled apology, much lower in decibels, follows his spitting outburst. I grimace, and the wine tastes sour over my tongue. The poor contractors. Of course he'll love having a crew to boss around and verbally abuse. Tiles seem like an odd thing to freak out over, but hey, whatever preoccupies him is good news for me.

Still, as his tirade continues, I can't bear to sit still and listen any longer.

I stand and wave, jiggling the girls a little. "Excuse me. I'm sorry." I present the contractor and Brent with my best smile, a few shades brighter than normal with bold red lipstick. "I couldn't help but overhear the conversation. Is there anything I can do to help? I do have a few friends in the industry. They might be able to hook you up."

"No thank you." Brent stares at me, the person interrupting. He radiates loathing until he gets a good look.

More than a decade has passed since we were in court, but seeing him again is too much. My blood boils, pumping fast and hot. I take a step forward, then another. Red fog floats into my vision, but he's clear in the aperture. I could kill him, right now. Jump over the ledge with a broken decanter and slit his neck.

Then his demeanor shifts, eel-like, to ingratiating.

I back up. Fix a serene smile on my face, hoping he didn't see my homicidal expression. Fucking Christ, I've already gone and ruined a first impression.

He offers an overbleached smile. "You must be my new neighbor! So sorry you had to hear that. This is the third contracting company I've gone through, and I swear, each one is worse than the last." He strides forward and offers his hand, contractor forgotten. "I'm Brent Wilder."

The contractor gives me a brief nod before ducking away and getting the hell out of Dodge. Well, there's one good deed for today.

"Oh my goodness!" I pretend to be floored. "*The* Brent Wilder? Wow! I just read about you in *The New Yorker*! You're that pharmaceutical guy, right? The CEO?"

"In the flesh." He grins.

I meet his hand, and he grips mine too hard, like he has to prove something. His hand is sweaty, and his nails are too long. It takes everything in my power not to wipe my hand clean on my jeans after I let go.

"Delilah Howard. I hear your company is doing great things. Weren't you the ones shipping a bunch of antimalarials to, like, Africa or something?"

"Yes, that was us." He rocks back on his heels, wearing a smirk. "We've got a phenomenal team, and it was the right thing to do. Philanthropy is so important to our culture at Prometheus."

"Right, of course! That's so great."

"So, are you renting?" He points to my patio. "Or did ol' Greg and Debra finally sell the place?"

"Renting for the time being."

"Throwing your money away, sweetheart." He *tsk*s and shakes his head, angelic blond curls catching the last of the day's light. "You should've bought."

Ah, yes. The unsolicited financial advice. I should've forked over seven million for the townhome. What was I thinking? For real, I should've made a bingo card before I talked to him. It would've livened up my conversations with this supremely boring man.

I look him up and down. He really isn't a bad-looking guy, all things considered. Empirically, I see why he made the 415's hottest bachelors list. He's tall and still has a swimmer's build, but all I see is the vermin beneath his skin suit, the empty blue eyes, like a demented, life-sized Ken doll.

"Oh, I'm not worried." I toss my head and smile, insouciant. "But thanks."

His eyes narrow at my dismissiveness, but a subtle glance at my chest helps his expression smooth out again. Not for the first time, I thank Mom for the great ta-tas.

Then I bite my lip and lower the synthetic eyelashes I glued on this morning. "You know, this might be forward, but I made a ton of food." I gesture to my platter of olives, goat cheese, charcuterie, blood oranges, grapes, sourdough. And, of course, the generous decanter of wine. "I don't suppose you'd care to join me?" I ply him with another demure smile. "I'd love to get to know my neighbor better. It's so hard being new in town."

Brent's eyes glow acetylene blue, and he all but leaps over the hedge separating our yards. "I'd love that."

Hook, line, and sinker. I turn and smile the smile of every Delilah before me.

*   *   *

Hours later, Brent's fair skin glows a shade of aubergine. With my generous refills, it didn't take him long to get drunk, and snippy besides. I expected this—he didn't seem like the sort to be a happy drunk—but it still takes considerable willpower not to roll my eyes as he drones on and on, spewing a never-ending litany of grievances, slights against his person, and mortal wounds to his ego. I haven't been trying to get a word in edgewise—all part of my role to play—but even if I had, I doubt I would've been able to.

"And then, when I asked her out, she had the nerve to tell me she's engaged." He sloshes more wine down his gullet. For a self-professed connoisseur, he's not taking the time to appreciate the subtle chocolate and blackberry notes anymore. "I mean, what the fuck? I'd been talking to her for weeks. Way to waste a guy's time."

"That sounds awful." I refill his glass. Really, someone should give me an Oscar for my performative himpathy. "Who does something like that?" How dare his new personal assistant be in a committed relationship and not spread her legs for Brent at the first available opportunity!

He leans closer, swaying. "Right? See, I knew you'd get it." He points at my general vicinity. "I had a good feeling about you the second I saw you."

I smile, bland and empty-headed. I doubt if he remembers my name. I doubt if he could fathom the ways he's shaped my world: everything from my profession to trust issues a mile wide.

As for my dry spell, we're not going to talk about that.

With a pang, I wonder how Daniel and Yoon So Ah are getting on. An image search of the heiress was not reassuring. She nearly matches him for height and was crushingly beautiful in a recent photograph from a charity event, with black hair that fell to her waist in a silky sheet and delicate, fine-boned features.

"Are you listening?" Brent pouts with a narcissist's awareness that my attention has lapsed, even though he's three sheets to the wind. "I said you looked familiar."

Danger, danger. It's possible he might recognize me from court ages ago. I smile brightly, wondering if he somehow sees past my disguise, though he doesn't look cogent enough to recognize himself in the mirror, much less anyone from his distant past. Still, better to cut our Meet Stab short.

"Sorry. Yeah, I hear that a lot. I guess I just have one of those faces." I fake a yawn and stretch my arms overhead, hoping he'll take the hint. "Anyway, it's been a long day. I'm going to turn in."

"You're not going to invite me over for a tour?" He smiles with purple-stained teeth to maybe show he's joking, but the humor is a thin veneer.

"To see my moving boxes?" I shake my head, laughing him off. "If anything, you should invite me over."

I'm genuinely wiped but hold my breath, waiting on his answer. It's taken a good bit of persuasion to lower his guard, and this would be the perfect opportunity. I don't think he'll notice me taking a few furtive pictures in his current state.

He hears the unspoken challenge, though, despite being drunk. "Sure, sweetheart. I'll show you right now." He stands. "After all, that'd be the neighborly thing to do."

"Fun! Okay. I'll drink to that." I clink my glass against his and pretend to gulp the rest of my wine, letting only a small splash reach the back of my throat. "Let's go!"

Inside his home, it's just as ridiculous as I expected. How many ornamental columns are too many? Or sculptures of scantily clad women? In my head, I tick off another bingo space, with women as objets d'art. Further proof money buys a lot of things—Daddy's money bought his exoneration, for one—but good taste sure as shit ain't one of them.

I follow him into the living room, noting the indoor cameras. It's dimly lit, with a men's club atmosphere, a weird, three-sided (oh you so fancy!) fireplace jutting from one wall, oversized leather chairs, and a zebra pelt on the floor. Mounted heads of exotic animals stare at me, lifeless. Between that and the deep-purple walls, I'm getting a real Vegas magician vibe. Maybe this won't be a total exercise in masochism—I could submit a photo to my favorite social media account for hideous interior design.

Brent turns and pauses, presumably to let me fawn over his trophies. Gross.

"You must be a hunter." I hide my distaste with dulcet, admiring tones.

He chest puffs. "Bagged this one last time I went to South Africa." He points to a probably endangered animal on the wall like he's fucking Gaston, and it takes all my self-discipline not to make a joke about compensating. I can't wait to tell Daniel what a tool this guy is.

"So, do you work much from home these days?" I ask, hoping he'll take the bait.

"Not especially." He cuts me a sharp look.

I lift a brow, exaggerating my surprise.

He backtracks, slicker than expected given how much wine he's had. "I spend more time at the office than I do at home. Should set up a cot and be done with it." He offers a deprecating smile. "You know how it is. Rise and grind."

I nod like I care about his hustle-culture nonsense.

Brent continues down a long hallway with too many chandeliers, then veers upstairs. I follow at a discreet distance and take photos on my burner phone of every room we pass, mentally mapping the floor plan and oohing and aahing at appropriate intervals as he whines about the slow pace of renovations, tile sourced from Morocco, salvaged lumber from some monastery in Spain, so many champagne problems in one place I'm surprised the entire home doesn't create a gravity-dense singularity and collapse into itself.

Unfortunately, no black hole opens to swallow the skin-suit monster for me.

Absent a black hole, I'd love to crush a few pipes, let gravity do the rest of the work, and watch his home rot.

Still, those are small things. Homes can be repaired (and the contractors wouldn't appreciate my fuckery). I grimace, wine sitting heavy in my stomach, discarding that option. If I want to end this monster's life as he knows it, I'll need to go bigger. Much bigger. Expose his company's fraud. Find the evidence, somewhere in this house, if Dr. Chang's hunch is correct. I didn't see an office on the tour, and the omission feels deliberate.

Back on the ground floor, I try to buy myself time to sneak around.

"Mind if I use the bathroom?" I ask. "That wine caught up to me."

He makes a brief moue of distaste before nodding. "Right down that hallway, last door on your left."

"Sweet, thank you. Be right back." I put extra sway in my step and pad down the hallway, checking each door I pass, hoping one of them might be his office. Might be the pin on the grenade I'll pull, blowing his life to bits.

The glow of a computer screen catches my attention. The office. I hazard a glimpse over my shoulder, but Brent's nowhere to be seen.

I dart in, phone at hand. Looking for anything valuable. I have minutes to make use of his ill-considered lapse. Maybe seconds.

Footsteps.

Fuck.

"Delilah?" Brent stands in the doorway, stone-faced. "What are you doing?"

"I couldn't help but admire the art." I wave to the wall, covered with a contemporary work, an abstract oil portrait of a woman, face and limbs distorted by lines of code. It's repugnant, like everything else in his home. "I'm not familiar with this artist, though."

Brent steps into the room. "You were taking pictures." There's ice in his voice, enough to float a few hairs on the back of my neck. How could I forget the flip side of delusional omnipotence: all-consuming paranoia? "Did you send them to someone?"

"Just trying to get an idea of your style so I can send it to my designer." My voice is too high. Like someone has a hand around my throat. I silence my phone and shove it in my jeans pocket. "She did an amazing job working on my condo in South Beach."

"I don't give a fuck about your condo." He holds out his hand. "Give me your phone."

I raise my brows. "I don't think so."

"It wasn't a question." He approaches me, looming, using the oldest trick in the book to try and intimidate. As if might ever made right.

"I'll delete the pictures if you want"—I raise a hand— "but I'm not about to give you my phone."

He stops a few inches from me, leaning over. Fury blazes in his pale-blue irises. It occurs to me he's not as drunk as he led me to believe.

Well, that makes two of us.

My knife, strapped to my ankle, burns through my jeans, but I don't move. Fail this test, and he won't respect me enough to let me into his inner sanctum. And that's where I need to be to hurt him, deep in the heart of darkness.

Then he throws his head back and laughs. "Oh my God! You should've seen your face." He wheezes like it's the funniest thing he's ever seen, a hiccupping hyena sound. "The artist is Kent Johnson. Good friend of mine."

If I didn't need to worm into his life, I'd split him balls to brain. I could do it in less time than it'd take to shout, *Eat the rich, minus Daniel!*

Instead, I laugh along. "Brent!" I hit his arm, scolding. "You really had me going there."

"Tell me the name of your designer," he says. "I'll reach out to her."

"Sure! What's your email? I'll send you her info."

He pauses, considering whether to allow me access.

Something in my vacant expression must convince him, because he lists his email. *Score!* Daniel will make quick work of his home security account with this. I send Amanda's contact information to Brent from my burner. She's an actual interior designer, someone I met at Noah's salon a few years ago. I briefed her ahead of time that a call might be coming her way, but told her to not do business with this person for any reason. If he follows through, she'll plead busyness and beg off the project, which will make him feel inferior and waste his time. I get my digs in where I can.

"And your number?" Brent asks.

I smile like a cat with the canary in my teeth. "If you need a cup of sugar, hmm?"

He bites his lip and returns my smile.

I give him the burner number.

Looking pleased, he stows his phone in his back pocket.

"Well, thank you for the grand tour. It was lovely getting to know you better, Brent." I wink. "Hope Amanda can help you out."

"Don't you need to use the bathroom?"

I shake my head. "I'll go at home. But thank you."

"Thank *you* for the referral," he says, Mr. Congeniality now that he has my number. "Let me walk you to the door. This place is easy to get lost in."

"No need." I back up, keeping my smile in place. "I'll see you around?"

His smile shifts, eyes gleaming with interest. "Count on it."

He likes the flirtation, that much is clear. It makes me nauseous, but as predicted, that's proven the quickest way into his good graces, so I'll have to keep it up.

When I'm clear of his home, prickling tension seeps out of my shoulders and neck. That was too close. Besides that, it's exhausting pretending to be someone else.

A glance at my burner phone shows it's close to midnight. As I lock my townhouse door behind me, my real phone chimes from the kitchen with a text. Daniel, maybe? Letting me know his date with the heiress was a resounding failure?

Not Daniel, but Gabrielle, of all people.

This sounds strange, but I got a weird feeling just now, like you were in danger? Or some kind of trouble? Text me when you can and let me know I'm paranoid.

I blink at the string of words on my screen, grasping at a response. Willing away the ache in my throat. How could she possibly know?

Then again, how could she have known when I broke my arm on the playground in second grade? Or the time a drunk driver almost made me wrap my car around a tree my junior year? Like Mom and her tarot cards and crystals in the back of her salon, Gabrielle's always seemed tuned to a different frequency. She's always looked out for me. If there were any justice in the world, I'd have been able to do the same for her.

As it is, I'll have to do my best with my version of retroactive restitution. Not that I can tell her what I'm doing. She won't approve. In fact, she'd be horrified. My parents too. *It's in the past, Dylan. Let it be.* It's only me who can't let go of the way this sonofabitch cracked our family open and dragged us through hell, shattering the future my brilliant sister should've had.

Her full ride to Cal, gone. My parents' meager savings, gone. Eaten by legal fees and medical bills, the cost of surviving.

Moving out of our home in the redwoods when the death threats to my sister came. We couldn't afford to stay anyway, and if there hadn't been money to send Gabrielle to undergrad to begin with, there sure as hell wasn't money to send me. Years later, she got her psychology degree at Cal Poly Humboldt by way of several grants, but mostly loans.

By some miracle, my parents remained together through it all, though I don't know how. Any marriage could've cracked under the strain. *I* cracked under the strain, hearing everyone cry through thin walls when we should've all been asleep.

I shake it off and type, *You're not paranoid, you're a good sister. Doing fine in the city but thank you for checking in anyway. Just sleepy.* 😊

Get some rest then 😘, she answers. *Little night owl. Thanks for letting me know you're okay.*

I stop fighting the tears, then, and let them come. My heart won't ever be quiet on this. The hurt runs too deep, a canyon dividing me before and after. Only an act of God could seal the gap. There's nothing to do but lean into the path I've chosen, full of wrath. Like a thermophile, I'll find new sustenance from the heat of my hatred.

A quick glance through my window reveals a dim shape on Brent's balcony. I might've known.

If there was ever a sight to dry my tears, harden my resolution, that'd be it.

In the bathroom, I peel off my eyelashes and remove my heavy makeup, brush my newly whitened teeth.

With the lamps in my bedroom on, drapes open, I peel my tank top overhead and let it fall to the floor, leaving my lacy bra on. Then I slide my jeans off my hips, exposing my skimpy boy shorts, angling my body so he's sure to have a view of my second-best end, if I do say so myself.

He'll wonder what he did to be so lucky. Marvel at the gift that dropped from the sky into his waiting arms. He'll keep wondering until I drive my knife into his neck and twist.

Not literally, of course.

Though never say never.

The thought brings a smile to my face, relaxes me enough to yawn. I crawl into my expansive king bed and use the remote to turn off the lights.

I'll be hearing from Brent soon. I all but guaranteed it.

While I'm looking at my phone, ready to send Daniel a text, let him know I'm no worse for wear and tell him the brand of Brent's alarm system, a typing bubble appears from him.

It's so late—though it's not unheard of for him to text at odd hours, the poor insomniac. I stare at the hovering bubble, wondering what he has for me.

The bubble disappears into the ether.

I send my message and wait and wait. And wait.

No reply comes.

8

*G*OOD *MORNING, SUNSHINE! I'm swamped with meetings this morning, but if you're available, I'd love to take you out for lunch, show you around the neighborhood.*

A text from good ol' Brent, the last person I want to talk to, greets me when I wake up. I groan and flop back on the pillow. High-thread-count sheets or no, I don't need a mirror to know I look worse for wear—I stayed up stupid late thinking about Gabrielle and wondering what Daniel typed and erased, then typed and erased. The chickenshit. Just hit send!

Still, obvious interest from Brent plays to my advantage. That's why I'm here, for God's sake. Not to sit and drive myself bananas pondering the contents of Daniel's indecipherable mind.

I sit up, wipe the loathing off my face, and type a suitably chipper reply.

Hey neighbor! 😊 *I'd love that. Still unpacking this morning, but maybe later for dinner?*

That ought to buy me more time to get myself ready, get my backstory straight. Get my meds lined up so I can search his home while he's occupied.

There's a long pause. I might've overplayed my hand, tried to make things more "serious" than Brent's aiming for. I nibble on a hangnail, wincing at the sting.

Dinner it is. What kind of food do you like? We can leave from my place. 6 PM.

Well, look at him trying to take my opinions into account. He must really want in my pants. I snicker and type.

Six is good. And I'm open to anything!

There. Let him read into that however he will. I bet he'll like the high-maintenance look + low-self-esteem + nonassertive vibe, because he's a worthless sack of shit.

Looking forward to it. Wear something nice, Brent says. *Nothing too revealing.*

Of course he'll tell me how to dress myself, like I'm a child. My grip tightens, causing the plastic case to creak. God, I *hate* him. I'll be lucky if I don't stab him before I'm done fucking him over.

I throw the burner phone on the bed, only to pick my other phone up when a text arrives.

Dinner at my place tonight? Daniel asks. *I'll cook. I managed to infiltrate his security and want to show you how it's done.*

I bite my hangnail, wondering why he's not spending time with the heiress.

You work fast, but no can do, I reply. *I have a hot date with Brent.* I add several vomit emojis in case he doesn't read my internet sarcasm.

There's a pause and I smile, imagining his gears turning.

You don't waste time, Lady Justice. When will you be free, then?

Not sure. I'll keep you posted? I don't mean to be coy, but I don't know how quickly things will move with Brent and need to keep my options open. I imagine he'll try the charm offensive and try to add another notch to his bedpost as quickly as possible, and that suits me too. The less time spent with him, the better.

Okay.

My, my. The "okay" with a period at the end? Stern Daniel is a force to be reckoned with. I should stay focused and not go out of my way to make time for him, but it doesn't stop me from typing a placating message anyway.

I plan to cut things short tonight, so I'll try to swing over later.

How will you cut it short, exactly? he asks after a minute.

If I don't tell you, you'll have plausible deniability. 😇 😈

All right, he says, *but for the record, I'm happy being your accomplice.*

I sigh at my phone and Daniel's general direction. Why does he have to say things like that and melt my cold heart into a sappy puddle? I can't afford softness. To slay the ogre, I'll need my armor well intact, thank you very much.

Still, I can't deny that the possibility of seeing Daniel tonight puts a spring in my step as I slip into my new uniform of ripped jeans, camisole, and heels.

The first order of business will be shopping. Delilah needs a cocktail dress for dinner. Something to knock Brent's head sideways, dull his senses, direct his thoughts where I want them. Brent might have wealth and the blessing of good looks and generations of privilege on his side, but I have weapons of my own too. With luck, they'll be more than enough to do him in.

* * *

At six PM sharp, I leave my home and walk next door, stilettos clicking on the pavement. My jade-green, long-sleeved, knee-length sheath dress with an open back and sheer black stockings do not at all fit the definition of "nothing too revealing," and if Brent has anything to say about it, he can pound sand. Or meet the end of my knife, currently strapped to my lacy garter belt.

"Delilah!" Brent opens the door, wearing a crisp ivory suit and a broad smile. "I'm so glad you could make it tonight!" He steps aside, ushering me across the divide with a deliberate hand across my back. Apparently, he likes the getup, despite his admonition.

He takes a second to scrutinize. "Your hair is pretty," he says inside, evaluating the loose waves with critical eyes. "But you should go blonder."

"Not sure how much lighter I could go," I say. "It's already pretty blonde."

"Platinum," he says, so sure I'll contort myself to fit his moving-goalpost prerequisites.

"Sure, handsome." I smile with all the sugar I can muster. "Whatever you think is best."

He nods, satisfied for the next thirty seconds or so.

I follow him inside his house, through the expansive kitchen he probably never cooks in to the multicar garage. The usual excess appears, several luxury cars so expensive each could house a family for a year. He clicks the button, and a convertible Beemer flashes orange lights.

"So, where are we headed?" I ask.

"Steak house," he says. "Hope you're not one of those hopeless vegans."

I roll my eyes to his back, patience thinning already. "What if I am?" I don't follow a plant-based diet, but if I did, I would've told him to fuck off. Actually, that would've happened about five minutes into our conversation the night prior.

He turns around. "You're joking, right?"

I shrug and smile. Socialite Delilah must play along. "You got me."

The frown deepens. "That's not funny."

"Lighten up, neighbor." I'm slipping from character, but God, there's nothing worse than someone with no sense of humor, incapable of the slightest bit of self-deprecation. "I love me some surf and turf."

Seeming to realize he's making an ass of himself, he smiles, but it looks like an effort. If I were really trying to win him over, it'd be exhausting, trying to pacify someone with the thinnest of skins. No wonder he treated my sister's accusation as if it were some deliberately cruel wound rather than, you know, facing the consequences of his own heinous behavior. It's always someone else's fault.

He peels out of his garage like it's on fire. At the steak house, the maître d' greets Brent by first name and makes a huge fuss getting us settled in a quiet, wood-paneled nook.

Brent soaks up the fawning like an incubus and smiles across the candlelit table at me. "This place has a three-month waitlist for reservations," he says, as if he's divulging state secrets. "Unless you're me. Aren't you lucky?"

"Well, I hope it lives up to its reputation." I smile sweetly and place my napkin across my lap, prim and proper. "My last boyfriend's father owned half the Michelin-starred restaurants in Europe, so fair warning, my standards are high."

Brent smiles into his wineglass, already filled with his favorite Tempranillo, but his eyes are cold. Like he's considering ways to dissect me, slowly.

I hide my laughter with a cough into my napkin. He might be cool on the outside, but I'm getting under his skin. The temptation to rile him more is strong, but I'll have to pace myself. Can't have him throwing a mantrum and storming off on our first date. When would I get to dump MiraLAX into his drink, then? And search his office while he's ocupado?

A long slurp of wine later, he leans forward on his elbows. "So. Tell me about yourself, Delilah." His sharp blue gaze is trained on me, as if I'm the only person in the room. His attention might be flattering if I didn't know I was about to endure a Spanish Inquisition.

I'm ready, though. All day, I solidified the details of my alleged identity, leaving a digital globe-trotting trail. It's more work than I need to do, but on the off chance Brent does investigate my background, it'll be suitably boring.

I take a careful sip of my own wine—Tempranillo for me too, because Delilah likes whatever her man likes—and launch into my spiel. "There's not much to know, really. My mom died when I was young. My father was a wealthy expat, and we lived all over the place. Europe mostly. When he died"—I look at my lap, blinking hard—"he left me more than enough to pursue whatever I wanted to do with my life. School, art, charity, travel. Sums up the last decade of my life, really."

Brent buys it wholesale so far as I can tell, nodding along.

"And what brought you to San Francisco?" he asks when I'm done. "More charitable endeavors?" The way he says it lets me know how much respect he has for good causes. To people like him, only fools would willingly part with their money. They could own the entire world and it still wouldn't be enough to satisfy.

"A bad breakup, actually." I let ice sneak into my voice, enough to put him on alert. "My ex agreed to take SoCal."

"So you're on the rebound." He likes this. Emotionally vulnerable means easier to manipulate. Or it would if I weren't ready to slip him meds that'll make him shit himself.

"I wouldn't put it like that," I say. "That makes me sound easy." I giggle and drink more wine.

Brent smiles, pure predation, and obsequiously refills my wineglass. Let him think I'm on my way to drunken debauchery. It'll make his expectations-versus-reality moment more bitter when the night does *not* end with me in his bed.

The wine bottle empty, Brent snaps his fingers, like he's some sort of Mafia don. "Excuse me, can we get a little help over here?" Then he glances at me, as if I'm supposed to be impressed with petty tyranny. I keep my smile in place like an over-Botoxed Stepford wife.

A tall, jacked server in her forties with a bitchin' bleached blonde undercut materializes and returns with a new bottle, apologizing about the delay. I bite my lip so I don't pipe up and tell her to take it easy. I'm sure waitstaff absolutely *adore* Brent. If I worked here, I'd make sure to drop the steak on the floor a few times before dishing it up. I prepare to leave an enormous tip for her trouble.

"What about you? What's your story?" I ask Brent when our food arrives. "I'm sure I could read up online and learn the basics, but I hope you don't mind if I ask you instead."

"My family is mostly on the East Coast. I came out to Cal for school, then dropped out when I was ready to start my company."

After you were expelled for assaulting my sister, you mean. The revisionist history is revolting. It's as if she never existed, not even as a small bump on his path toward preordained greatness. Not that I expected him to confess outright, but anyone could see the allegations on his Wikipedia page, under "Controversies." What a fucking euphemism.

I force myself to smile. Lower my steak knife back to the table. It would've been so easy to slam it in the thin skin between his thumb and forefinger. Pin him down and watch him writhe.

I take a deep breath and clear away the red bleeding into my vision. "And you've been unicorning all over the place since." The thready note in my voice could be admiration, overwhelm in the presence of genius.

He laughs, looking pleased. "What can I say? Prometheus has been a dream come true. There's nothing a strong vision and hard work can't accomplish."

Hard work and a shit ton of intergenerational wealth, but I'm just splitting hairs. I dig into my petite filet mignon and use the segue of food to question him further, my phone recording all the while. I don't know if he'll answer, but I hope he'll love the opportunity to brag a little more.

"What's on the horizon for Prometheus? Anything exciting?"

He considers his rib eye and then looks up at me, wine languor gone. "Who wants to know?"

". . . Me?"

He chews his steak, considering. "Well, naturally, we have several new products in the pipeline." His smile is a sneer, hitching up the corner of his mouth. "But I wouldn't want to bore you with the science."

Well, well. Looks like I hit a nerve. The eager way he pounces lets me know he couldn't wait to take me down a peg.

"Fair. I am an art history major, after all." I throw back more red, hoping I look like a buzzed wine floozy. He might still confide a few useful details if he thinks I'm too dumb to even condescend to. Just another founder hounder out for his gold.

I wait a few more beats, but there's no apology for insulting my intelligence. "What should we talk about, then?" I try to keep the bite from my words, but my patience is running thin. "May I have an approved list of topics?"

"Well." He clears his throat. "You could tell me about your family."

"There's no one, really, aside from an aunt." I'm prepared for this probe into my past. "But mostly me."

"I have you all to myself?" The abuser in the making lifts a pale brow. No family means fewer people to notice when he pulls me away from them, an ever-widening divide.

"Looks that way." I smile at his obvious pleasure. "Aren't *you* lucky?"

"To serendipitous neighbors." He lifts his glass. "Though I must say, I feel like I've known you longer."

Unease sends shivers across my skin. His words are warm, but my paranoia lifts another notch.

I lift my glass and meet his toast. "Well, when you have a connection," I smile as if I can't believe my remarkable good fortune, "you just know."

He sits back, looking pleased.

Dinner is a rare delight, so long as I don't think about what's probably been done to our food thanks to Brent's nasty behavior toward waitstaff. Unfortunately, it takes forever for him to drink enough to need to use the bathroom. When he finally excuses himself, I fish the laxative out of my handbag and quickly pour the powder into the cap under the table.

We're in a secluded nook, walled off from the other restaurant patrons, but I still hesitate. If someone sees me drugging his wine, it's over.

Just as I'm about to dump the huge capful of "medicine" in, the server appears to clear our plates.

I freeze, gaze locked with hers.

"I'm doing this for the good of humanity." It's both the absolute truth and the only thing I can think of.

"That I don't doubt. Also, thanks. You won me ten bucks." She lights up with a crooked grin.

"I did?"

"I had a bet going with the other servers. Knew damn well there was something else going on here. Smokeshow like you, hanging out with that colossal douche?" She shakes her head and lowers her voice. "A word to the wise: Wilder harasses the female waitstaff every time he's here. I volunteered to take this table because he doesn't give me any shit."

"Hmm. I wonder why." I gesture to her ripped forearms, covered with exquisite ink.

Her grin returns. "All that's to say, we're ready to call a rideshare for you if you need to run. Just blink three times."

"Did we just become best friends?" I laugh. "I really appreciate the support, but don't worry, I know who I'm dealing with. I'll take care of him."

She evaluates me a beat, then takes my plate, green eyes twinkling. "I'm sure you will." As she backs away to the kitchen, she makes the Katniss three-finger salute. "But I didn't see anything."

I'm smiling so hard when Brent comes back. Naturally, he can't help but think he's the reason—of course he thinks this song is about him. Nothing in the world has told him different. Not yet, anyway.

"Do you want to come over after this?" he asks. "I'd love to show you more of the work done on the reno."

I'm sure you would. "By the way." I consider my wine, pretending not to have heard his question. "Did my designer ever get in touch with you?"

"No, actually." He twirls his wineglass, restless.

"Really? How odd." *Don't laugh, don't laugh.*

"Yeah, well." He leans forward on his elbows. "You'd think she'd want another client, especially someone with my profile, but some people are just lazy, I guess."

Before I can set the record straight on Amanda's work ethic, even if it's breaking character, he interrupts. "But you didn't answer my question. Do you want to come over?" He directs one hundred percent of his focus to me, twitching with anticipation. As though I'm another cut of meat he can't wait to carve up.

"I don't know." I sip more vino, hoping he'll do the same, and meet his hungry gaze across the table. "What will you think of me if I do?"

"I'll think you're a woman who knows what she wants."

It's a decent line. I pretend to buy it, as if I can't help myself. "Sure. I'm a hard sell, huh?" I make myself laugh. Keep it light, keep it vapid. "You better drink up, then."

He downs the rest of his red, and I glow happy pink for all the wrong reasons. This will be fun to watch when I go to Daniel's and hack into Brent's home security.

"You don't want dessert, do you?" he asks.

I could take the question any number of ways, but I'm sure he's critiquing my weight. It might have something to do with his unsubtle comments about my "hearty" appetite and the fact that I finished my steak. Heaven forbid I eat to satiety. I'm fit as a gymnast, curvy and muscular, but sure, guy. Go ahead and try to crack the foundations of my self-esteem. The irony is that if I hadn't eaten well, he'd have found a way to critique that too. Might as well enjoy my meal.

"Of course I want dessert," I say, mostly to annoy him. He won't dare contradict me if there's sex on the table. "I always have my cake and eat it too, Brent."

He frowns but acquiesces when our server reappears with our dessert menu. While he sips black coffee and looks on disapprovingly, I devour my chocolate cheesecake and don't share a single bite.

CHAPTER

9

I'M FULL AND content when we leave the restaurant. He shouldn't be driving right now—I still smell the alcohol on his breath, even at a distance—but somehow we make it the few blocks home without getting into an accident.

Inside his garage, I ready myself for the onslaught, adrenaline flowing. His laxative won't take effect that soon. In the meantime, I need to be ready for the wheedling and whining and coercion.

Or violence.

He leads me up to the main floor.

I spy the front door and pace toward it, pretending to admire the enormous painting by the entryway. He follows, a few steps too close.

"I had a nice time tonight." I turn and face him. Neutral. Noncommittal. "Thank you for taking me out for dinner."

"I did too, babe." He leans in, caging me against the wall.

Babe? Ew.

Then he mashes his mouth against mine. He's aggressive, lips hard, trying to force my mouth open. I gasp for air, and he takes it as encouragement, panting with excitement, pressing me against the door.

After a few awkward seconds, I push against his chest.

Finally, he breaks off, breathing hard, eyes unfocused.

I could be anyone. Anyone with a hole he can fill. There was nothing personal in the kiss. It was a battle to see who might capitulate first.

"Will you stay for a drink?" He seems nervous, maybe because I haven't said anything. The words are clipped, broken off. His gaze hasn't left me since we stepped outside the restaurant, like he's afraid I'll wise up to the danger he presents and run.

"No thank you." Inwardly, I curse and thrash, smarting with disappointment that I'll miss this chance to investigate, but I can't stay here. Not when the fine hairs on my body are afloat. "My head still feels heavy after all that wine." He drank most of the two bottles, but it's a convenient enough excuse.

"No to the drink, or no to staying?" He shifts to high alert, panicked energy radiating around him. Like a child about to have a new, shiny toy taken away.

"Both." I smile brightly. "I'll see you later, neighbor. Good night." I sidestep the cage he's made and edge away, aiming for the door.

"Wait a minute." He grabs my wrist, hard. A man who knows his strength and doesn't check it. "I thought . . ."

I look at his hand, then at him. "You thought?"

"Fucking tease," he slurs. Murder brews in his glazed irises, control slipping. "You wanted to come over. You *let* me think that. Throwing yourself at me."

"Did you get that impression?" I wrench my arm away, blazing with hatred. "Whether I have sex with you is *my* prerogative, Brent. It's not something you're owed. In case you forgot."

Several tense moments pass. My hand hovers over the knife strapped to my thigh.

Then he breaks.

"You're right." He grimaces and looks at his shoes, affecting a chastened demeanor. "I shouldn't have pushed. Tell me I didn't ruin things?"

"I don't make any promises." Regrets over drugging him? Hell no. I'm just sad I'll have missed a chance to snoop and find the original data. The countdown with Rhys has begun, and this setback hurts. "Call me. Or don't." I open the door and click down the front steps.

Walking away is a gamble—he might decide I'm too much work, go find someone else to manipulate—but I'm betting big he'll relish the challenge. I count under my breath. *Five, four, three—*

"Delilah, wait." Footsteps clatter down the smooth marble steps. He catches my arm again, gently this time. "Listen. I didn't mean what I said. I've had too much to drink."

Yes, you did. You've had enough wine to let me see the monster. Your real self.

I sigh and summon a patient smile. "That's fair."

"Can I call you later? Try this again?" His hand strokes up my arm, eyes big blue pools. He knows how to turn on the charm when he needs to. I'm sure it's worked well for him before.

He still hasn't apologized, though. I wonder if he's capable.

"Yeah. I'd like that." I force another smile.

Looking placated, he leans in for another kiss. A chaste one this time, sober and closed-mouthed. Then he backs away, smiling broadly. Hope springing eternal.

I wave and keep my smile plastered on as long as I can.

Then I take the long way back around my block to cool off, so I won't march back over and set his house on fire while he's on the porcelain throne.

Inside my townhome, I text Daniel. It's later than I planned, but maybe he'll still be up.

May I drop in?? I add a few prayer hands emojis. *Or is it too late?* I'll have to sneak out so Brent doesn't notice me departing, but I'll worry about that later.

Anything for you, Dylan, he says. *Come on over.*

No emojis or other inflection. It's too easy to read the statement as is. *Anything for you, Dylan.* Too easy to think he means it. My smile is real as I step out of my stilettos and sigh with relief, swapping them for flats. I'm tempted to change out of my dress and stockings, but I don't want to waste any more time. Better to focus on brushing my teeth, washing the taste of Brent out of my mouth, and swiping on gloss.

Outside, I order a rideshare, setting my pickup location as the cul-de-sac at the end of Vallejo Street, well out of Brent's sight.

There's no light from inside Brent's house. I think I'm safe, but if he asks, I can always say I had to run out to pick something up, cough-cough-that-time-of-the-month. The horror of menstruation will shut down any more questioning. Still, I lock my front door as quietly as possible. Better not to rouse more suspicion.

With a final glance over my shoulder, I take off, clattering down the Lyon Street Steps like I've escaped Alcatraz.

* * *

It's a quick ride to Daniel's place on Webster. He meets me in the gorgeous black marble lobby of his building, still wearing his work clothes, but he's swapped out contacts for black, thick-framed glasses, a lethal turn of events I wasn't ready for.

Closer, however, he looks tired. Dark smudges of lavender glow beneath his eyes. Up late with the heiress? I'd be surprised if so, but my mind travels the slick channels of jealousy anyway.

Even tired, he's silly handsome. Erudite, rumpled Daniel is a welcome sight after spending too much time with Brent, after my setback. I quicken my steps, a big smile stretching across my face.

His eyes widen when he sees my dress from multiple angles. "How was your date?" His voice is taut, just like the muscles around his mouth.

"Así así. Yours?" I smile like I don't know what he's upset about. He has no right.

He frowns and gestures for me to lead the way upstairs, so I hike up my tight dress to free my thighs and hoof it.

He makes an odd, choked-off sound. Like he took a punch.

"What's up?" I ask.

His gaze darts back up to my face, a suspiciously blank expression on his.

Realization dawns. I look at my leg, seeing the lacy seam of my thigh-highs peeking out beneath the hem of my dress. My face heats.

"My bad." I pull it down, resigned to a slow climb up the stairs. "Can't take me anywhere, can you?" I smile over my shoulder.

Daniel follows my lead, walking slowly, scowling.

"Well?" I ask, desperate to shift the conversation. "How's the heiress?"

His voice is low and full of shadows in the echoing stairwell, sending goose bumps down my spine. "She's lovely, like I remember. Smart, kind. Beautiful."

"Lucky man. So Ah sounds like the complete package." I catch my breath on the landing of the fourth floor, then push into the hallway and wait by his door.

"She would be if I loved her."

A thrill shoots through my veins. Pure, uncut opiates, a warm wave flowing to every small capillary. Still, I face him and say what a friend should.

"Give her another chance, Haas." He shouldn't whine. If all goes well, he'll marry into one of the wealthiest families in South Korea. He could do so much good with the largesse, more than he does already. Certainly far more than he could slumming with me and my petty attempts at retribution. For God's sake, I couldn't even complete my first mission with Brent.

Daniel looks down at me, backlit by the glow of the recessed lights in the hallway, black hair turning espresso brown. His mouth works, as if he's trying out words and rejecting them. Trying and giving up. So much of himself he keeps hidden.

"I could listen to anyone else say that," he finally says. "But not you."

"What do you mean?" I can barely hear over the roar of blood in my ears.

He's close, leaning down. So close my back touches the cold metal of his door and his warmth reaches me from inches away, seeping through the thin fabric of my dress. I breathe shallowly, waiting and wondering, neck and face blooming with heat. Not even the chill of the door on my bare skin cools me off.

It'd be like this with him in bed, I think. Blistering focus, hot enough to blast away all the walls and mazes and trapdoors on the way to my heart. He'd find a way.

"I mean . . ." He swallows, and his gaze drops to my mouth.

It's so quiet in the dim, hushed hallway. Just the soft rustle of his clothing as he steps closer, well into my space.

Just my heart crashing against my ribs.

I take a shaky breath, trying to clear away the lust saturating my blood, but it's a mistake. He smells divine, warm clothes tinged with lemon, anchored by something deeper, cedary, basal. Irresistible.

Tipping my face up to his is the most natural thing in the world. We know each other, our angles and dimensions. I wait, jaw tilted, hoping for something I can't even articulate, much less voice aloud.

That's not true, really.

But how to tell my best friend I want him to devour me? How to say I ache to disappear inside him? I'd let him do anything he wanted, anything he asked. I'd let him consume me, body and mind. My trust in him is bottomless.

The realization relights my frontal cortex. Slows my lizard brain roll. I could never go down this road with Daniel because I'd never recover. I'd lose myself.

More importantly, he's not for me. A beautiful woman traveled across the Pacific to marry him, and if I were Yoon So Ah, I'd hate me. Hate me for interfering. For not letting go gracefully. For not letting go at all, from all outward appearances.

"Haas."

His eyes are closed, a firm line drawn between his brows. A vein in his forehead stands out. "Yeah?" His Adam's apple bobs, and he opens his eyes, blinking.

"Should we go in?"

Rue curls the edge of his mouth. A dimple divots his cheek. "We should."

I ache to reach and push the heavy black hair away from his face. See what swam in his eyes seconds ago, before I spoke. Too late now. His serene mask is back, high color in his skin gone, as if the last seconds of exquisite torture never existed.

Meanwhile, my hands are still numb. Unfair, considering he didn't even touch me. I grimace as he unlocks the door and ushers me inside his home. Riding the knife edge with him hurts, but the masochism is strong in this one.

I take off my shoes. He does the same, setting our comically different sizes by the door.

"Can I get you anything?" he asks. "I know you ate already, but something to drink?"

"Water would be great, please." *To pour over my head.*

"Sparkling?"

"You know me well." I borrow his words as he hands me a tall glass of fizzing water.

The only source of light is the fire flickering in the gas fireplace, lending a warm patina to everything in the apartment. Too intimate by half, but it's too late to tuck tail and run. Dammit.

While he settles at his desktop abutting the floor-to-ceiling windows, I gulp the water down in greedy bursts. Hoping the ice will cool me off, lighten the flush of arousal across my neck and chest. It's not visible under my high-necked dress, but it glows across my skin, scarlet splotches marking me as well as any brand. Serves me right for the X-rated thoughts filling my brain, pushing against my skull, demanding to be acted upon. *For God's sake, Dylan. Get a grip.*

Water consumed, I pad over to him and lean over his shoulder. "So, what do you have for me?"

He types away, long fingers rolling over the ergonomic keyboard in a smooth, rippling motion, entering lines of code I couldn't begin to interpret. For him, it just seems to be another language mastered.

"Ta-da." The screen flickers, then a video feed appears. Daniel glances back at me, gauging my reaction.

"Straight to the fuck boy's palace," I say. "Holy shit."

10

"**G**ODDAMN! WOW!" I squeeze Daniel's shoulder and cackle like a harpy. It's enough to blunt my disappointment about the aborted mission. "Well done, sir."

Daniel smiles ear to ear, the rare variety he keeps on reserve, deploying like weapons. "It wasn't too tough."

He's too much to look at, so I study the screen filled with Brent. "Sure, my dude." I huff another laugh and try to stifle a carbonation burp. "Don't make me feel any more technologically inferior."

"Do you want me to show you how?" He stands and offers his chair.

"Please." I adjust my dress and sit.

With patience that shouldn't surprise me, Daniel kneels at my side and gives me step-by-step instructions to enter code and access the camera feeds. It doesn't take long—turns out Brent's never updated the camera firmware and left it vulnerable with a backdoor entrance other hackers discovered a while ago.

"Happens more than you'd think." Daniel shrugs. "Sometimes we have to work hard; other times we take advantage of laziness."

When we portal into the Palace of Privilege, Brent is on-screen, front and center.

"Oh! There he is!" I clap my hands together, delighted.

Daniel breathes, "A first try, no less."

I meet his dark gaze, glowing under his approval, then focus on Brent.

Brent's on the phone, and we can hear every word—but even if we couldn't, the half-lidded expression on his face would tell me everything I need to know. He's talking to another woman, beseeching, hoping for a booty call after plan A fell through.

Or maybe looking for someone else to bring to this Friday's sex party. I was underwhelmed the last time I attended one, at an entrepreneur's villa in Napa several years ago, but then again, I hadn't had Molly like many revelers. Tellingly, no sexual paradigms were harmed during the night, despite the highfalutin talk from the venture capitalist who invited me. It was the same old tired, patriarchal bullshit, all the men masters of this small, odd universe, all the women of a certain age and attractiveness vastly outnumbering the men. Weirdly, all the men were heterosexual—nary a dude hooking up with another dude. The women, of course, were expected to be more flexible. Yawn.

I have to laugh the longer we listen to Brent's pleading. "And here I thought I was special," I say in mock disappointment. "What a bastard."

"We don't have to keep watching." Daniel lifts his glasses and rubs his eye, wincing. "Or listening. I just wanted to show you how to do it from your home."

"Well, we might see him run to the bathroom, so don't cut the feed yet."

Daniel looks at me, thick brows lifted in surprise. He turns toward the black-and-white video and bites the inside of his cheek, holding in a laugh. Then he gives up and throws his head back. "You bad girl."

What I wouldn't give to hear that sound every day. I fold my arms across my chest. "Not to worry. He had it coming."

His smile fades. "In what way?"

"You don't want to know."

"Yes I do."

"Tough shit." I shrug. "You don't need to worry about it."

"I thought that was my job." He cracks another bitter smile, an arrow straight through my sternum. When did he start looking so sad? Could it be my fault, the clueless hanger-on disrupting the otherwise happy, Apple commercial life he might enjoy? "Worrying about my wayward friend."

"It's not that I don't appreciate it." I speak to the dark-green, glittery toenails I repainted, willing the tightness in my throat to go away. The polish is much more Dylan than Delilah, not that Brent would ever notice. "I don't want you to fret. I promise I'm okay." I make myself meet Daniel's eyes, so he'll know I mean it.

He chews his bottom lip, radiating skepticism, face taut with concern.

"All right," he says, wisely backing off. "But if he hurts you in *any* way, you'll tell me. Right?"

"So you can go over to the Emporium of Bad Design and blow my cover? No, Haas." I laugh without humor. "Just no."

"There are other ways," he says. "None of which I'd hesitate to employ. Just say the word."

I look past his shoulder at the panorama of city lights, tiny constellations in the dark. What would it be like to watch the sun rise from these windows, filling his home with sunshine, illuminating him again, contour by contour?

Why do I keep burning for something I can't have? His whole future is lined up already, neat rows of black-and-white dominoes. No room for a chaos entity like me.

It doesn't stop me from demanding, "Why are you so good to me?"

The words are out before I can stop them and followed by deafening silence.

Daniel doesn't look away. "Do you have to ask, Dylan?" His voice is hoarse, like he just finished one of his runs up and down the vertiginous hills of Fog City. "What do you want me to say?"

"I'm sorry." I shake my head. "I don't know why I . . ." Why is it so impossible to be around him sometimes? We go from light and sunny to excruciating pressure in seconds, as if all we had to do was reach a hand into the water to touch the bottom of the ocean. No doubt my unhelpful revelation—I want him, so much, have been aching for him longer than I can remember—has something to do with our newfound awkwardness. "I'm sorry I asked."

"No." He stands up fast, pushing the desk chair away, but winces as he does. Now I notice it: his entire face is pinched with pain. Has been all night, despite his hiding it well. "Don't be."

"Are you okay?" I ask. Torn between concern and self-preservation.

He nods, but he's not very convincing. "All good."

"No, you're not." I push him back down. "Sit. What's going on with you?"

He slumps into his chair, shaking his head, but even the small movement makes him wince again.

Looking resigned, he rolls his head my way. "I get these excruciating cluster headaches. They come on in the middle of the night, like there's a hot coal in my skull." He rubs the offending eye socket, brows crinkled.

I bite my lip. "How long has this been going on?"

"Since I got promoted." His smile is wry. "Stress makes it worse. Which makes sense. There's been a lot of that lately, with Oma and everything. Dad is not handling it well. She's our glue, you know? And it's just . . . a lot."

My eyes water. "I know exactly what you mean." When one person in your family suffers, everyone does. So is the way of things when you love.

"And tech feels toxic sometimes. The sixty-, eighty-hour workweeks. The douchebags and their egos." He sighs. "Why are people, Dylan?"

"Beats me. I'm just glad to be in business." I knew he logged insane hours sometimes, but that kind of grind stuns even my workaholic soul. As does the fact that he's always made time for me, even when he had none to spare.

"I love coding," he continues, "and working on big projects, managing a team, but sometimes I think if I have to move, I'll miss my family, but I won't miss my job." He glances at me from the corner of his eye, frowning. "To Seoul, that is."

I ignore the sharp stab his eventual move spurs and edge closer, leaning a hip on his desk. "You've dealt with these headaches for two years. My brother in Christ, why have you never said anything?" To me, anyway.

"They're episodic, thank God, but *suffer in silence* is my trademark." He musters a weak smile for me before he closes his eyes again, head resting on the padded back. "You know that."

"I'm so sorry." I crack my knuckles. "If I'd known you were hurting, I would've left you in peace and not barged in with my nonsense. You already have so much on your plate—"

"Your safety is not nonsense," he croaks, eyes still closed. "And it's not your fault, Dylan."

Damn you, Daniel. I wish he'd knock it off with his sweet nothings. Stop taking a blowtorch to my frozen fortress.

"Still." I lean closer, a hand outstretched. I can't stop myself from touching him. Trying to help. Seems like the least I could do. He just looks so miserable. "Could I maybe try to . . . ?"

"Try to what—" He startles as he feels my fingertips on his brow, then holds himself still as a statue, unbreathing. "Oh."

"I did work as a massage therapist for a while. I might be able to help?"

"I remember." The corner of his mouth folds in a smile. "Jill of all trades."

"Is it okay?"

"Yes." He speaks so softly, I almost miss his sigh of assent.

I carefully remove his glasses and place them on his desk, then trace the straight slash of his eyebrow with the pad of my thumb, feeling the small, tense muscles relax under my gentle pressure.

"That feels . . ." He groans a little. "It hurts, but it feels good too."

"Should I keep going?"

"*Please.*"

I start light, bracing one hand on his shoulder, the other on his temple. In slow, sweeping strokes, I cover the tender high points of his face, lingering at his temple, over his brow bone, working into his hairline and scalp. His skin is burning hot, fine-grained, silken under my fingertips.

"Maybe you could freelance?" I offer.

He shakes his head with a small huff of amusement. "I like health insurance."

"Are you sure?" I try not to smile. "There's probably a crystal for this."

"And steady income." He beams, broad and real, eyes still closed.

My breath catches. I pause a beat, dazed.

"Well, you got me there," I say as soon as I'm able, and continue my work.

Minutes or hours pass, and the stiff muscles become pliable, his shoulders sagging with the weight of relief. His mouth has parted ever so slightly, revealing the true shape of his generous Cupid's bow again. His breathing has changed, shifting to deep, measured pulls. Even his pulse has slowed, a lazy throb at the base of his throat.

I can't look away from the soft shape of his lips in the dim light.

I could kiss him.

I think he'd let me.

I think he'd let me slide onto his lap and sink my hands back into all that dark hair and hold on tight as I took what I wanted.

I make myself let go. "Better?"

"Dylan." He opens his eyes, looking up at me with his own hazy, indecipherable expression. "Thank you. That felt . . ."

"I should go." My voice is too loud in his hushed apartment.

Cowardly, but if I stay any longer, I don't trust myself to do the right thing. I've had too much wine. Too much play-acting with Brent to put up necessary walls with Daniel and pretend he doesn't mean everything to me. Even now, the words dance on the tip of my tongue, a nonsensical jumble of *I want you, please let me, mineminemine.*

I back away like he's fire, almost falling over my feet. The late hour and the alcohol make me clumsy and conspic-uous, like a hermit crab wrestling with a new, too-large shell.

"Dylan." He lurches upright and catches me with an arm around my back before I trip on the corner of his sofa. "It's late. Stay here for the night."

His hand is so warm, I swear his fingerprints brand my skin. I gawp at him like a beached fish and try to find a reason to say no, but my brain hurts and I'm not thinking clearly around him. I wonder when I stopped.

No. He belongs to someone else. How could I forget?

I slink out of his hold, twisting away. His handprint glows on the small of my back. "I can get a ride. No big thing."

"Stay here." With a hand on my shoulder, he nudges me in the direction of his room. "I'd feel better if you did. You take my bed, and I'll sleep out here."

"If I stay, I'll have to do the walk of shame back to my house." I look up at him. He looms like a large shadow. "So far as Brent knows, I'm at home and pining for him."

His hand falls, and he sighs, imbuing the sound with testiness at the reminder of Brent. "Fine. Let me at least drive you back, then?"

"No need." I skitter past the edge of the couch and hurry toward the door. I'm seconds away from making a terrible decision and seeing if the rest of his skin beneath his prim button-ups is as flawless as his face. Acres of hammered gold waiting for me to explore. I slip on my flats and reach for the door. My hand is shaking.

"Dylan. Just wait."

I turn around, hesitant. So afraid of myself I don't even want to look him in the eye.

"I didn't mean to scare you off. Or make you uncomfortable. Are we . . ." He swallows hard. "Are we good?"

"We're always good." I try to smile. "Like I said, you get a pass for pretty much everything."

He doesn't return my smile. Just looks at me, steady and unrelenting, as if he can make me confess the dumb things tumbling around in my head. Dumb, because even if he were mine for the taking, I don't know how a real relationship would work. All I've ever had are meaningless flings. Throwaway fucks I couldn't care less about. The second anyone got too close, I straight-armed them off the cliff and into the bay. Cruelty, thy name is woman.

"Good night, Haas." I wrench the door open and run from his home.

CHAPTER

11

IN THE MORNING, I feel every ounce of wine left in my system. My mouth is drier than the Mojave, and most importantly, I'm pretty sure I came within seconds of making a colossally bad decision at Daniel's last night. Again, the firelight spelled my doom. That or hormones I can't wrangle.

Or his aching vulnerability, trusting and malleable under my hands, giving himself over to me.

"Temporary insanity."

I fling off the covers, slump out of bed, and open my laptop. I was still buzzed when he gave me instructions, so God knows whether I'll remember the magic words. Checking to see how Brent's night went might boost my mood, though.

Several abortive attempts at hacking Brent's home security later, I haven't managed to crack it.

"For Bjork's sake." I slam the laptop shut and toss it to the end of the bed, disgusted with my incompetence. The only thing standing between me and direct access to the House of Hauteur is my pride. Guess I'll have to ask Daniel again for help. Considering how well the last visit went, though—*What the hell happened there?*—I'd better try hacking a few more times before I plead my case with him.

I flop back into bed and stare at the frescoed ceiling.

"I didn't imagine it, did I?" The way Daniel tried to convince me to stay. The heat in his irises, like embers. A shudder racks my shoulders, and my insides twist at the memory. Something has changed, altering our structure. Like we built a bridge on either side of the strait between us, working toward a golden spike.

Information is a gift, I tell my clients. When you have all the information, all the variables, you can choose your actions accordingly.

I might've oversold it. For example, wondering if your best friend wants you the same way you want him could be, in fact, intolerable. We've both made choices leading us away from one another, walking parallel paths, never crossing lines.

"Daniel." I sigh his name, the way I've wanted to for ages. "What have you done to me?"

*   *   *

After caffeinating, right down to business with two cups of coffee, I open my laptop again. I'm due for a check-in with Dr. Chang, to let her know how things are going re ruining Brent's life. No huge strides to mention yet, but it's early days. Since I declined to put out last night, I bet he'll be back for more.

After I hit send on my email apprising her of my progress, an email from my favorite journalist pops up in my in-box. Amazing I almost forgot about him in the hustle to ingratiate myself with Brent.

"Rhys Morgan, you persistent motherfucker." I open the message, jittery. I overdid it with the caffeine. It's either that or this wily investigative journalist raising the hackles on my neck. Has he changed his mind on waiting for two weeks and decided to publish now?

I miss my kayaking buddy. Can we meet—off the record 😊—*and just talk?*

"Off the record, my ass." I close my email.

Then I open it again, finally noticing the attachment he included. Damn my curiosity. I click it.

It's . . . a proposed target for Lady Justice. A failed gubernatorial candidate who's been credibly accused of sexually harassing underage girls. Rhys has pages and pages of documentation, going back a decade, and an actual bullet list of reasons this person should be the next person in my cross hairs. An olive branch, albeit an odd one.

"I'll be damned." I sit back, popping my knuckles.

He knows who I am, and he means to . . . help? It's a lot like Daniel's quiet entrée into my life.

Maybe it's the coffee singing in my veins, but inspiration strikes like dry lightning in the desert, firing me up.

Instead of shutting Rhys down, what if I let him know who my current target is? And why I'm hunting Brent? For God's sake, it's Theranos worthy. He might even get a Pulitzer for it. More importantly, if I brought him into the fold, maybe Rhys could be an ally instead of a would-be adversary. It seems like he might be angling for that, anyway.

Then again, it could all be a trap.

Can he be trusted? Daniel's voice asks the million-dollar question. I already know what my cautious partner in crime would say about this proposed alliance—feck *no.* But I'm not accountable to him, only to myself.

With new determination, I create a fresh file on my laptop and begin my keyword search, fingers flying over the keyboard.

My burner rings. I sigh in disgust when I see Brent's number and let it go to voice mail. Let him sweat. After all, he did call me a fucking tease.

In an hour, I know more about Rhys than he does. His articles share a recurring theme: rooting out corruption. Exposing those who abuse their power. Everyone from dirty cops in LA to private military cartels to politicians in the pockets of their extremist donors. (Which is to say, most. Slime.)

Heart pounding, I reply to Rhys's email with a time and place, a coffee shop closer to my real home in Sausalito. Can't risk running into Brent around here. If Rhys wants to meet me, he'll have to do it this morning before I change my mind and think better of it.

I get a reply within minutes.

I'll be there. Looking forward to seeing you again, Dylan.

I snort. "I bet you are."

Let's hope he's ready to join me on the hunt for the white whale.

* * *

I take public transit across the Golden Gate. It's a gorgeous fall day, the kind we dream about all year, with clear blue skies and views stretching to infinity.

The beautiful weather does nothing to ease my nerves, though. This whole enterprise could go sideways if he decides to publish and reveals my identity before I've had a chance to mete out the justice Brent deserves. I jiggle my knees, unable to be still on the forty-five-minute bus ride from Pac Heights to Sausalito, sweating through my thin silk blouse.

Still, my spirits lift as I hop off the bus by the yacht harbor, comforted by the familiar sights and smells, the cool breeze, the brine of the ocean filling my nose. This is my territory, and if Rhys has any sense, he'll take the golden fleece I'm dropping in his lap, run with it, and leave my alias the hell alone.

I'm purposely early, setting up shop in a corner of the coffee shop where I can see everyone's comings and goings. I order a rich, decadent honey lavender latte and sip from my heavy travel mug while I rehearse what I'm going to tell him.

A few minutes after our meeting time, Rhys barrels in through the door, breathing hard as if he ran the whole way. His gaze darts around the small café and passes right over me. A frown mars his face as he knits his eyebrows together.

I laugh and raise a hand in acknowledgment.

He does a double take, brows rising to his sun-bleached, coppery hairline. Nice to know my disguise is working. After ordering something for himself, he slowly approaches the table, like he's afraid I'm a rare breed of coffee shop monster.

"Hey, Rhys. Have a seat."

He folds himself into the heavy red chair. "You look . . ." He swallows, seemingly at a loss.

"Delicious?" I offer. No doubt I present a different picture in my new armor than in my neoprene.

He huffs a laugh. "I was going to say different, but delicious also applies." Tongue pressed to the inside of his cheek, he appraises me, hazel eyes flitting over the getup.

"Flatterer." I hid my grin in my mug. "But that won't get me to spill."

"Can't blame me for trying." He folds his arms and leans on his elbows. "I've been following your"—a pause—"career, for a long time now."

"That makes me sound notorious." I lift my brows, hoping he'll explain.

He shrugs. "Word travels, especially when everyone has a camera in their pocket. People meeting spectacular falls from grace, in ways too good to be true? You could call it instant karma—"

"Should've put that on my business card." I snicker into my latte. *"Instant karma, keep me on retainer."*

His mouth quirks in a charming, crooked smile. "You could call it instant karma, sure, or you could wonder how the deplorables of the world came to meet such just ends."

"And you did the latter."

"Seemed to me whoever was at work was doing a better job holding people accountable than the justice system, much as it hurts my pride to admit it."

"I wouldn't sell yourself short. I saw your recent articles." Now's the time to initiate the negotiation. Bring my offerings to the table. "Like the misappropriation of public funds in Yolo County? The police chief with a six-figure salary for a town with a population of three hundred?"

"How could I forget." His wide mouth flattens into a frown, and he blows out a frustrated breath. "That little town is *still* tied up in legal battles, but at least the public knows where their money went."

"To say nothing of the target you sent me," I say. "That was an impressive dossier."

Rhys looks up, a little shy, a little proud. Like a dog dropping a dead bird in my lap. "Seems like he'd be the perfect target."

I set my mug down and lean forward, summoning my courage. I want to believe him when he says he admires me, but if I leave myself vulnerable for what could be bullshit, I deserve having my cover blown. "What if I told you"—I grin at my Morpheus opener—"you could expose a scandal ten times bigger than that?"

Rhys blinks. Then he shakes his head, smiling. "You're yanking my chain."

"Not at all. You know what I do. Why do you think I've made such a drastic costume change?" I glance at my designer duds and lower my voice. "I'm on the hunt."

He chews his lower lip, eyes bright in his suntanned face. "Who's the target?"

"I'll tell you, under one condition."

"What would that be?"

My heart beats in my throat, my palms sweat. "That you don't reveal my real identity." I hold out my iPad and a nondisclosure agreement.

"Of course. There's always a catch." He sits back with a snort.

"You're kidding yourself if you thought I'd go along with your plan to expose me. For God's sake, Rhys," I hiss. "I'd go to jail."

He swallows. Looking pale beneath his freckles. Was he prepared to go through with it, even if it'd ruin me? I can't tell, and it makes me nervous.

"If you're impressed with my work," I continue, keeping calm, "and it sounds like you are, why not leave me in peace?" I sip the latte, savoring the sweet, wild flower honey on my tongue. "Besides, the person I'm pursuing is a much larger catch."

"So, this is your counteroffer?"

I nod.

"And all I have to go on is your word it'll be worth my while." He shakes his head again. "My editor is going to string me up."

"Will you please look at the larger picture? We're talking fraud on the scale of billions, Rhys." I set my mug on the table with a clank. "Really, you ought to be thanking me for the tip-off."

"Who is it?" he repeats, with iron in his voice. "Kinda hard to tell what the bigger picture is unless I know that much."

"Can I trust you?" I offer him the iPad again. "That you won't dox me?"

After a pause that swells and expands, he nods and signs.

"It's Brent Wilder," I make myself say, over the pounding in my temples. "The CEO of Prometheus Pharmaceuticals."

Rhys's eyes widen until I see the whites around his green-and-gold irises. "Holy shit. You weren't joking about your target being higher up the food chain."

Chills race down my spine despite the warmth of the sun pouring through the large windows. Like water from the Pacific poured over my blouse. "I have no room for error."

As the words leave my mouth, I realize how true they are. I've swum far out to sea, far beyond sight of the shore. Either I'll grow gills and scales and serrated teeth and drag Brent under, or he'll do the same to me. There's no doubt in my mind he'd kill me and feed me to the great whites if he knew who I was and what I aimed to do. I love Shark Week, but not that much.

I smile at my grim gallows humor, but the reprieve is momentary. Even with Daniel to help, and possibly Rhys, this case will take every bit of my money, smarts, and skill. I cannot fail.

"The connection to Brent . . . who's your client?" he asks after a moment. "I assume it's an employee. Or a former employee?"

I zip my mouth shut. "Client privilege. Anonymity of the strictest variety."

Rhys nods, as if he expected as much but knew he had to try anyway. "Fraud, you said. How so?"

"You've seen those stupid billboards, right? The woman smiling in a meadow? 'Good-bye to the blues'?"

"Yeah, they're everywhere."

"Well, he falsified the clinical trial data on the antidepressant he's pushing to the world, promising to end major
depression as we know it, despite the fact it increases suicide
risk by a large margin." I down the last of my latte. "That
whole spiel about his mother suffering from depression, thus
spurring him to find a 'cure'? Crock of shit. There's money
to be made, that's all."

He leans back in his chair, folding his arms against his
chest. "Surprising, but then again, not really. I only know
him tangentially, but I always thought the guy was a total
schmuck."

"That's one word for it." Unbidden, the memory of last
night's horrible, teeth-clacking kiss fills my brain. I wish
I could scrub him off me, but no matter how I brush my
teeth, I still taste his rancid wine breath.

"Now I think about it, another colleague, Katie, was
ready to do an interview with a woman who'd worked at
Prometheus. I always figured there was sexual harassment
going on. But it happened right around the time the paper
changed ownership and the story was scrapped." He taps his
lips with an index finger. "I should talk to Katie, see what
she says. Aside from your client, though, is there anyone else
I can talk to? Anyone who'd be willing to go on the record?"
Rhys asks. "I can't take this to my editor with nothing but
an anonymous, vague source and no evidence whatsoever."

I crack my knuckles. "I don't know for sure, but likely
not. I'll ask around, but you'll have to do some digging of
your own, I'm afraid."

Rhys grimaces. "Making me earn my salt, huh?"

"I pointed you in the right direction. I have every reason
to believe it's only a matter of time before this story leaks. If
you get the jump and blow the lid on his operation, you'll be
the one to expose one of the most malignant narcissists on
the West Coast. You'll make international news."

Rhys pauses for long beats. "No pressure."

"No pressure." I smile in earnest. "But you'll have my help along the way."

"A partnership." He strokes his couple days' grown-in beard, glinting auburn. "In other words." Eyes narrowed, he meets my gaze across the small table, asking questions, searching for answers.

"Yes." I investigate my empty mug. "And I don't make the offer lightly. But others have pointed out I could stand to delegate, so consider this my attempt at sharing the shit pie."

"How could I say no when you put it like that?" he asks dryly. Then he laughs, full throated, and tosses back more coffee. As I wait on an answer, his smile disappears and he rubs at his worn, sage-green T-shirt, like he feels the rib-crushing pressure to stop Brent too. Anyone with a con-science would.

"So what do you say?" I ask when I can't bear it any-more. "Will you help?"

"You still need to work on your pitch." He casts a quick smile. "But . . . in honor of the girl who stood up for me when I most needed it, I'm in."

I sigh, tension oozing from my neck and shoulders. I didn't know much I wanted another ally until I had one.

"Is this where I say 'You have my pen' or something like that?" He smiles again. "How does this fellowship work, exactly?"

"Nerd." I roll my eyes, though I'm more than a little touched. I wonder if anyone else remembers me the same way. If anything I've ever done has made a difference in the grand scheme of things. If Rhys is to be believed, there may be a chance.

I clear my throat and push away the philosophical thoughts. "I don't know how this fellowship of fuckery is going to work, but thanks for signing on, for starters. I'll talk to my client to see whether they would be willing to go on the record, but I can't make any promises. Brent has everyone sign some pretty intimidating NDAs."

Rhys nods. "Standard operating procedure, but still discouraging."

"Sure, but it's possible others might be willing to come forward. Anyone who's met Brent and has a spine has to hate that guy. He's left a substantial trail of destruction, just by being himself. Let's use people's resentment, yeah?"

"Experience says it's a good place to start." He sounds amused. "People love talking about people they hate."

I stand and offer my hand. Rhys does the same, looking down at me, seeming very young and . . . determined. He hasn't lost his way, yet. Become disillusioned, like me on my worst days. The thought gives me hope. Maybe this reckless initiative won't blow up in my face.

"Let's drown this sonofabitch," I say.

Rhys takes my hand and gives it a firm shake, all humor gone. "I won't let you down, Dylan."

My heart squeezes without warning.

It's scary, inviting others into my strange little world.

Scary . . . and wonderful.

12

WHEN I GET back to Pac Heights, it's already late afternoon. I spent too long at my houseboat, stalling as I watered my many plants, but having time away was crucial. Time to consider my next moves with Brent. How to get into his house again while he's out of commission.

I tip my driver and spring out onto the street, excited to check in with Dr. Chang and update her. Excited, too, to try to hack Brent's security again and learn how the rest of his evening went.

As I near my townhome, however, a large package on my front step catches my gaze. I haven't ordered anything, so my suspicions are instantly piqued.

Inside, I cut the box open, and the heady fragrance from dozens of peach roses fills the sleek, subway-tiled kitchen. More confused than ever, I pluck the note from the arrangement and read the chicken scratch.

Delilah,

I know I messed up. Let me make it up to you?

—Brent

"Huh." I drop the note on the counter. "I'll be damned."

I've gotta say, I didn't expect this, but maybe letting him stew put enough fear in his tiny lemur brain to alter his usual modus operandi. Enough to make him pretend to be someone he's not. For someone like him, even an apology is a tool for manipulation.

A glance through the sliding glass door lets me know Brent's already out there on his side of the border, waiting. No doubt expecting my exaltation after he dropped hundreds of dollars on dinner last night, and more still for such an extravagant bouquet.

After putting the roses on the counter—I'll leave them with Noah at the salon; he'll appreciate them as the hopeless romantic out of the two of us—I rummage unsuccessfully for something to eat, wishing I didn't have to face Brent.

"Tits up," I tell my reflection in the glass door. "Knives out." Then I pop open another button on my blouse and step outside.

"Howdy, Brent," I call across the hedge, infusing my voice with friendliness.

"Delilah! My favorite neighbor." Brent lifts his head and waves me over. "Join me!"

He seems to be in a mighty fine mood. I'm instantly on high alert, pulse picking up, temples throbbing.

Gritting my teeth, I step over the hedge between our yards and join him on his patio.

He's sprawled on a deck chair, pale-blue dress shirt unbuttoned and untucked, wine in hand, looking deceptively at ease. "Wine?"

"Just a little for me." I can't keep up with his binge drinking. Between our steak house date and the unseasonal heat, deprived of fog, I'm still dehydrated.

He fills my stemless glass to the rim. I pretend not to notice, smothering my frown. I can't put my finger on what's making me ill at ease. Maybe it's the way his light-blue irises track my every movement, like he sees beneath my clothing. Or how he seems too convivial.

"So, how was the rest of your night?" I ask.

The quick frown etching his face tells me everything I need to know. I bite the inside of my cheek. I *have* to get my hands on that footage.

"It was fine," he says. "Did you get the flowers?"

Abrupt change in topic? Yeah, he spent time on the shitter. "I did! That was a nice surprise." I try to sound awed. "Thank you so much."

"It's nothing. Have you thought about what I proposed?"

"Trying again?" In an ordinary life, I would've already been buried by the sheer volume of his red flags, one after another. To secure his trust, get inside his home, and find the data, however, I'll have to dive further into this dysfunctional mess. Pretend I can be bought with several dozen roses and his bullshit nonapology. "I don't see why not."

"Good." He smiles and lifts his glass in a toast. "Because I want you all to myself."

He's known me all of a few days, but it comes as no surprise. It's all part of the abuser's profile, a blitzkrieg designed to overwhelm and lock down the target.

"Is that right?" I meet his toast and lift a brow, hoping I look flattered and maybe a little saucy. "You don't want to share me?"

He cuts me a dark look. "No." Then he reaches into the pocket of his suit jacket on the back of his chair, retrieves a small, cream-colored envelope, and slides it across the table to me.

"What's this?"

"Open it," he says, as if I'm dumber than a box of rocks.

I bite back my snarling retort and take the envelope. The paper is smooth and heavy. It's an invitation to a Halloween costume ball thrown by a local, high-profile environmental organization.

"I'm the guest of honor. And I want you to be my plus-one."

"Uh, wow." He must've struck out on his first choices. This was not part of my plan, to put it lightly. I operate best in the shadows, placing my invisible chess pieces. Alarm trickles into my arteries drop by cold drop, an icy slush despite the heat of late afternoon. "You sure you want me there? This is a big deal."

"Of course I want you there." Like he didn't call someone else the second I was out of earshot after our date. Our one and only date. If my liar radar weren't honed to a precise, obsidian edge, I'd never know he wasn't sincere.

"Don't you think this is moving fast, though?" Even Socialite Delilah would question.

"If you don't want to go, just say so." His affable mood disappears like fog in the sun.

Oh, shit. It'd be funny if I hadn't crushed the brittle eggshell of his ego without meaning to. He's caught on I'm not as invested in this burgeoning relationship as I should be. My loathing must seep out in unguarded moments. I'll have to do a better job acting.

Seriously, though. How is it possible for someone so volatile to run such a huge company? And they call women emotional. If a mercurial temper is the extent of his credentials, I'm pretty sure he could hand the reins of Prometheus to me.

"I . . . well, I guess I—"

"Don't waste my time," he snaps. "I thought you were different, but if you're going to play games, you can get out." He stands and takes his wine with him.

I stand and rush after him. "Brent, wait. Please." I reach for his arm.

He stills and looks down his nose at me, pupils enormous despite the angle of sunset light. "What, Delilah?"

He's ashen and sweaty, skin shiny in the lamplight from his home. He smells different too, a vinegary tinge I can barely stand long enough to do the necessary task of proving my adoration. Strung out on uppers? It'd go a long way toward explaining his explosive shifts in mood.

"I do want to go with you to the ball," I say, with lowered lashes. "I was just surprised. Will you please take me?" I stroke his forearm, letting my nails lightly scratch his skin, an unsubtle preview. A little abject begging ought to do the trick. Let him think I'd ever grovel.

He looks at my hand, touching him, then at my face. Whatever he sees must convince him his departure was hasty.

"Of course, babe." He smiles at me like a benevolent king.

"I've never been to a costume ball like this before. Who will you go as?"

"Alexander the Great."

"Ah." I cover my mouth and chin in a show of contemplation, trying not to laugh. Could've called that one a mile away. Next he'll tell me he only has Ayn Rand and first-edition Hemingway on his shelves. If he's searching antiquity for inspiration, Caligula would be the better fit, but I won't be the one to pierce his fantasy. Not yet anyway. I'll have to share my commentary with Daniel instead.

"Who should I be, then? In keeping with the theme? Cleopatra?" I can get down with a bad bitch who knew how to rule and brought two Roman generals to heel.

"Well, if we were really going to be accurate, you'd have to be a concubine." He smirks.

Is it too soon to shank him? "Or Hephaestion, Alexander's bodyguard." I give him a honeyed smile. "And erstwhile lover. I don't mind going in drag."

Brent returns my smile, but there's fury in his irises. Toxic masculinity, bro. It's a hell of a drug.

"Cleopatra is fine." He sensibly cuts his losses. "But your costume has to be appropriate. Important people will be there."

It takes everything in my power not to shove his wrist back and break it. "I'm sure I'll find something." Probably a navel-grazing, diaphanous sheath held together with a few creative bits of metal. It was hot in Alexandria, after all. "It's tomorrow, right?"

"Yes, tomorrow."

"Plenty of time." I smile, though putting together a whole costume in twenty-four hours will be a massive crunch. I have a suitable wig already, and the right makeup, but finding accessories might take some work.

Going to the event itself will be risky too. If he makes introductions, that'll be more people to poke holes in my false identity. Still, this could be the perfect setup. If I play the trophy part well, I bet his guard will finally be low enough to leap over. Once I've drugged him and gotten into his home again, it's going to get ugly. I'll tear it down to the foundation to find the evidence if I must.

"Glad to hear it." He leans down and kisses me, tongue plunging into my mouth.

I hold my breath and do my best not to gag.

Finally, he pulls away. "My driver will take us over at seven. Don't be late."

"You're not going to invite me over now?" I ask teasingly, in a remarkable feat of endurance.

He looks me over, considering. Then he shakes his head, looking not at all sorry and definitely smug. Just as I planned. Everything must be his idea. "I would, but I've still got tons of work, babe." He leans down and kisses me again, aggressive and insistent. "I'll make it up to you tomorrow night. Promise."

"I hope so." I blow him a kiss. "See you then, handsome."

When his back is finally turned, I let my smile slip. The muscles in my cheeks are sore from the act. I sip more wine, trying to look unhurried, then saunter back to my temporary home.

Inside, I kick off my sandals and wipe my mouth, washing it clean with a several gulps of sparkling water. Then I race upstairs to my bedroom and throw open my laptop.

Before I can try to hack his home security again, however, I see an email from Daniel with several attachments.

I sifted and found the money shots, so to speak. You're welcome.

—DH

I crack a grin and open the first video. Goddamn, does that man speak my love language, bizarre though it may be.

In the clip, Brent doubles over and runs from the kitchen—yes, runs—to a bathroom. Twenty minutes and several flushes later, he emerges, looking pale and downright angry, only to turn right back around and slam the door shut again.

By that point, I'm laughing so hard, I can barely see the video. This one hundred percent makes me feel better about bailing on the risky situation the night prior, missing the chance to search his home while he was otherwise engaged.

I type a quick reply to Daniel before I can censor myself.

We're an odd pair, aren't we? But I adore you anyway. Many thanks for this heartwarming compilation. A real morale booster!

Your bad influence,

Dylan

Too much, but I've downed enough wine and gleeful schadenfreude to shed several layers of my good sense.

A few minutes later, a reply.

Anything for you, Dylan.

Damn him. I bite my hangnail. I keep getting real *As you wish* vibes every time he says that, and I really don't know what to make of it.

Sobered, I close the laptop and shake it off. "Me and my wishful thinking."

I walk out onto the balcony and slide the door shut quietly behind me, my inner night creature stirring with the coming dusk. The sky is still hazy pink with wildfire smoke, but I have a sultan's view from my perch in Pac Heights, with the Greco-Roman Palace of Fine Arts glowing in the twilight, the Golden Gate shining behind it, and the ocean a giant, shimmering mass of lavender beyond, dissolving the border between water and sky.

I turn my gaze to the lights in Brent's ostentatious, tasteless home. Sooner than he knows, the lights will be off, because he won't live there anymore.

It's time to move into deeper water.

13

I START THE DAY caffeinating and reaching out to anyone I know looking for a pharmacologist. There's bound to be *someone* in the Bay Area not afraid of Brent and needing Dr. Chang's expertise.

A call back arrives while I'm crossing the Gate. Dr. Maritza Sanchez, another client of Noah's, is looking to bring a chief scientist on board for her biotech start-up. I take mental notes as she fills me in on the job requirements, thrilled to have a lead for Dr. Chang already. Buoyed, I waltz into Noah's salon with the roses.

"You trying to steal me away from my hubby?" Noah asks with a grin. "These flowers are amazing. Like your hair, if I do say so myself."

"Never ever, and yes, you're an artist." I grin and wrap an arm around his wiry shoulders. "Just don't want them to go to waste."

He's right, it's a lovely bouquet. Might as well be appreciated by someone who'll like them. I don't plan on letting Brent ever see the inside of my house, so he won't know one way or the other. I set the large vase on the reception desk.

"Uh-oh." Noah tucks his scissors into the pocket of his trim black apron. "Whose heart are we breaking today, Dilly?"

"He doesn't have a heart, so we're good."

Noah smirks. "Bad girl. Can I live vicariously through you?"

"Sure!" I lean against the front desk and send him my best smile. "Any makeup pointers if I want to be Cleopatra?" I do a decent job with makeup on my own, but he's the real pro. When I need the big guns, I always go to him.

"Somewhere to be?" He hands off his current client to another stylist for her shampooing and leads me to the back of the salon where he keeps his trunk of makeup.

"Costume ball tonight." I plop down in the director's chair. "And I need to make someone regret all the decisions they've ever made."

His thick brows lift, revealing the gold in his irises. "Never let it be said you lack ambition."

I shrug. "All in a day's work. So, what do you think?"

"You want to be Elizabeth Taylor again, huh?" He scrunches a speculative brow. "I bet I can make it happen. Can you come back around four o'clock?"

I kiss him on the cheek and beam. "It's a date."

* * *

"It's perfect."

I swirl the gold sateen gown around my ankles. I'll need heels to make the length work, and it's a little tighter in the chest than I'd like, but otherwise, it's an exceptional find. It dips low in front and plunges positively indecently in back. The beading across the bodice is extravagant, with narrow seams of green, black, and gold faience that gather at my shoulders. When I move, I shimmer like something elemental under the lights. "But I'm going to need lots of tape, aren't I?" I laugh, covering myself.

"I suspect so, but what a small price to pay." Maya's reflection in the three-paneled mirror grins back at me. They're the proprietor of this hidden gem of a store, and they look it, dressed head to toe in vibrant jewel tones, so beautiful against their dark-brown skin. "Then again, maybe not." They purse their lips, considering. "Maybe a low-backed teddy?"

"Ooo! Now you're talking." I swish back and forth, reveling in the fabric swirling around my ankles. "I have just the thing. Thank God. I'd be so sad to not wear this!"

"Well, I had a feeling this was what you'd be looking for, Miss Femme Fatale. By the way, I'm loving your hair. I've never seen it lighter like this."

"Thank you! Just having fun being the girl next door." I smile back. "And you've never let me down before." I turn and give them a hug. "Thank you so much for setting this aside for me."

"You're lucky it's still here—a dress like this won't stay long."

"That I don't doubt." This snug shop is my favorite not-well-kept secret for finding extraordinary designer castoffs from San Francisco's .001 percent. I've sourced more than a few business-related costumes from this little consignment boutique.

"C'mon." Maya nods to the cases of jewelry sparkling under the lights. "If you're going to be Her Highness, you're going to need bling."

"Twist my arm, why don't you." I grab my wallet and prepare to leave my retirement fund behind.

An hour later, weighed down with my gilt treasures, I hop on a cable car and ride it back up the hill. From there, I get on the bus and head to a Korean women-only day spa, my favorite place in the whole city, and check in for my appointment with my fake name.

The afternoon passes in a sensual haze, a full-body scrub followed by a gold gel wrap, a massage, and a shampoo, a ritual I suspect Cleopatra herself would've endorsed. Afterward, I lie prone in the clay sauna and push Brent far from my brain. Later, I'll be focused and "on," but after this week, this time is for me and me alone.

Well, maybe Daniel can tag along too—the man lives rent-free in my head, after all. I can't help but think he'd like this place if he were allowed. He tolerates the heat far better than I, cool and sphinxlike even when climate change threatens to ruin the good thing we've got going on in the Bay Area.

When it's time to leave, I step out into a haze of wildfire smoke, heat, hot wind, and a blood-red sun.

"Jesus Christ." I haven't needed a heavy-duty mask for smoke in a while, but I dig in my handbag for the one Daniel gave me last summer and gratefully secure it over my mouth and nose. The fire in the northern part of the state must've grown by leaps and bounds, or else the wind has dramatically shifted, funneling all the smoke toward the bay. "Goddammit."

I'm so preoccupied with the dystopian (quotidian?) skies, it takes me longer to notice the white van parked across the street. I'm sure I saw them when I was at Maya's store too. Awareness pierces my post-spa bliss, a sharp thorn.

Brent.

Shit. He didn't give any indication he suspects me. This doesn't bode well for my hopes of getting him to loosen up and trust me. I pretend not to notice the van and continue my walk back to the salon on Divisadero for my makeup date with Noah, trying and failing to put myself at ease as the van turns and crawls along.

Well, two can play this game.

On the next block, I veer into a lingerie boutique. As if I'd ever wear it for Brent, but maybe this bit of theater will get back to him and assuage the misogynist.

I admire the fine confections of lace and silk, biding my time until the van disappears. Then I pay for my purchases, small frills only I will appreciate.

Relieved to be in the clear, I climb back on the bus to head west. I breathe the stale scent of my mask and lean my head against the window, grateful to be out of the smoke and no longer inhaling poison. If only everyone had the same luxury.

My hands ball into fists on my lap. *I'm going to make you regret this, you entitled piece of shit.*

*   *   *

Brent knocks on my back door half an hour before he said he would. It's a good thing I'm already dressed in my gown and ready to roll.

I slide open the patio door, fixing a politician's smile on my face. "Brent! You're early!" He looks patently absurd in his warrior armor, like a seven-year-old trying his new Halloween costume out for size.

He eyes me up and down, mouth hitching in a smug smile. Then he steps in without invitation, bringing a waft of smoky air with him when he doesn't bother to close the door. I shut it quickly, trying to preserve some semblance of air quality.

As soon as it's latched, he flips me around and kisses me without warning, walking me back step by step until the kitchen counter digs into my lower back. He's forceful, pawing at my dress, his movements jerky. Angry, almost.

My martial arts training takes over. I stagger my feet, counterbalancing his weight, and free my arms. He's too close to kick, but I could strike with a backhand fist or a palm shove and break his nose.

He also tastes awful, breath sour with alcohol, like he hasn't brushed his teeth all day. If he were someone I loved, I'd be worried about him. As it stands, I'm glad his demons are talking extra loudly. My sister shouldn't be the only one plagued by memory.

"Easy there," I say against his mouth, after a few tense seconds. If I shove my knee to his groin before we even leave for the soiree, might be tough to, uh, play the honeypot. *Keep it light. Let him down easy.* "We have all night, Alexander."

He pulls away as I hoped but doesn't let go of my upper arms.

"Where were you today?" he demands. "I tried to get a hold of you."

"Did you? I'm pretty sure I didn't get any missed calls." I know for a fact he never called me. With a quick side step, I break his hold on the pretense of grabbing my burner phone on the kitchen counter. "To answer your question, I was running errands, trying to get my costume ready." *And plotting your demise, but that's a technicality.*

I can tell he wants to press the issue, tongue stuck to the inside of his cheek, but if he does, he'd have to reveal he had me tailed today. Possibly longer. It's troubled me all day, wondering if he knows I met up with Rhys earlier in the week.

"What do you think, by the way?" I lift a brow and make a slow spin. "Not bad for short notice, huh?"

"It's great, babe." His gaze is heavy lidded. "You look super hot."

And who said romance was dead?

"Well, of course." I grin like any self-respecting coquette, pressing my palms to his chest. "I wanted to look good for you."

He smirks, looking pleased. Then studies me, a few beats too long.

I hold my breath.

"Maybe it's the wig, but I swear you look like someone familiar," he says. "I just can't place where."

"I feel the same way." I ignore the shrill warning sounds going off in my head and force myself to look up with adoration. "Like I've known you forever. My spirit guide said we probably met in a past life and that's why."

He looks mildly disgusted by my woo-woo bent—an inspired choice if I do say so myself—and shrugs. The carelessness of someone with no curiosity and all the answers. "Are you ready to go? Or do I have to wait for you?"

"Just about." I smile blandly and refrain from reminding him at knifepoint he's half an hour early. "Let me grab my clutch and I'll be set. Make yourself at home in the meantime."

I turn and dash upstairs as well as I'm able in the form-fitting dress. I pack the things I'll need into the tiny, beaded clutch—cash, card, fake ID, burner, meds for my boy Brent, lipstick, and shiv—and ease downstairs in my strappy gold stilettos.

"I don't see the roses anywhere," he says when I rejoin him. He sits in the armchair, foot tapping. His tone is nonchalant and his gaze is focused on the umber sky, but fury radiates from him, a burning force field.

Maybe he knows I took the roses to Noah—hence the ire.

Then again, it could be his paranoia. I didn't see the van until later in the afternoon, after all.

"They're upstairs." I lean over his shoulder and whisper in his ear. "In my room. I wanted to keep them close. See them when I wake up in the morning."

"Will I get to see them later?" He turns and meets my gaze.

The whites of his eyes are bloodshot. Could be the smoke from the wildfires. Could be the coke.

"That depends on you." And on his tolerance for anti-histamines. If all goes according to plan, he'll be out cold in his bed before he realizes I'm not in it with him.

Looking placated, he stands and offers his arm. "Let's go, then, babe."

*   *   *

An uncharacteristic burst of nerves hits me when Brent's driver pulls up at the entrance of the immense five-star hotel in Nob Hill. The Ionic columns glow orange in the early dusk from the smoke, and the scene of limousines depositing costumed guests against the backdrop of sienna skies—as if everything were normal!—takes on a bizarre quality. What are we doing here? Congratulating ourselves on this sorry situation? Really?

"I assume your company has made sizable donations, if you're the guest of honor?" I ask Brent as we roll to a stop, trying to ease the awkward silence.

He shrugs. "Tax write-offs."

"Ah." I nod knowingly, as if it's something I do all the time too. "Smart."

Of course he wouldn't ever use his money from a desire to do good. If he wanted, he could end homelessness in the city. Feed anyone who's ever felt the persistent gnaw of hunger. Pay for every student's college tuition in the Bay Area. Open rehab treatment centers. Save us from ourselves, deliver us into a better future. But no. His cares extend only as far as he does. Probably—I size him up—no more than four inches.

Goddamn, I can't wait to see this piece of dung behind bars and his ill-gotten gains given to another. Literally anyone else, but hopefully many others.

As we exit the limo, the flashes from several cameras blind me. I send the photographers my best famous-for-being-famous smile and link my arm through Brent's. A few reporters ask Brent who his Cleopatra is and whether he's going as Mark Antony.

His face flattens in annoyance, and I have to look away before I laugh. Naturally, he finds the idea of being Cleopatra's boy toy offensive. He'd rather sulk and make an ass of himself than be upstaged.

His lapse is quick, though; I have to give him credit. He lights up under the attention from the press, soaking it in like a demagogue at a rally. After he sets the record straight about his personage and the woman on his arm—"Just a friend" he says, enjoying his coyness—and promises to have news about Prometheus soon, we finally mount the steps arm in arm and get out of the smoke and falling ash.

Inside the hotel's opulent lobby, I breathe deep, trying to clean the awful ashy taste out of my mouth and throat.

Head a little clearer, I get the lay of the land. From the nearby ballroom, a string quartet playing an awesome arrangement of "Somewhere Only We Know" filters through the controlled hum of chatter.

Brent's tied up talking to pretentious-looking Not in My Backyard sorts, so I make my grand entrance into the ballroom without him. I gleefully lift a slender flute of bubbly and a canape from the tray of a passing server as I go, thanking him along the way. The smoked salmon rillette melts in my mouth, and I moan in appreciation. If I have to suffer next to a violent narcissist, I might as well eat something tasty.

The ballroom is lit in shades of deep red and gold, with chandeliers casting sparkles across the walls and floor. Between the dramatic decorations and the swirl of vibrant, over-the-top costumes, I feel like I've dropped in at the Met Gala.

Movement from my peripheral vision catches my attention. A group of four has entered the fray. The tallest among them looks familiar, to say the least, despite his costume. Dracula, maybe? The gold brocade waistcoat hugging his lean torso and dramatic, floor-length black cape would suggest so, as would the smoky eyes and thin trickle of blood painted to run down his chin and beneath the sharp bevel of his jaw.

Daniel. And his date, Yoon So Ah, Dracula's bride in lacy white.

"Oh, sweet Christ on a cracker," I wheeze. I've lost my voice from the smoke.

Capes and eyeliner, bro. Who would've thought that'd be the thing to raise my core temperature? I really need to have a sit-down chat with my id, but this is not the time.

They walk alongside an older couple I assume are his parents, dressed as a regal queen and king in shades of gold and black. His mom is petite, shorter than me even, and carries a cane. Daniel's arm is linked through hers for additional support, long strides shortened to match hers. The sight of them, two dark heads bent together, makes my heart give a sharp, painful squeeze. My God, this love is hurtful. A fearful, hurtful thing.

My breath comes faster. *Oh, shit. I . . . I love him.* The knowledge was there all along in the shallows, waiting for waves to roll it to the shore, but my timing is the worst.

I want to look away, but I don't. "This *can't* be happening," I say to no one in particular.

"What's not happening?" Brent asks, joining me.

I turn and smile, fake as his bot followers on social media. "Nothing. Just getting a little hungry."

He eyes my half-drunk champagne. "One glass," he says. "And don't take off again." He squeezes my wrist, too hard. "I don't like having to search for you."

Hell if I'll follow either bit of that "advice." Especially when—oh God, Daniel's seen me.

He looks at me across the room, taking in my risqué gown, and it's as if everyone else has disappeared.

I don't move, can't breathe. My skin is unbearably hot, despite so little being covered. Brent speaks to me, but he sounds far away, on an island, voice muffled by the thunder of the ocean.

Daniel's shock melts away, morphing to determination, his entire body angling in our direction. He takes a few steps toward me before being called back by another person, distracted for the time being.

I know him, though. He'll absolutely introduce himself to me and Brent if I don't find a way to evade. And I might be a decent actress, but I don't think I'm good enough to pretend I don't know him from Adam. Damn him.

"Sure, babe," I say to Brent, sweet as syrup. I have no idea what he said, and it doesn't matter. He just wants my subservience. "Whatever you think is best."

He smiles, mollified to see me so amenable. "Good. I have to make the rounds. Will you be okay on your own for a while?"

I don't want to introduce you as my date, he might as well have said. Naturally, it's fine if *he* wants to mingle, but heaven forbid I have the same freedom. Still, I'll be glad to be rid of him.

"Of course. I know my way around a gala." I sip more bottled starlight so I can watch his skin pink with irritation. He turns, frowning, and goes back to his glad-handing.

Thankfully, he didn't notice my panic at watching both spheres of my life crash together in spectacular slow motion. Like galaxies colliding, there's bound to be wreckage.

As soon as Brent's back is turned, I down the remainder of my champagne.

This night just became far more interesting.

14

TWO HOURS LATER, I've still somehow managed to avoid Daniel, So Ah, and his parents, ducking behind pillars and spinning circles around the Bay Area's elite. It might be funny if it weren't imperative. I *cannot* meet his parents sporting the raciest dress I've ever worn—I'd expire on the spot. Melt from fatal mortification.

After dinner, however, the one glass of champagne and all the water I've been drinking have caught up to me, and I stand to excuse myself from the table.

"You're going to miss my speech," Brent says, in a tone suggesting there'll be hell to pay if I do.

"Sorry, *babe.*" I give him my best apologetic smile, already backing away. "Nature calls. I promise I'll hurry."

Before he can say anything else, I put distance between us, clickety-clacking in my heels.

I'm just past the ballroom entrance when a deep voice says, "If I didn't know any better, I'd say you were avoiding me."

I stop in my tracks and turn.

There Daniel is in the shadows, looking like he leapt straight out of my fantasies.

If I could see my blood, I'm certain it'd be shimmering with heat. As it is, warmth blooms everywhere across my neck and chest, into my face, all the way up my scalp.

"Can you blame me?" I fold my arms.

He steps closer, looking amused. The points of his artificially elongated incisors press into his full lower lip, and once I notice, I can't tear my gaze away.

"Don't trust me to speak extemporaneously?" He removes his black leather gloves, one finger at a time. In my one-track mind, the subtle movements are foreplay. Would that everyone could live in such a blissful unreality. "I bet I could've come up with something."

"I don't even know what that word means. Also, I have to pee. You're holding me up."

"By all means." He does laugh then, and waves a hand for me to continue. "You did look like you were doing the dance."

I swivel on a heel and march into the bathroom.

Inside, So Ah leans against the white marble counter, reapplying her lipstick in a shade of blood red. My stomach hollows out and I blink several times, momentarily stunned by how gorgeous she is in person, like I've crossed paths with a gothy unicorn.

In the mirror, she notices me gaping, and her face lights up in recognition. "Dylan, right? Daniel's friend?" Her English is flawless, just a hint of an accent.

"Um, yes, hi!" I do an awkward wave. "That's me. And you're Yoon So Ah, right?"

She nods. "It's wonderful to meet you." Her smile is wide and beautiful, much like Daniel's. How lovely they look together, standing side by side. How right.

"So nice to meet you too. Daniel said you went to grad school together?"

"That's right. I got my MBA while he was in engineering."

"Must be nice to see him again," I venture.

"We always kept in touch." She pulls her long, silky hair over one shoulder. "But yes, it's been great to see him in person again. His parents too. They're so sweet. I'm so glad his oma could come out tonight."

"I bet she's glad for a change in scenery too." I pick at a hangnail before noticing her noticing and stopping, awkwardly dropping my hands. "Well, I hope you have a great visit in the States." My bladder can't hang on much longer. Neither can my self-confidence. I feel like a short and trashy homunculus next to her, though it's no fault of hers. She just exudes class and poise. "With good news at the end of it, maybe?"

So Ah looks me up and down. Not in a condescending way, though I imagine she'd do so to great effect, but more of a considering pause. "Daniel says you're his best friend. The person he trusts most in the world. I hope . . ." She bites her lip. "I hope that means we can be friends too? He's a pretty good judge of character."

It must've taken guts for her to admit all of that, if the way she's wringing her fine-boned hands is any indication. How can I not like this person?

"Of course! Maybe if you have time before you head back to Seoul, I can take you out for breakfast? Where are you staying?"

"The Ritz-Carlton. I'd love to meet up for brunch." She smiles again and sighs. "Maybe you can even help me crack that shell of his. He's always been private, but I thought maybe it'd be easier, having known each other before . . ." She trails off.

Her vulnerability makes the guilt pool in my stomach. It's in my nature to want to help people. I wouldn't have picked this odd profession otherwise.

"You bet." I speak past the tightness in my throat. "I know a good brunch place nearby the Ritz. And yeah, he does have thick walls, that Daniel."

She nods knowingly. For a second, she looks like she might cry.

She's so different from who I expected, the typical cut-throat, future CEO on the rise. I wish I hadn't judged her before I met her.

"It was so nice to meet you," she says. "I'll find you later and we can exchange numbers."

"It was great to meet you too. And yes, come find me later!" *Just not in front of Shithead.*

I wave good-bye and lock myself in a stall.

"Oh, for fuck's sake." The tears well up out of nowhere. "What am I doing?"

She's so in love with him. And she's trying so hard to be good to him. Win him over. The least I could do is remove myself from the picture, but instead, I'm going to befriend her as well, like a lonely drunkard at a party exchanging numbers with any old rando. I pinch the bridge of my nose, stemming the rush of tears. It'd be a crime to ruin Noah's exquisite handiwork, an expansive black cat eye lined with shimmery gold.

After I wash my hands, I stare hard at my reflection. I look more familiar indeed, with dark eyebrows drawn in and my blonde hair hidden by a black wig, but I loathe this teary-eyed version of myself. "Tits up. Knives out."

It'll be a dick move, but I'll have to beg off from the brunch date with So Ah. The last thing I need is to delve deeper into this already-tense arrangement between me, her, and Daniel. My business depends on clear-eyed deci-sions and quick thinking, neither of which I've been doing lately. And Daniel's sense of duty to his parents will forever preclude anything we might share together. Now that I've seen his mom, I realize just how important it is that he follow through with his promise. So why walk a road to nowhere? He could be happy with So Ah, if only I'd get out of the goddamn way.

When I have my act together, I tiptoe back to the ballroom and take my seat.

Brent has assumed command of the podium and drones on and on about his commitment to the environment. If I weren't already drowsy from the champagne (small-people problems), I'd be well on my way to falling asleep.

With everyone's attention focused on the front of the room, though, it's time to dispense the diphenhydramine. I reach into my clutch and dig out the preground powder, six pills' worth, then take Brent's mostly full glass as my own, bringing it to rest on my lap. No one will question me. Looking at Brent the entire time, gaze turned lovingly upward, I drop the powder in his glass and swirl.

When the powder's dissolved, I take a tiny sip. Plausible deniability. The aftertaste is bitter, but I doubt he'll notice. For someone who wanted to control how much I drank, he had more than enough for both of us.

Twenty minutes into this soliloquy, and he's still only partway through the story of his summit to Everest and how it brought him closer to nature and in touch with his own spirituality, yada, yada, yada. Once again, I should've made a bingo card to liven up my evening, this time for New Age Bullshit. There's no mention, of course, of the three to four tons of carbon dioxide his flight to Kathmandu dumped into the atmosphere. No mention, either, of the Sherpas tasked with carrying his seventy pounds of crap five miles high into thin air, cooking his meals, and setting up his tent so he could be the big man.

A gentle tap on my shoulder keeps me from completely checking out and leaving.

I look up, startled to find Daniel slipping into Brent's vacant seat without a sound.

"What did you say to So Ah?" he asks, without looking at me. "She was really upset when she left the bathroom."

"Nothing unkind." I shift, taken aback, then irked at his accusatory tone and presence. If Brent sees him, there'll be consequences. I may well be envious of her, my aura shining sickly green, but he ought to know I'd never take shots at another woman. The world is hard enough without operating from a bullshit scarcity mindset, clawing at each other over men. For God's sake, there are always more fish in the sea.

None like him, though, a small, unwelcome voice pipes up. Someone who, by his own admission, shunned the women-as-objects mindset so pervasive among the new-money technorati who couldn't get laid in high school.

Daniel shoots me a skeptical glance, one brow skewed.

I suppress the urge to stab his calf with my stiletto.

"I mean, we introduced ourselves in the bathroom, talked about you guys and your parents for a minute, and she said she wanted to meet up with me later, maybe grab brunch near her hotel, but that was it. I don't know why she'd be upset, but it wasn't anything we said to each other." I sip some water. "Also, you should *not* be sitting here."

Daniel chews his lower lip with the fangs, thinking. Then he says, "Okay. I believe you."

"Good." My smile is tight. "Now, shoo. Go take care of your mama."

He frowns and slinks away, much like the Count himself, swift and agile.

When Brent is finally done congratulating himself and the tepid applause starts, I come back online, rise to my feet, smile and clap. *Isn't my man amazing?* I tell everyone with my over-the-top standing ovation.

He returns to the table, skin flushed, basking in the glow of everyone's more-polite-than-genuine admiration. How do they clap at all? Am I the only one who sees this man for the flesh-eating bacteria he truly is?

"Let's go," he says.

"Aren't we going to stay for the dancing?" I feign surprise.

He shoots me a broad smile. "No."

The first inklings of alarm dump into my stomach, icy hot. If he doesn't drink the champagne, extricating myself will become magnitudes more difficult. I could claim self-defense if needed, but involving the police really isn't an option. My false identity won't stand up for more than a minute.

"I thought we were spending time together after you had to work last night." I try for a pout. "Besides, I bet other people will want to talk to you after your amazing speech."

"So what? I did what I needed to do here." He gathers his phone.

"At least finish your champagne." I hold out the flute invitingly.

He shakes his head. "No. I've already had enough."

Really, this of all nights he finds restraint? My hackles lift with frustration. And fear.

I thought I could sleep with him if I absolutely had to, to get into his good graces, lower his guard, but I've broken into a nervous, acrid sweat. The idea of being stuck beneath him is enough to lace a corset around my lungs, squeezing and squeezing.

I look around for a way to stall, buy myself time, but I've already used up my bathroom excuse. The small bit of antihistamine must've dulled my thinking too. I'm so off my game it's terrifying.

Across the room, Daniel's gaze meets mine. He reads my involuntary body language like a book—angling away from Brent while he pulls my elbow, forcing me along.

No, I mouth.

It doesn't matter. Daniel's already on his feet, picking his way around the tables and people, eating up ground with those long legs. Seconds later, he's in Brent's face, over-enthused, reaching out to shake his hand. "Big fan, big fan. So great to meet you in person. I didn't know you were a mountaineer!"

Brent looks bemused but thaws under Daniel's worship. A narcissist never says no to a potential neophyte. He stands up straighter, though Daniel still has a few inches on him. "I've been an alpinist for a few years now. Are you into climbing?"

"I tackled Denali last year, and I've been wanting to give Everest a shot. Feels like this would be a good time, now the Sherpas finally stopped their strike." Daniel rolls his eyes.

Even I'm shocked at how quickly he shapeshifts, assuming a douchey, entitled-bro persona. He's bloody brilliant. The dig about Denali will rankle too. No slave labor permitted.

"Right." Brent shakes his head, not looking at all sorry for the twenty-six people who died in a massive avalanche trying to earn a living catering to selfish twats like him.

"So, tell me what it was like on the summit." Daniel glances over his shoulder at me.

I've been so busy watching him, I didn't realize Brent let go of my arm. Only now does the joint throb. He grabbed hard enough to bruise.

I swallow my pride for the second time this evening and take the assist.

Thank you, I mouth.

He nods, infinitesimal.

When my back is turned, I dig my burner phone out of my clutch and pretend to take a call, finger pressed in my free ear as though to block the chatter from the gala. My blood races when Brent calls after me, but I give a remorseful wave and keep moving. I'll text him later with the terrible news, whatever it may be.

For now, escape is the only thing that matters.

CHAPTER

15

IT'S DARK AND smoky when I return to my houseboat after taking a circuitous route to lose anyone tailing me, sky roiling scarlet over the lights of the city. Feels like there should be noise to accompany the brimstone night, but it's quieter than usual. Subdued. Every creature seems to sense the menace on the wind, hunkering down with their families and young. It's only the night creatures like me remaining awake. And alone. It's just me, candles, and my gas fireplace, small puddles of light here and there on the boat.

My location services are turned off, and I silenced my burner on the way home, but a glance at the screen shows two missed calls from Brent. He's not concerned about me; he craves control. I slipped through his groping fingers yet again (with much thanks to Daniel), and there'll be hell to pay, but I can't right now.

I could kick something, I'm so frustrated I lost my chance to get into his home. Instead, I type a quick message.

I'm sorry I had to bail tonight. My aunt had to evacuate because of the fires, and I don't know if she made it out in time. I'm staying at my cabin until I know more, waiting for her to get here.

It could well be true. The last I checked, the fire was tracking east, but changeable winds could've driven it toward my mom's sister's house. God, I hope Helena is okay. I hope we'll all be okay. Nights like this, I can't help but think we're doomed. The thought of Daniel's little one someday wearing a mask because of the smoke makes my heart hurt. And clench with an urge to protect, an instinct I won't examine too closely.

I see three quick dots as Brent starts to reply. Then they disappear.

He doesn't even pretend to be sorry. Just another reason to be glad I left him high and dry, even if it set me back. How far am I willing to go to slay a monster? I thought I could wear my chain mail and harden my heart, but when every cell in my body wants to be as far from him as possible, I don't know how I'll do what needs to be done.

I have underestimated him and overestimated myself.

I wonder if this will be the first mission I'll fail.

I grimace and unclasp my heels, wincing as my arches stretch in contact with the radiant-heat floor. Then I unbutton my shimmery gown, letting it pool around my ankles, and step out of the warm fabric. It's a stunning dress. I wish I could've worn it for someone I care about.

Daniel.

I can't believe the way he rushed in, putting himself bodily between Brent and me. Somehow, he knew I was shaking in my stilettos. I'm so damned lucky to have a friend like him. Would anyone else have stood up for me like that, or would they have let me be dragged away?

I flop on the foot of my couch and press the heels of my palms to my eyes to stop the tears boiling up, smudging the heavy shadow with skin and salt water.

His best friend . . . the person he trusts most in the world.

No. I can't go there. Not when So Ah looked so crushed when we met in the bathroom. As if she had everything she ever wanted, except the one thing that mattered.

You and me both, girl. I stand and sigh, trying to tame my stormy heart. My mouth curls in a smile that feels a whole lot bitter. A successful job. A family that loves me from afar. But no one to share the good and bad with. After Gabrielle suffered, after she walked through a shadowy no-man's-land between the living and dead, I closed myself off and made sure no one got close enough to hurt.

Still wearing my black lace teddy, I tread to the bathroom and slip into my silk robe. Then I remove my wig, returning it to my Moira Rose collection, and wipe away Noah's artwork.

The distinctive plink of raindrops on the metal roof makes me freeze. Could it be?

I turn off the light and hustle downstairs, back to the living room. Outside, the droplets splatter onto my deck and the ocean, silver in the light from everyone's homes.

The rain. The *rain*.

After months without, I can't miss this religious experience.

I slide open the door and step out into the drizzly nirvana. I lift my arms and face to the sky, receiving my benediction.

Already the air smells better, petrichor filling my nose. Already I'm clean.

And cold. I shiver, goose bumps pebbling my skin, the silk clammy and stuck to my body, but it's worth it. God, it's so worth it. I feel like Andy Freaking Dufresne breaking out of prison.

A loud knock booms at my door.

I jump back inside the house. The silence after the knock is expectant. Like someone knows I'm home.

My heart rate skyrockets. Brent? Did he follow me?

I tiptoe to the door, jumping when there's another loud knock.

"Jesus *Christ*," I hiss. I grab my favorite knife from the desk drawer and hold it close to my chest. Then I peer through the peephole, ready to send Brent to the ER. Or slice him to ribbons and toss him overboard for the great whites. I'm sure they'd appreciate the midnight snack.

"Haas?" I don't recognize my own voice. High-pitched. Breathy.

I throw open the door.

He stands under the eave like a gift from the rain itself. His shoulders lift and fall too fast, like he ran all the way from the hotel to my home. His cape and waistcoat are gone, and the rain seeps through his white, high-collared shirt, plastering it to the expanse of his shoulders. His hair isn't neat and slicked back anymore, threatening to fall forward into his eyes again, and his skin has taken on a glazed gold sheen. His gaze drills into me, black and full of heat.

He glances from my knife back up to my face, presumably still frozen in a rictus of alarm.

Whatever kinetic energy spiriting him to my home seeps out of his body, loosening the hard set of his jaw and making his shoulders sag.

"I'm sorry," he croaks. "I should've known you'd be . . . on high alert, after Brent."

"That's a nice way of describing my utter terror."

My voice sounds scraped and hoarse, like it did when I had bronchitis eons ago, when my business was still fledgling and I worked all hours, trying to claw out a living. Keep up with demand after Ruth helped me get the ball rolling. It caught up to me, all right—I couldn't talk or even move without hurting. The only thing that kept me going was . . . Daniel. Bringing me homemade gomtang, beef bone soup, every day. He left it at my door each morning before he went to work. The next day, an electric blanket. The next day, more tea than I knew what to do with. I couldn't do much, but knowing the soup was waiting got me up and moving. I'd text him *Thank you, Haas*, to which he always replied *Anything for you, Dylan*. I couldn't keep much down, but the heat and umami comforted me when nothing else would. Brought me back from the brink when I wasn't sure how to do it on my own.

I grip the doorframe to steady myself from the strength of the memory washing over me. What a myopic moron I've been. How could he have been right under my nose this entire time? Unassuming but determined, altering my structure bit by bit, like a black hole siphoning nearby stars.

"I should've let you know I was on the way, but I didn't know I was coming here until I was already across the bridge," he says.

"How'd you know I'd be here instead of Pac Heights?"

A one-shouldered shrug. "Just had a feeling."

"Why are you here, though?"

He meets my gaze again. My pulse leaps and skitters. I could not mistake the look in his eyes for anything else. Pure, undiluted desire. Mirror to my own. Every bit of my body feels light enough to float away, disappear into the rain.

"Will you set Dark Sister down first?" He smiles, a little unsure. The uncertainty compels me, draws me in. There's nothing more attractive than someone who knows not to take anything for granted. That, and he remembers the decidedly dorky name for my knife, because of course he does. I couldn't make this guy up. "And we could talk?"

"Where is So Ah?" I can't let him off the hook that easily. Even if his hair is messy and disheveled, eyes still smudged with traces of eyeliner, smoky and intense. He looks like himself still, but with the volume turned all the way up. My litany of excuses to turn him away grows thinner by the moment. Goddamn it all.

"At her hotel. Tomorrow, she'll fly back to Seoul."

I have to lift my jaw from the floor before I can answer. "What? Why?"

"Can I come inside?" The rain's still splattering his shirt. Dripping down his long neck, traveling the broad wing of his collarbone, collecting in the hollow of his throat.

I shake my head, not trusting my voice. It's as if he's really a vampire and once he's permitted entry, vaulting past the threshold, I know I'll never be able to say no to him again.

He opens his mouth. Closes it. The trickle of blood is gone, and so are the long incisors, but his teeth are still white and glowing in the dim light.

"She said she knew I'd never look at her the way I do you." His voice sounds ground up, weighted with emotion.

It's so quiet. Just rain. Breathing. Heartbeats.

"Daniel." His name rolls off my tongue like an offering. The way I speak in my dreams.

He inhales deep, eyes wide, searching. "I wondered when you'd say my name like that. I've waited . . ." He shakes his head. "Lifetimes. Hoping you would."

"It's over with her?" I have to be sure.

He hesitates. Considering the secondary, tertiary consequences. The family he'll be disappointing. How I wish I were enough for him, the way he is for me. My whole world and everyone in it.

Then he nods.

Thank fuck. Maybe I can be enough, if only for a night. Just one night.

My hands tremor, but I reach for him. Tracing the placket of his shirt, the iridescent mother-of-pearl buttons.

His warmth reaches my fingertips despite the chill and damp.

He sighs, shuddering. Dissolving, even at such a small touch.

I never knew what power was until this moment.

My control evaporates. I grab a greedy fistful of his fine shirt and pull him across the invisible boundary. *Yes*, I say with my hands. *Yes. Yes, forever.*

He stumbles past the entry, toe of his oxford catching on the frame, but rights himself with the preternatural grace of a cat.

I shut the door behind him, lock it, and push him against the back. Inside my small home, he's completely still, immense, absorbing all the light. At odds with my volcanic desire, or at least doing a better job tempering his.

"Dylan?" He steps forward, hesitant. "We should talk—"

"Hush." I push him against the door again and brace myself on his chest while I stand on my toes to kiss him.

His lips are soft, hot. Lush. And unmoving.

Undeterred, I pull away and get to work on his buttons. I want him bared, all of him. He smells divine with wet skin and hair, the water bringing out the scent of his citrusy, cedary shampoo. "Just let me—"

"No." He takes me by the shoulders, firmly, but gentle, and puts space between us.

His hands are warm through my robe, and I miss the heat when he lets go. The candlelight flickers across his sharp features, casting them into shadow and bas-relief. I blink up at him, daunted.

"No, what?" I demand. Brimming with impatience. With aching, terrible need.

"I won't touch you until I know I can. Until you tell me what I can do, or not do." His voice is deep enough to feel in the soles of my feet, traveling up my legs. Higher.

"Anything," I say.

His breath leaves in a small puff, and his eyes are so dilated, I barely see the dark-brown iris any longer, just the thinnest edge ringing his pupil. "Anything?"

"I . . ." *Love you.* "I trust you. If something doesn't feel good, I'll tell you. Otherwise?" I shrug. "I'm yours."

He blinks once. Twice. Then a slow smile folds the corner of his mouth and grows.

I smile back, happy to see him happy. Like a child, my joy is that simple.

Convinced of his welcome, he takes off his shoes and sets them by the door. Such a simple gesture shouldn't be so appealing, but it is, attention to detail and consideration wrapped together in one tidy act.

"What about you?" It's strange to have this conversation with someone I've known so long, setting up boundaries of this variety, but I'm dying to know what's inside his mind.

"What have I told you all along?" His smile grows another degree. "Anything for you, Dylan. Whatever you want to give, I'll take."

Without further ado, he picks at the buttons of his shirt and rolls it off his shoulders, letting it fall to the floor.

I hold my breath, realizing I've never seen him shirtless before. A short-sleeved shirt at most in the summer. My imaginings weren't far off, however. Whereas I'm sure he was lanky as a teen, he's grown into his frame as an adult, body solid and sleek. Two decades of cycling and weight lifting and trail running in Marin have kept him in unreal shape, such that I'm self-conscious in my short robe.

"Christ," I say. "Are you for real with this?"

"With what?" He seems genuinely puzzled, the impossible man.

I wave in his vicinity. "If I had a body like yours, I'd be naked all the time." All that biological art hiding beneath his three-piece suits—like a present waiting to be unwrapped—makes more heat gather between my thighs.

He shakes his head. "The traffic is bad enough without you stopping it."

I roll my eyes and try to hide my smile. "Stopping it in a bad way."

"In a good way." He's already begun a slow perusal, gaze lingering here and there.

I should feel naked standing in front of him with nothing but the merest whisps of wet fabric clinging to my body, but I don't, because the only sensation is familiarity, rightness. I stand taller, glowing under his luxuriant inspection, self-consciousness ebbing away. Enough to undo the tie on my robe and let it fall.

His eyes widen, his hands fist. "This was what you had on?" He moves so fast, I don't have time to answer before his hands are on my neck, my breasts, caressing, just this side of rough. "Dylan . . ." His voice is choked. "You'll be the death of me."

He breathes slow and deep. Decelerating after his lapse. Determined to savor, it seems. Then he rubs warmth into my upper arms, still flecked with goose bumps, and up my neck.

"Your skin," he murmurs, knuckles grazing the edge of my jaw. "I've never felt anything like it."

I send up a silent prayer of thanks to the kind, very thorough ajumeoni at the spa for turning me velveteen. "You should talk." His skin is fine-grained, glowing with health even in the faint light.

"You were out in the rain?" His hands drift to my hair, sifting it through his fingers.

I nod, embarrassed by my water fairy moment. "I love the first rain of the season."

"Me too." He tucks a wet strand behind my ear. "It always smells so good. And then the world feels new again, doesn't it?" Before I can answer, he leans down, nose skimming up the length of my shoulder. "I can smell it on your skin." Then he places a warm, open-mouthed kiss on the tender spot where my ear meets my jaw.

I shiver from his breath floating past my ear, breaking into fresh goose bumps. I was ready for urgency. For messiness, mindlessness. Not his slow, cerebral seduction. Everything he does is deliberate, though. Why would this conquest be different?

Carefully, when I'm sure my hands have warmed a little, I place them on his abdomen. His bare skin is hot to the touch, pulsing with life. The texture is like satin, smooth and supple.

He stiffens.

"You're so warm. My hands are still probably icicles." I pull them away. It's not like me to be deferential, but then again, I knew I'd never see other guys after I had my way with them.

With Daniel? God knows what the night—or morning—will bring.

"Don't." He catches my fingers, places them back where they were, at the lowest rung of his rib cage. I can't peel my eyes away from the handful of veins crisscrossing his abs, disappearing beneath the dress pants. "You can keep going."

His voice already sounds ragged. I wonder how long it's been for him. Longer than my unholy, self-imposed drought? Probably not. Encouraged, I trail my fingers down the firm ridges of his stomach, listening to his breath quicken the lower I go.

When I reach for his belt buckle, however, he tips my face back up, lifting my chin with a single finger. He's smiling, as if he knew exactly where I'd been headed.

"Easy, tiger."

He cups my jaw with both hands, holding me like I'm made of water, liable to slip away if he's not careful. He leans down, pressing his forehead to mine, breath skating across my face, short and choppy. I lift onto my toes, absorbing his exhalations, taking him into my blood.

Our lips are inches apart. I can't think about anything other than closing that miniscule gap. Finally learning the true taste of him. His nearness floods me, heightening every sense to unbearable degrees, blowing every fuse.

"Daniel."

"Hmm?"

"Kiss me," I say, pretending it doesn't sound like a plea.

"Anything for you, Dylan." Still smiling, he brings his mouth down to mine.

16

THE LAST THING I see before I close my eyes is the wolf-ish flash of Daniel's teeth in the corner of his mouth. I already know the image will be seared into my memory.

He surprises me by aiming elsewhere, delivering a teasing kiss to the tip of my nose. Another at the corner of my mouth. More on my cheekbones, feather light.

With each pass, I squirm, wanting more contact, more force. More.

His laughter leaves a puff of steam against my cheek.

Then his lips press against mine, soft and perfect.

I gasp at the unexpected pressure, inhaling the sweet, peppery bite of cinnamon as I breathe him in. The kiss is so different from Brent's toxic invasion, it makes my eyes water with something too much like adoration. I have never been kissed like this. Like I matter.

A small, hungry noise builds in my throat, escaping when I break away a fraction.

Daniel's control snaps.

He kisses me again, hard, angling my jaw to get deeper.

I can't help but reply with a bite to his lower lip, sinking my teeth into him. He tastes so good, better than I ever could've imagined. And I did, waking up in the middle of the night after dreams that would damn my soul forever.

His hands rove everywhere, pressing into my spine, arching me toward him. A moan rises from deep in his chest and coaxes my mouth open before I know it's happened. The tip of his tongue grazes mine in a delicious swipe and my ears ring with the change in blood pressure.

Single-minded, his hands travel low, pulling my hips flush to him. His erection juts into my stomach, pulsing, warm even through fabric.

Fused, he walks me backward, never breaking our kiss.

My legs catch the edge of the sectional and I fall back, breathing hard, light-headed, not sure how I wound up there. It's like my brain melted on the way, blinking in and out of awareness.

Daniel stands tall, backlit by the fire like some vengeful god of the underworld.

Shivers course through my body. Is it the damp lace or the way he's looking at me, like he's going to consume me whole?

I sit up before he can devour, somehow plucking the important information out of my lust haze. "I have an IUD, but I don't have condoms."

He takes it in stride. "I brought one."

I raise a brow.

He has the good sense to look a little abashed. His skin tone isn't the sort to betray a blush, but color fills his skin, turning it rose gold.

"Cheeky," I say.

"Hopeful?" he counters. "Prepared?"

"Nuh-uh." I laugh. "Don't try to rebrand this one, sir."

He smiles, fiendish. "And if I brought more than one? What would you say then?"

For the first time in my life, I'm without words. I swallow, hoping to find them. "Do you need one? For STIs?"

He shakes his head.

"Me neither. I was tested a while back. There hasn't been anyone . . ." I cover myself, wishing I knew how to stop rambling. "Like I said, it's been a while. A long while." I sit up. "So, I guess the, uh . . . option is there, if you want to . . ."

"To come?" His voice is all gravel. "Inside you?"

I nod.

He breathes out, then looks up. "Would you feel better if I wore a condom?"

"Probably." My smile is tight. "Don't want to be the case study exception. Especially now."

A shadow flits over his face. "Then I will."

I heave a sigh of relief. I can't imagine becoming pregnant with everything going on. Trying to protect myself as well as another life.

Daniel takes advantage of my pause and kneels to clasp my ankles, long fingers overlapping. His palms are hot enough to lift the lingering goose bumps from my skin. He continues upward, kneading warmth into my calves, the tendons surrounding my knees. When his hands reach my thighs, prizing them apart, I stop breathing.

He looks up, meeting my gaze, eyes liquid and heated. "Lay back."

There's something in the quiet, fierce tone of his voice that makes me acquiescent, compliant. I obey, head falling back on the soft cushion.

"Instant agreement?" His fingers trail up the inside of my thigh, chased by a warm kiss. "Must be a first."

"Guess you just needed to get me naked." I struggle beneath his secure hold, trying to inch my way closer to him, aching for friction. Everything from waist to knees throbs and tightens.

"You don't know how long I've wanted to." His voice is a curl of smoke, breath fanning across my hyper-flushed skin. His hands roam up and over my teddy and reach beneath the delicate straps. "Let me?"

"Please." I sit up and obligingly lower the thin straps over my shoulders.

He peels the wet fabric down my body, dropping it on the floor without a glance.

The silence while he takes me in is freighted. I resist the urge to cover myself.

"Just look at you." He swallows hard, Adam's apple shifting. "Dylan, you're so lovely."

He shakes his head, gaze heavy lidded, unfocused. "So lovely."

He drops to his knees again and kisses me. One arm goes around my back, the other under the heavy weight of my hair, fingers wrapping tight around the nape of my neck.

He feels so good against my bare skin, I can't help pushing up against him, pressed chest to chest. His body is so different from mine, so unyielding. I sink my fingers into his dark hair and tug. His hair is cold at the ends, still damp, but warm at the roots and soft as mink.

Daniel groans and pulls me even tighter, like he wants to crush us together.

His lips drift to my neck, pressing kiss after kiss down the length, then across the top swell of my breasts. When his mouth closes over a tight bud, laving it with his tongue, I whimper.

The sight of him bent to taste, cheeks hollowed, dark hair obscuring his eyes, makes liquid fire race south. The sensation gathers and surges the longer he goes on, leaving me shaky and gasping.

He resumes his work on the other side. Each pull with his tongue winds me up more. A fine mist of sweat collects in all the depressions of my body, and my whimpering grows louder and louder. It feels indescribably good, like I could climax from the pressure of his mouth and teeth alone.

Breathing hard through his nose, he abruptly pulls back.

I look up, dazed, wondering what stopped him from carrying me away. Wondering if I'll live to see the other side of this fever dream. My skin glistens everywhere he touched me.

He widens my legs, spreading them to fit his shoulders.

I don't have time to take a breath before he parts me with his tongue, mouth so soft and hot I cry out. Stars dance in and out of my vision as he picks up where he left off, one decadent lick after another.

I writhe on the cushions, hips rocking, grasping for something to anchor to.

"Daniel," I gasp. I don't know what I'm asking for. Begging for mercy? Relief from the fire filling my body with each passing second?

He groans against me but doesn't pause or ease up. Not even a little.

I let my head fall back, panting. Watching the candlelight cast our twined shadows across the ceiling. Consigned to my fate, one moan after another spilling out of me.

The vibration from his baritone hums of approval travel deep inside, fueling the fire degree by degree. Jesus, God. I pull his hair—too hard—but I've lost all finesse. All remove. I won't withstand this.

Then I have to laugh, because it's just as I suspected. Feared. If given half a chance, my mild-mannered friend would turn into a fire god in bed and immolate me on the spot. No wonder I held him at arm's length as long as humanly possible.

The laughter catches his attention. He lifts his head, brows drawn. Looking fearsome. "That bad?"

His lips are puffy. Wet with me. I blink, still not quite sure how this surreal sequence of events came to be. Flung onto a plateau of arousal I didn't know existed.

"No," I say, because I have no filter. Not anymore. "It's better than I imagined."

Comprehension softens his face, followed by determination, hardening the planes of his cheeks and jaw. "You imagined?"

"More than you know."

In answer, he slides a long finger into me, stroking and caressing.

I gasp at the unexpected invasion. Even a single finger is a stretch, muscles shifting and tightening around him. Drawing him deeper.

"Does it hurt?" he asks.

I shake my head. "You feel so goddamn good." I squeeze on him, hard.

He growls against my skin and bends to resume his thorough devastation with lips and tongue. Between the firm suction and the added pressure from his fingers—oh God, he added another—it's not long before me he's worked me into near-constant shaking, vibrating with tension.

"I can't . . ." I arch my back, lifting my hips closer to his mouth. "Daniel, it feels . . . Fuck, I'm so close."

His grip on my thigh tightens, pinning me down, steadying my frantic movements. He groans into me, hot and loud.

My hold on space and time grows hazy. Everything else falls away. The only things anchoring me are his mouth and hands. Firm, upward strokes, working in concert. Driving me into another plane of existence, suspended between torture and release.

Bright heat rolls up my toes, my legs, gathers under my ribs. The agonizing rush keeps going, pushing me up and up. "Oh my God." My entire body is resonant and taut, like a glass harp tuned to a pitch beyond human hearing.

Then the glass explodes, shattering me along with it. I sob, hips bucking, nails digging merciless crescents into Daniel's forearms.

He doesn't ease up, tongue still teasing and fluttering. The orgasm rolls on and on, waves of ecstasy shimmering. I close my eyes and surrender, letting the delirium consume me until I'm boneless.

When I've stopped quaking, he pulls away. His dark eyes are glazed, and every breath looks like a struggle, tendons in his neck strained. "Dylan, I need you." He palms himself, groaning. "Please, let me fuck you."

I shiver, hearing him say such a filthy word in that precise way of his.

"Yes," I say. Like he didn't deliver me to another dimension minutes ago. "Hurry."

He fumbles with his belt buckle, struggling. Then, frustrated, he yanks it off with a clean snap.

Jesus Christ, he looks like he's in agony. A pressed coil, bursting with potential energy.

The button on his pants is the next casualty when he rips it open and stands to step out of the stiff wool, revealing long, built legs and the firm outline of his erection through the silky-looking boxer briefs. When he drops them, kicking the fabric away, a small nip of apprehension cuts into my admiration.

"I don't know if I—"

"If what?" He pauses, breathing hard, like he remembers he's supposed to be listening to me.

"It's been a long time," I try again.

He catches my meaning and glances down, then back at me, and I know I'm in trouble. "Well. Only one way to find out."

He drops to his knees and begins a slow slide, filling me inch by precious inch.

"Ohhhh." The pressure is unreal, muscles stretching to accommodate. Mere seconds later, however, a deep glow builds inside. A dangerous thrill, powerful enough to render the rest of the world as dull background noise.

"You're so wet," he hisses, sliding another inch. "Ah, fuck."

"Daniel . . ." I wince, but it's so good, I can't tell him to stop.

Nevertheless, he holds himself still. Every vein in his chest and arms stands in relief. "Are you okay?"

I nod. It's beyond my current vocabulary to describe the bite of pain and pleasure, how they work in concert, obliterating everything else.

"You can do it," he says to my neck. "Just take . . . a little more."

He's right, like he usually is. The last bit of resistance gives way. A groan gusts out of him as he sinks to the hilt, head lowered, brows knitted like he's in pain. Then he looks at me, eyes flashing obsidian.

Our gazes lock.

He goes still and quiet. I do too. Not pushing, not thrusting. Not so much as a breath.

The moment is so voltaic, I'm surprised it doesn't burn down my boat.

As it is, everything could go up in flames around us and I'm not sure I'd notice. There's too much awe floating around us, filling the air. The longer I look, the more of the universe and all its secrets I see inside his blown-out pupils. How could I have let this man walk a parallel path for so long?

"Dylan." My name sounds like a prayer. "You're so . . . *so* tight."

"Daniel." I'm shaking, but I lift my hands to his face, touching the strong bones, framing his clean jaw.

I don't dare say more. God knows what ludicrous things might spew out of my mouth. I might tell him I liked his cape, and the following record screech would for sure *for sure* ruin my night.

He begins to move. An easy, experimental lift and release, flexing the muscles in his back and hips.

Even that small, delicious effort is enough to make my vision blur. He's so hard inside me, massaging everything he touches.

He groans and brings his mouth down to mine, delivering a hot, open kiss that steals all my air.

Then he rears back, eyes wide, mouth parted in horror.

"What?" I demand, alarmed by his expression.

"The condom," he rasps. "Dylan, I'm sorry." He starts to withdraw.

I wrap my legs tight around his back, locking him in place.

"Change your mind?" He's already picked up the thread of movement again, the smallest of smiles dancing across his face.

"Looks that way." I shift, welcoming him deeper. "You can thank my drought."

He groans, then smiles in earnest, popping both dimples, a diabolical glint in his eyes. "All work, no play for Lady Justice?" He leans down, words a fiery rush past my ear. "I'm going to make you feel good, darling." A kiss on my throat punctuates the promise. "So good."

I answer with a squeeze, urging him on. "Please."

He's as good as his word. With every deft thrust and roll of his hips, the coal burns hotter inside, flooding my body with new heat. Sweat coats my skin and I start to clench around him, involuntary pulls tugging him deeper and deeper.

"Fuck," he mutters, face buried in my neck and hair, pausing for a moment. I feel his smile against my throat. "You'll kill me if you keep that up."

"It's not . . . on purpose." I pant for air as he picks up again. "You feel . . . God, you feel good."

Face etched with grim determination, he pulls my hips high, positioning me at a new and helpless angle.

Each stroke lights up something deep inside, turning me to a creature of raw sensation. I curve and grind against him, determined to meet each push.

He curses again and reaches to caress the twitching bundle of nerves with his thumb. All the while, his abs flex and torque, thrusts never losing speed.

I turn my head and moan into the pillow, undone by even the slightest added abrasion. It's too much. He's too much, razing me from the inside out. Minutes float by in a fog of arousal so acute, I don't know how I'll live through it.

"I can't," I say. "I can't hang on." The pleasure builds and crests with such speed, it steals my breath.

Daniel's answer is to lean over and draw a taut nipple into his mouth.

The soft tug and swirl of his tongue synced with every stroke feels like a deliberate attack. "Harder." I grip his head to hold him in place. "Please."

He groans into my aching flesh and gives and gives, driving into me. I feel him swell and lengthen inside, if such a thing is possible. His breathing is labored, uneven. Seconds away from release.

The knowledge he's on the knife edge catapults me up and over the final barrier. "Oh," I breathe. "Oh my God . . ."

The wave pushes me higher and higher and higher. When it breaks, I cry his name, dizzy with euphoria.

His thrusts grow irregular, frantic. He grunts and tries to pull away. Out of me.

"No," I gasp. Still riding the last shuddering swell of climax. "Don't. I want you to—"

Daniel gapes at me, frozen for one agonized moment, every muscle rigid.

Then he wrenches himself away. With a broken sound torn from his throat, he spurts onto my stomach, one hot pulse after another after another.

He falls forward, chest heaving, bracing himself with one arm on the back of the couch. Sweat coats his skin, highlighting the broad planes of his chest and shoulders. His eyes search mine out, a thousand unspoken things swimming in his gaze.

I reach for him, desperate to touch, to reassure. To leave trails of love all over his skin and push the hair out of his eyes.

"I'm sorry," I say helplessly. My face and neck burn with residual shame. "I shouldn't have put you on the spot. It just . . ." I shake my head. "You felt . . ." I can't bring myself to say the words out loud. That he made me feel better than I ever have.

He shifts forward, leaning over me, and brings his lips to mine, sweet and silky. "No, Dylan. You don't have anything to be sorry for." With a free hand, he pushes the hair out of my face, lifts my chin up so I have no choice but to meet his eyes. "Even if there's only a fractional chance of conception, I know how you feel about it, and I mean to respect that."

I blink, eyes watering. "Okay." The best I can do, given the love this good man has laid at my feet.

Then he looks around, brows furrowed, presumably searching for something to clean us up with.

"Use my robe." Better than ruining his fine clothing.

He smiles in thanks and reaches a long arm to retrieve it, then wipes me down with the precision of a surgeon. He does his best with the flimsy garment, anyway. Afterward, he pulls me up against his chest, arms wrapping around my back, rubbing circles up and down my spine.

"I don't want you to worry." He breathes into my hair. "Promise I won't cut it so close next time."

Next time. It doesn't seem like a good time to mention how unworried I am. Like my basal brain already settled the matter before cognition could catch up. *Dylan, you are so, so fucked.*

Instead, I tip my head back, doing my best to look skeptical. "Next time, huh?"

He bites his lip, expression caught between plaintive and ready to call my bet.

Then, because he's Daniel, he says, "If it please the lady." He shoots me a luminous, thoroughly winsome smile. "If not, I'll take my leave and fling myself into the bay."

I muffle my laughter against his chest. "Only one of us can be theatric." I look up again. "Stay a while, then. If you want?"

He nods, all humor gone. "I want."

For long minutes, we hold each other, lost in a world of our own.

The sound of rain returns when my breathing settles, pattering the metal roof, louder than the slowing throb of his heartbeat under my cheek. In the distance, sirens howl. Slowly, the mundane creeps in along the borders of the sublime, fragments of outside, other, ordinary working their way into the magic we've created.

What have we done? I can't wrap my head the enormity. We created an entire future in one act. An alternate universe shining with promise, even on a dark, stormy, smoky night. Nothing short of a revelation.

I pull away and stand, sweat-slicked body gliding against his, and pull him up so he's not on his knees anymore.

"Come upstairs with me?" I ask, head tilted back.

The smile starts in his eyes, crinkling the corners. "Yes, darling." His hands frame my face, and he leans down to press a soft kiss to my forehead. "Anything for you."

I could withstand a thousand temptations, but not this. Not his lips pressed to the thin, delicate skin beneath my hairline, warm and possessive. The tender gesture destroys me. I blink back tears, mortified at my own susceptibility.

I'm already lost in him. Hopelessly, miserably lost.

17

W HEN I WAKE, bright sunshine slants into my bedroom. For breathless seconds, I lie still. Last night seems like something I dreamed, an overheated imagination fusing with frustration and edibles to produce something surreal. What a time to be alive.

And I call Noah the romantic.

I roll over with a snort of self-censure bordering on terror.

When my eyes refocus, my heart leaps into my throat, blood flowing fast and hot.

I knew Daniel was still with me—the unbelievable warmth is not mine. His arm is thrown across the small gap between us, gripping my hip, pulling me in. My bed and skin smell like him, lemony and musky. But to see him in my sheets, black hair like a shock of ink on my pillow . . .

No one should be so beautiful in the unforgiving light of late morning. No one should be so beautiful after keeping me up half the night either, but that doesn't stop him from glowing in the sunlight, golden and fine as precious metal.

I'm in over my head.

The thought washes over my brain like the waves lapping at the hull of my boat. Gentle. Insistent. I can't fight the tides, and I can't help but love him more the longer I study his unguarded face, lashes pressed like dark half-moons on his cheeks. Listening to his steady breathing, one even pull after another, torquing the muscles in his shoulders and back in a way I can never unsee.

I said *one* night. I meant it when I said it.

Now? I feel like a kid eyeing the proverbial cookie jar, wondering if I can sneak another.

Daniel stirs.

I freeze. If he opens his eyes, he'll catch me being a first-rate creeper. Not the way I'd like him to start this day. Or ever.

Then he sighs, shifting, and the easy breathing continues.

I'm not surprised he's exhausted. The man knows how to work, but my God, I never could've predicted the deviousness. My chapped lips spread into a smile, glad to feel whisker burn stings everywhere, blooming under the heavy comforter. My insides, too, bear evidence, raw and pleasantly sore, skin chafed and hot and sensitive. I wouldn't be surprised if a few bruises shadow in too. The imprint of his fingers on my thighs, maybe. The places where his teeth met my skin and my skin inevitably gave, yielding to him.

Good.

I want proof. Proof I didn't hallucinate this entire, earth-shattering experience.

I reach out, hand hovering over his back, as if drawing his warmth up to my cold palm.

"You're a cover thief." The sleep-rough version of Daniel's voice makes my stomach do an odd little flip.

"What?" I jerk my hand away and pull the duvet up to my nose, which isn't helping my case, but his sudden, sentient reemergence throws me for a loop. Still, the contrarian in me says, "No, I'm not."

He rolls over, a smile in his eyes, and gestures with a long arm to his bare upper body before returning it to my hip.

As though I need another excuse to look my fill. "Well, maybe."

"You kept rolling and rolling, like a little sea otter wrapping yourself in kelp." He laughs and groans and arches, stretching from end to end like a cat.

"Dammit," I grunt, trying to distribute the covers, but I'm hopelessly tangled. "Guess I'm not used to having someone else in my bed."

He pushes upright and scoots closer to me, a sweet smile soothing the rough edges of my embarrassment. That and the sight of scratches I left in his skin. "Will you hold it against me that I stayed?" His voice is teasing, but threads of uncertainty edge his words.

I shake my head. "If you can handle my cover theft."

"Somehow"—he leans down and places a warm kiss on my forehead, branding me, wrecking me—"I think I'll live."

Will I? is the better question. He looks so relaxed. So . . . content. Every movement fluid, replete with satisfaction. A facet of him I've never seen. It's possible no one has. I watch an exceptional gift, unfolding in real time.

How will I ever go back to Brent now? It's enough to make my throat cinch tight.

No. He doesn't belong here. Not in my—our?—haven. I push Brent away, barricading him. That bastard doesn't get to share in this. Not even in my mind.

"How did you sleep?" Daniel asks, pulling me out of the morass.

"When did you know?" I ask instead.

Daniel stills, shutters. He knows exactly what I'm asking. "You won't like my answer."

I scoot closer, curl up in his lap. Like I can force the words out of him if I just let my breath skate across his collarbone. "Why not?"

A shiver makes his shoulders quake, lifts goose bumps across his skin. His hearing has always seemed sensitive; it doesn't surprise me he'd like a bit of ASMR. He folds me in his arms, erection pressing against my thigh, body like a hot coal. A haven built just for me.

"C'mon," I whisper past his ear, wicked now that I've found his trigger. "Tell me."

He shivers again but shakes his head, looking amused. Hands brushing warmth into my arms, my shoulder, my neck. "You go first. Then I'll tell you."

"Fine." I pout, racking my brain for a good answer. Then, like a shift in the tides, the memory floods me. "Remember when we dealt with that dirtbag landlord? The one who stole deposits and tried to get CPS involved when that mom stood up to him? You took us to that little speakeasy afterward to celebrate, the swanky place above the Chinese restaurant? Where the bartenders were all wearing white tuxes." I grin. "I felt like we stepped onto a movie set or something."

Much of that night is a blur—my first and last tangle with Scotch-heavy cocktails—but a few details lodged in my brain like barbs, never to be removed. The statice blooms I tucked into my half-up hair. His black tonal pinstripe waistcoat and the rolled sleeves of his white oxford, exposing welded muscle. The color of the drink Daniel ordered for me while he served as DD, a lovely lilac concoction in a coupe glass with a deep-purple pansy garnish, named Lotusland. It was tart and sweet and strong enough to make my eyes water. I was so jazzed when the singer with a gardenia behind her ear belted out a sultry "Lilac Wine" around midnight, as if the evening had already been written, and kept exclaiming about it to a patient Daniel, much to his amusement. We stood so close, his body leaning over mine, heat seeping through the silk of my cowl-neck dress. The scent of him reached me in the packed bar, bright citrus notes underpinned by cedar and amber. I couldn't look away from him, the way his skin glowed in the light from the neon tiger on the wall, like he, too, was lit from within.

After he dropped me off at home, I sweated and yearned and abused my vibrator a few times and didn't fall asleep until the sun was already high in the sky and blamed it all on the alcohol, like anyone else swimming the Nile. "I never looked at you the same way again," I say to his skin.

"So." I tip my head back and bring my gaze to his, wondering if this deep dive will ring a bell, or if I swam alone in those murky, estuarine waters—neither friends nor lovers but a strange amalgam of both. "Did I reach too far back in the vault?" I try to keep my voice light.

His expression has changed. Alertness tempered with remembrance, softening the sharp contours of his face. "I remember it well." A small, pleased smile lifts the edge of his mouth. "That was a good night."

"You always find . . ." I sigh into his shoulder. "The best places."

"Any excuse to see you in silk," he purrs past my ear.

"I wanted to dance with you."

"Just as well we didn't." Amusement laces his voice. "I probably would've crushed your feet with my derp moves and ruined my chances once and for all."

"You mean to tell me you weren't scouted to join a K-pop group?"

"It was a modeling agency. My freshman year at Stanford."

"Of course it was." My laughter sounds hoarse and ragged. Crazed. "Do you have to be so extra?"

"Would you rather I wasn't?" His fingers trail the juncture of my hips. Teasing. Testing. "Should I back off?"

"Don't you dare." I smother my smile in his neck. His pulse pounds under my lips, contrary to the cool and calm he exudes. "Now, you fess up. When did you know?"

He breathes deep, then he pulls back to meet my gaze. "From the beginning, Dylan."

I blink, sure I've misheard him. Five years is a long time to hold a torch.

He can't be saying that.

"Weren't you dating someone at the time?" Like I don't know already. She was a coworker of his, in development, whip-smart and gorgeous and crazy fit from all her Peloton action. I still made a file for her in case she ended up being a jerk. Even then, I didn't want his feelings hurt.

"I was, but it wasn't serious." He swallows. "Not after we met."

"My compliments to your poker face, sir." Even after waiting for composure, my voice is weak. Throttled. "Why didn't you ever say anything?"

"What would I have said, exactly? *Please love me?*"

"It might've worked." I sound defensive to my own ears.

Daniel smiles, bittersweet, and shakes his head. "I couldn't make you feel anything you didn't want to feel. That's Nice Guy shit, and you know it. I didn't have an ulterior motive, I just . . ." He sighs into my neck. "I cared about you. Even if you didn't feel the same way, I was happy to be in your orbit."

I search his face, waiting for him to follow up with something. Moderate the intensity. Anything.

He doesn't.

Of course not. People always step away from the truth, but he never has. His dark, unflinching eyes assess the world as it stands, not as we wish it, not as it should be. It's part of what drew me to him in the beginning, and the reason I still like him so much.

Across the bay, the fog rolls in and the deep blast of the foghorns on the bridge travel across the water. A warning, perhaps, but I was never much good at heeding them.

He doesn't mean it, though. He can't. That would assign more meaning to this carnal undertaking than either of us can afford.

For the first time since we woke up, he looks nervous, the muscles along his jaw tightening. "Last night was . . ." His mouth works, searching for words and tossing them out. Then he gives up and meets my gaze, a V between his brows, as if hoping I'll fill in the gaps. Describe the impossible.

I pick up his hand, tracing the pattern of raised veins and smoothing the fine, dark hair. Having this conversation is like picking our way through the aftershocks of a massive earthquake, struggling through rubble to find solid ground. I consider lying, diminishing, but I can't.

"It was good, Daniel." I flip his hand over, close my eyes, and press my lips to the center of his hot palm. "It was so good."

His fingers flex against my cheek, stretching to my hairline. "You were there too?" His voice is rough again, filled with sand. And wonder. "With me?"

Wherever "there" was. Maybe we found Lotusland after all.

I open my eyes, meet his gaze. Dark, unfathomable. "Yes."

"What does that mean?"

I can't help but smile. Of course he'll look beneath the surface and try to identify the currents; it's just in his nature.

If only I had a good answer for him.

I lean into the warmth of his hand, letting him support the weight of my tired brain. "Brew us coffee, and I'll try to give you an answer? And make up for the fact I legit fell asleep on you last night?"

"Can't argue with caffeine first." His smile morphs into a yawn, and it shouldn't be so endearing, but mussed-hair, naked, drowsy-eyes Daniel—so very human, so different from his sharp three-piece suits—is a sight to behold. "And you don't owe me, Dylan." He leans over to kiss my temple.

With that, he lifts and walks away, down the hall to my bathroom.

There should be something marring him. Aside from my scratches, that is. There's nothing, though. Just grooves of muscle anchoring his spine and back dimples and concave cheeks and runner's legs.

I sigh loudly, not the least bit calmed, and flop back onto my pillow.

So far over my head.

18

DANIEL WEARS MY apron when he cooks, tying it around his trim waist. My apron and his wrinkled dress pants and nothing else.

I admire him through the sliding glass door from my patch of midday sunshine on the deck, not sure what I did to be so lucky. The cushions are still wet from the rain, but between patches of fog, the sky is a blessed shade of blue, smoke cleared, air cold and clean, raising goose bumps as the wind sneaks through my robe. And Daniel is in my house wearing a frilly apron, considerable day-after stubble framing his lips and shadowing his jaw.

He slides the door open, wearing his glasses.

"You brought your specs, hmm? This is sounding more and more premeditated."

His smile is a brief, unapologetic flash, fading as soon as it appears. He holds out my burner phone. "Someone wants to get a hold of you." He holds out the offensive chunk of metal and glass and transistors.

I already know who it is. His tight jaw shows me he must've caught a glimpse too.

"I'm sorry." He looks guilty as I reach and take it from him. "I didn't mean to pry. It was annoying, back-to-back, and then I worried it might be your family or something."

"Don't be sorry." I turn away to sift through the missed calls and texts. Daniel has no way of knowing I haven't spoken to my parents for months. Unlike him, I am not a good child.

By the looks of it, Brent didn't sleep last night either.

What the fuck, Delilah? Where'd you go?

Seriously, THAT'S why you left? What fucking cabin?

Even if that's true, you should've told me where you were going. It just sounds like you're lying.

You need to tell me where you are and who you're really with.

Fucking bitch.

Fine. FINE. Don't fucking tell me.

Don't bother crawling back tomorrow, whore.

I pace the deck. Shards of glass pierce my stomach, burrowing inward. I need to face him, but does he know where I escaped to last night? Could his surveillance team have tracked me down? I planned to tell him more about my aunt if he asked, but that excuse might not hold water if he's having me tracked. Is my cover already blown?

"Shit." I tuck my phone in my robe pocket, suddenly gloomy when I should feel well fucked.

Daniel hasn't moved from the threshold. "What is it?"

"I think I have to go put out a fire." I wave the phone at him, more bitter than I meant. "Several missed calls say so, anyway."

Daniel steps outside, still wearing the apron, and slides the door shut behind him.

What will I do with this soft, hard man and his verisimilitude? "It's cold," I protest.

"I don't feel it."

Not *I don't mind* or *I don't care*, but *I don't feel it*. What an apt way to describe this potent reality. I swear I could dive into the water and let it evaporate around me, clear a path all the way to the Golden Gate. We both sipped one hell of a cocktail.

"And no, you don't have to go." He spits the words out like chips of granite. "Fuck him. He doesn't get to summon you."

I fold my arms. "You know better than anyone why I have to go back. Why I have to smooth things over. Or try, anyway."

"Dylan . . ." Daniel sighs. The wind shifts his hair, blows it into his face. He pushes it back, eyes narrowed in annoyance. "He'll punish you for taking off. For leaving him high and dry last night. Why can't you see that?"

His patient tone borders too close to condescension. He may be the smartest person I know, but I can't stand it when he proves it by asking questions I can't answer. "How, then? How do I get close enough to hurt him?" I stare daggers.

"Does it have to be you?" he counters. "Can't it be someone else?"

I shake my head. The old anger has returned, filling my cells one by one. Priming me for battle. "No one could be more motivated than me."

He sighs again, shoulders sagging, and closes the distance between us. "Help me understand." He leans down, beautiful, dark-brown eyes filling my frame of vision. Demanding entry. Demanding to see the bottom of my ocean, strewn with wreckage, carcasses, and bottom-feeders.

He'd never look at me the same way again if he knew how deep my hatred for Brent tracks. How far my fault line runs, a rift stitched together with gossamer and sea foam.

When I remain silent, he pulls away, raking hands through his hair. Angry.

Defensiveness creeps up my spine, all my justifications rising to the fore. I sip my cooling coffee, letting the bitter taste roll over my tongue. Why forgive when I could *not* and use this unholy rage for something useful? For fuck's sake, taking down pricks for a living is better than any therapy. Not to mention lucrative. And more effective than the usual wheels of justice, clogged with corruption and a surfeit of good ol' boys bound by tacit agreement to never hold their own accountable.

"You don't want to know," is all I can say. "Trust me."

He shakes his head. "I can't believe you'd still . . . after last night . . ." He faces me, mouth pressed in a grim line.

On the one hand, he has a point. We did unspeakable things to each other.

On the other . . .

"Just because we had sex doesn't mean I answer to you." The words come out sharper than I intend.

I turn and stare at the shorebirds and the waves and their bright crests before I say anything else with too much malice. I don't want to argue with Daniel, but then, I've never had to justify myself to him or anyone else. I live my life that way for a reason: to protect people from getting hurt. Revenge is a nasty, messy business, and I have made many an enemy.

"How well I know it."

His voice is much closer. I hadn't heard him approach and can't suppress a shiver when he lifts hair from my nape and kisses the juncture between my neck and jaw.

He holds himself there, breathing, tickling the fine hairs on my neck. The kiss sinks into my skin, ribbons of heat unspooling from the sole point of contact. Within seconds, it reaches my center.

A small, plaintive noise falls out of my mouth without my permission. "This feels . . . unfair."

"Why's that?" he whispers against my skin with soft lips, all innocence.

I close my eyes and tip my head to the side, offering my neck for his consumption, not caring that every neighbor and a few pelicans can see. All my annoyance has fallen away, replaced by the lure of him, a new gravitational body.

"You." I gasp when his teeth skim over my carotids, nipping. "You are not fair."

"Mmm." His tongue swipes a small patch of thin skin, soothing the bite. "All's fair, Lady Justice. Don't tell me that's not your MO."

Before I can answer, he turns my chin and seals his lips to mine, not bothering to be gentle. I swivel to face him and stand on tiptoes, matching his frequency, anchoring my hands in his glossy hair.

When I reach for his waist, he catches my hands, a smile pulling his lips taut. "Easy, tiger."

I drop my hands, sulking. Then I look up.

"Did we just have a fight?"

"I think so." He chews his lower lip.

"Can it be over now?" All I want is to shoo him inside my home and see the rest of him in better light.

"No." He sounds amused. "But I'd settle for a ceasefire." Then he picks me up to straddle him and carries me back inside. I wrap my legs around his back, reveling in the bare heat of him against my core.

He deposits me on the kitchen counter, standing between my legs, kissing me until I can't see or think about anything else. Nothing but having him inside me. My blood feels hot, and my inner muscles make small, wrenching pulses, closing on nothing. His erection strains against the wool pants, and I eye it with interest.

"Are you hungry?" he pulls away enough to ask.

"Yes." I grip the back of his neck and tug him down to me again, crushing us together.

"For breakfast?" His voice sounds distant and muted, like he's speaking to me underwater. "I was going to cook up some eggs, if that's all right?"

"Fertilize them instead." I do my best to say it with a straight face, if only to make him clutch his pearls.

"Oh my *God*, Dylan." He buries his face in my neck, laughing into my hair, shoulders shaking. The laughter travels into my skin, through my ribs, filling the spaces between heartbeats. "Have I ever told you I never know what you're going to say?"

"Maybe once."

"I love it." His eyes are hazy when he shifts, meeting my gaze again. "But you'd better be careful, tiger. I may take you at your word." He pulls the lapel of my robe, exposing my neck and most of my shoulder and arm, leaning down to kiss my throat, then my collarbone. Lower.

"Don't listen to a word out of my mouth." My voice doesn't hold much conviction. Not when he works me up like this. "You know I'm an incurable liar."

"So I do." He growls. "But I still like it."

He pauses, thumb on my elbow, still as a statue.

"What's wrong?"

He nods to the joint, mouth set in a flat line. Remembering.

There's a bruise there too, but not from him.

Brent's fingertips left a pattern of purple on my forearm, complete with small crescents from his overlong nails. Just as I knew they would.

"How could you even think of going back to him?" Daniel's gaze is riveted to the small, hideous marks.

The anguish in his voice makes my eyes water. A stupid, involuntary response, one I thought I'd burned out of me ages ago. The heaviness of unspent arousal settles into my bones, weighing them down.

So much for our cease fire.

19

I DON'T ANSWER DANIEL.

He pulls away and braces himself on the opposite counter, shoulders rising and falling, faster and faster. "The thought of you . . . of him touching you. *Hurting* you the way he hurt your sister, with the knife . . ." He shakes his head. "Dylan, I don't think I can—I can't handle it."

I have never seen him like this. Devolving. Breaking.

Overcome, I slide off the counter and press my cheek into the deep groove of his spine, arms wrapping around his waist. His skin is hot to the touch and his heartbeat drums into my ear, quick and frantic.

He startles, then softens into my hold, one hand gripping my clasped ones.

"How did you know there was a knife?" I ask, throat tight.

"I Googled her case. What little there was, anyway. And kept digging from there."

"Well." Inside, alarms trill, warning me I'm close to shutting down, the way I always do whenever I veer too close to Gabrielle. "Yeah. He left his mark, all right."

"Tell me you won't go back. Promise me."

"Daniel . . ." I let go, wooden. "You know I'm not going to promise that. I already made promises to my client, as well as my sister, even if she doesn't know. I can't give you what you want on this."

"The sister you never talk about?" He turns, casting me a supremely judgy look. "Does your family have any idea what kind of work you're doing? The danger you're in?"

I move to the other side of the island, buying room to deflect. "Last time I checked, I wasn't the only one keeping their family in the dark. I mean, have you told your parents So Ah is headed back? That things are over with you two and there won't be nuptials after all?" We both have fragments to pick up after the messes we made. He has no right to question my motivations or my relationship with my family.

He sighs, a short, staccato burst. Seeming to resent the reminder. "No. But I imagine they'll have heard already." His voice is as dry as tinder. "The auntie network is formidable."

"Maybe you should talk to your elders, then, and apprise them of your decisions in the last twenty-four hours." I retie my robe and fold my arms across my chest. "While you're doing that, you can let me get back to work. I have to finish what I started."

He studies me, taking in my defensive posture. The likely mutinous set of my jaw.

His brows furrow, and he looks so sad, a man watching his hourglass sand flow away, time on Earth disappearing one grain at a time.

I look away; it's unbearable. I can't stand letting him down. Not when all I ever do is try to crack him open and pry a real smile out of him. My greed knows no depths where he's concerned.

"I hate this timeline," he finally says.

Our running joke when everything seems heartwarming and heartbreaking by turns. Our faith in humanity restored by the good works of some, shattered by the selfish acts of others. The schism leaves him reeling. Not so much me, Ms. Machiavelli, but Daniel . . . yes. He understands darkness as well as the next person, recognizes it with his own perceptive gaze, but never as well as me. Never seems to comprehend why everyone doesn't do the right thing by others.

Of course he doesn't understand. My heart would be heavy, too, if it were made of gold.

"Me too." My voice sounds scratchy and my eyes water, perilously close to ugly crying.

"Then why choose it? It could be different, Dylan. Everything could be different."

I close my eyes. Force steel into my spine. "Someday, I hope it will make sense for you. Until then, you'll have to trust me. Trust that this is . . . something I *must* see done. I won't be able to let it go. Not until it's well and truly over."

He shakes his head, as if he can't wrap his considerable mind around my words.

Then he unties the apron, sets it on the counter, and picks his crumpled white shirt off the floor, sliding his arms through. The shirt is missing a few buttons, but he doesn't seem to notice or care.

Tendrils of panic root me to the spot as I watch him piece himself back together. Rolling socks over prehensile toes and slipping on his polished shoes. Returning to the mundane. Assembling his shield, such as it is, to face the world.

"Daniel . . ."

He leaves, closing the door behind him with a quiet snick.

It's the quietness that ruins me. A rude slam would've been better.

I burst into tears, hot and explosive.

My knees weaken, and I fold from the hips, clutching my sides. It feels like my innards have been scooped out and dumped into the water, chum for the sharks. I hold tighter, wondering if I've already managed to blow it with him. It'd have to be a new record.

After a few minutes, the heavy gasps and god-awful wailing—is there anything more humiliating than this?— quell my tears and dry them on my cheeks.

"Fuck this." I've never let anyone make a mess of me. Never let anyone hurt me. Daniel doesn't get to be the exception. Even if he did indescribable things to me when the rest of the world was asleep.

Even if I love him so much I hurt.

Proof I shouldn't have let him in to begin with.

"Out of my system now. I'm good." I cinch my robe, holding my insides together. "I'm good."

How dare he assume he knows better than me? Why can't he take me at my word when I tell him this is important?

I pound the rest of my coffee, cold now, and pour the rest from his mug down my throat as well. Bit by bit, my crushing tension headache disappears.

"It's like he's never watched anyone he loves suffer," I tell my succulents. Never been buried alive by grief. Never had to fight to crawl his way back out of a hole that kept filling with earth. It's easy to let go and let live when you don't know how ugly monsters can be.

I march back to my room, searching under my bed for a photo.

Gabrielle and me on her high school graduation day. She wore a black cap and gown, gorgeous with her auburn hair flowing down her back. She left her classmates in the dust with her grades, graduating valedictorian. She looks so happy in the picture, her arm around my shoulders. Full of hope.

I press the photograph to my chest. "It was really us."

Anyone would be forgiven for not believing it. The photo is a portal into time before the light was gone from her eyes and a mean scar snaked up her neck and face.

I will never forgive. *Never.*

Charged, I throw on wide-leg jeans and a blue midriff T-shirt. Then I floof my hair—the just-fucked bedhead is really working today—brush my teeth, and wash my face, cooling the heated patches from my crying. I layer on makeup like a shield, giving myself a smudged smoky eye and glossy lips. Then I leave, slamming my door. I would eat something, but I'm not hungry. Not for food. Not for love. For vengeance, goddammit.

I want this done with.

I want to see Brent in jumpsuit orange and know he'll be prey in his next life.

If I sell my soul in the bargain, it'll be currency well spent.

* * *

The neighborhood is quiet when the bus rolls up in Pac Heights. I leap out onto the sidewalk, sunglasses on, hips swaying.

Just as I'm about to head in, my phone rings. I dig it out of my bag and smile when I see it's Dr. Chang.

I push the keypad code and let myself into the townhouse. When I'm inside, I answer the phone and chirp, "Good morning, Doctor! I'm so glad you called! I just heard from a friend, a Dr. Sanchez, who happens to be looking for a chief scientist for her biotech startup, and I could not wait to tell her I had just the woman—"

"Did you leak my name to the press?" Her voice is icy.

"What?" I press my phone closer to my ear. "No, of course not. My confidentiality agreements are ironclad. I protect my clients' anonymity at all costs."

"Then why did I get a call this morning from a journalist with the *Chronicle*, wanting me to go on the record with Prometheus's wrongdoing?"

I lock the door and lean against it, taking one breath. Then another. *Goddammit, Rhys.*

"I do know a journalist who's interested in Brent's misconduct," I say carefully, "but it's important you know I did not expose your identity. I told him I'd ask if you were willing to speak out, but it was a long shot and he'd have to look elsewhere to start. If I had to guess, that's maybe where he got a hold of your contact information, from another former employee?"

Dr. Chang is silent for a long time. "I know who it probably was, then." She sighs. "Why do I feel like the lid on this is going to blow open and screw us all over before we can find the real data, and Brent will still be the last one standing?"

"For whatever it's worth, a scientist of your stature going on record about company culture would be a huge, powerful move, even without the evidence." I wipe my sweating forehead with my free hand. "And the more people you can convince to speak up, the better."

"I can't." Her voice is tremulous. "They're threatening me with legal action, and I still don't have a job—I can't be labeled as a troublemaker—"

"Legal action?" I chew my lip.

"A court summons, if I don't turn over proprietary research I don't even have."

Fuck. "Dr. Chang, I'm sorry. I should've seen that coming." I press between my brows, trying to smooth the straining muscles. Trying to fight the sense of everything unraveling. "It may be time to bring a lawyer on board. I know someone—I'll have her reach out to you immediately."

"I can't pay for a lawyer." She sounds like she's on the verge of tears. "You don't know what you're asking of me."

"Listen. Whether we like it or not, Brent has changed the game, and I know what I'm asking. I don't suggest going to the press lightly. Or hiring a lawyer. If not the one I know, a free one. Regardless . . ." I pinch the bridge of my nose. "There's something to be said for exposing the rot to the light of day, rather than trying to eliminate it from the shadows."

I can't believe those words left my mouth. Who am I?

"Will you think about it?" I ask when the silence grows. "Just think about it and let me know?" Too pleading, but I don't have room to play it cool. Taking down a person of Brent's outsized standing will require attacks from multiple fronts. An overwhelming surge he can't buy, lie, or bully his way out of.

"I'll think about it," she says.

"That's all I ask. As for the job search, I've been working on that too. I'll email you the details?"

"Okay." Her voice is no more than a whisper.

I bite my lip, hard, hoping to put strength into my voice. "How's it going, aside from that? Are you still being followed?"

"Pretty sure I am, yes. You'd think he'd get tired of me puttering around the house and going to the grocery store, but . . ."

The headache returns, pounding over my temples. "I'm so sorry. Is the security team I hired still working out well for you?"

"They're a little intimidating, but I'm glad we have people here, even if I don't know how to explain any of this to my kids." Her laugh is short and caustic. "God, I just want all of this to be over."

"It will be. We're working toward that every day." I crane my neck, looking through the window, trying to see if the monster next door is in residence. I could ask the construction crew on the sly and see if I can sneak in if he's not home. This might well be my chance to find the data. "Speaking of, I may have a chance to do fieldwork."

"I'll let you get to it, then."

"Keep the faith, Evelyn."

"You too."

I hang up and slide my phone into the back pocket of my jeans. The day is crisp and cold after the rain. I shiver when I step outside, sweat cooling, wishing I'd brought a jacket, but if Brent is home, my skimpy top will probably buy goodwill. I pick my way through my courtyard and let myself into Brent's yard, listening to the threads of conversation in Spanish from the laborers.

"Buenos días!" I wave. My Spanish is rusty, but I remember a little from backpacking the Camino de Santiago. "Está el señor Wilder en casa?"

The man's thick eyebrows rise to the brim of his bright-yellow hard hat. "No, miss. He's been gone since last night."

"Ah." I nod. "I think I left something at his house the other day. Would you mind letting me in to have a look? I won't need more than a few minutes."

He shifts from boot to boot, looking uncomfortable. "I'm not sure if—"

"If he asks, we'll say I insisted on being let in, okay? I didn't take no for an answer." I meet his gaze. "Blame it all on me, bien?"

After a long, tense silence, he gives a curt nod. "Vamos."

He leads me past the scaffolding and deafening clatter from construction equipment. On the way, I send Daniel a hasty text. *Don't suppose you could take his security cams offline for the next ten minutes?* I add a sad-puppy-eyes face and prayer hands emoji.

I don't expect a reply. Not after the way we left things on my houseboat. Daniel hardly ever gets mad—not like me, lurching from one emotion to the next like a toddler, quick to anger but also quick to forgive—but when he does get angry, he stays that way, hot like cast iron long after the heat has been turned down.

My phone vibrates. *Consider it done.*

I blink against the well of tears. God, I must be about to go on my period. Even the simplest of generosities is enough to rattle me.

Either that or I'm crazy about him.

Thank you, I type.

Do what you need to do, then get the hell out of there, he replies.

Okay, yeah. Still pissed.

I will.

The foreman ushers me into the quiet stillness of the monster's den. "Be quick."

I try to give him a reassuring smile. Brent's toxic atmosphere has permeated everything in a mile radius, instilling everyone with fear. "I will be. Thank you."

As soon as he closes the door, I veer down the hallway, wending my way toward Brent's office.

I expected neuroticism, everything in its appointed place like it was before, but his workspace looks like a tornado blew through. Papers are strewn everywhere, like he took a stack and shoved it off his desk onto the floor.

I kneel and pick up a few pages. The dates look about right, nearly six years ago, as do the numbers of participants—small still, likely phase one or two for the clinical trials. Might this be an early look at Risederon, before it was named? Or is it some other drug?

I keep reading.

It's a tricyclic antidepressant, referred to as N-methyl-nortriptyline, 20mg. I read down the list of batch numbers, patient numbers, investigators. At the bottom, there's the name of the sponsor: Prometheus Pharmaceuticals.

I sift through pages of information on the patients and dosages, drug metabolization, bioavailability. Outcomes compared to placebo. It's just as Dr. Chang said: headaches, hallucinations. Suicides. Allowance that this incarnation of the drug presents too many safety risks to continue with trials.

My heart beats faster.

I've found it. The real data from the original clinical trials. The golden ticket, the thread to pull, unraveling an entire company.

"Christ," I hiss.

I snap picture after picture, documenting one page after another.

A door slams somewhere in the house, followed by quick footfalls.

"Oh, shit." I freeze like I've been doused with ice water.

It could be the foreman, but if it isn't, any attempt at escape would lead me right back down the hallway, face-to-face with Brent.

I dive into the closet and close the door after me as gently as I can. It's pitch-black after the bright natural light from the huge windows in his office, overlooking the bay. I move deeper into the constricted space and crack my toe on something hard and metal. A safe? I wince and bite my lip, trying not to make a sound while my toe throbs.

The footfalls draw closer and the door to the office opens with a bang, sending all the papers flying.

Terror seizes my throat. My hands are numb, tingling. I'm sure he hears my telltale heart beating through my ribs, through the walls, sealing my doom.

Brent slumps down in his chair and starts typing on his keyboard.

When stars float in my vision, I sip air through my nose, buying myself time before I black out from asphyxiation.

If he finds me, it'll be over. Everything I hoped for, everything I struggled and fought for. There's no way I'll be able to explain my presence—I'll go to jail for false impersonation. But how long can I stay here before he either notices me or moves to another room? It could be hours before he gets up.

I hold my breath for another interminable stretch, willing stillness into my limbs, but I'm light-headed from too much caffeine and low blood sugar. Minutes pass in suspended dread. All the while, my phone burns like a hot coal in my jeans. I can't remember if it's still set to vibrate, but even that noise would be audible in his quiet office.

I reach into my pocket, moving so carefully, monitoring every rustle of my clothing. Every breath.

Before I can silence the phone, the home security alarm blares.

I jump, muffling my shriek with a hand.

"What the fuck!" Brent shoves away from his desk, metal casters screeching on the hardwood floor. "Diego!" he roars. "Did one of your guys trip the alarm again?" His heavy footfalls leave the room, but his furious voice still carries down the hallway. "I swear to fucking God, all of you are gonna have a visit from ICE if you can't get your shit together!"

When he's for sure down the hall, I open the door, peering. This is my chance, but all Brent has to do is turn around—

My phone vibrates.

I tripped the alarm. Get the fuck out of there, Daniel says. *NOW*.

CHAPTER

20

I OBEY DANIEL'S ORDER, forcing my terror-stiff muscles to move and abandon the dubious safety of the office. Every part of my body feels hot. My heart pounds forcefully, throbbing in my ears.

Brent's voice carries down the hallway, still blistering the foreman.

I wince. "Dammit." The last thing I wanted was to get him in trouble with that bastard. I'll have to make it up to Diego and the rest of the crew for the trouble I've caused them all.

But how to escape?

A soft whistle down the hall behind me makes me jump.

"Aquí." A much-younger Hispanic man with deep-set brown eyes waves at me to follow. "Rápidamente!"

I hesitate, but it's either follow him or try to edge past Brent in the living room while his attention is fixed on Diego.

Instinct propels me down the hall, following the younger man. He leads me through another series of interconnected rooms walled off with plastic tarping, down to a bedroom suite with French doors opening to another secluded patio.

Outside, the ivy hedge is tall, bordering on all sides. Enviable privacy, but I don't know how I'll tear through it.

I look back at the man still standing in the doorway, wondering if there's some portal to Narnia I'm missing.

"Eres pequeña!" He points in frustration to a small part near the roots below the dense hedge. "Aquí, aquí!"

I crouch and peer through. Daylight shines on my patio on the other side. A tight, scraping fit, but I think I can do it.

"Gracias. Muchas gracias!" Relief surges through my body, all the way to my toes. I give the man a brief hug, which seems to surprise him, but the random kindness of strangers never ceases to amaze me.

"Vamos," he says, with a panicked look back inside the house. "El señor cabrón viene."

I dive into the gap, crawling my way through the sodden ground, scratching my arms and bare stomach on the branches. Hoping no black widows drop into my hair.

Finally, I'm through to the other side, to my patio. Covered in mud, T-shirt torn, scratched and bloodied. I tuck my feet under and crouch low, beneath the ivy, hoping Brent won't be able to see me from this angle. If I can just get to the door . . .

Brent calls my name. Not sounding accusatory but not friendly either.

If it were the former, I'd duck and run, and deal with the consequences later. But the latter . . . I think I can handle.

I stand and rip out a few dead vines of the ivy, holding them in my fist like armor. "Hey, neighbor! What's up?" I smile brightly.

From his side of the wrought-iron fence, he looks me up and down, eyes narrowed in seeming annoyance at my bright-eyed, bushy-tailed tone. "Eavesdropping?" He hops over the low border into my garden.

"Couldn't help but hear the alarm, but no." I brush a few dead leaves from my jeans with a free hand and swipe my forehead for good measure. "Just doing yard-work, trying to clear my head. Why? Something happen next door?"

"Greg and Debra already have landscapers." The idea of working outside for the fun of it seems so foreign to him, so puzzling, I have to bite the inside of my cheek not to laugh. Oh, you sweet summer child.

"I know, but I like to garden." I set the dead vines aside. "There's something about getting my hands dirty, I guess."

If he hears the double entendre, he doesn't acknowledge it. He just stares at me, finally seeming to notice how filthy my clothing is. The fact I don't have any tools or gloves or—

I pick a few errant weeds, tearing them up, roots and all. "Is everything all right? You seem off this morning, babe." Deflect, deflect, defect.

"You didn't return any of my calls or messages or texts last night." He catches my wrist, gripping hard.

I hear it in his voice, the high, strained notes. Like he's grasping for the last strands of his control.

"I'm so sorry." I smile sweetly and place my dirt-caked hand over his, which has the predictable effect of making him let go, looking disgusted. The sniveling germophobe. "But I didn't get any of your calls until this morning. The cell service for my cabin is really spotty."

I can tell he wants to argue, but instead he moves on to his next point of contention. Grilling me. "And your aunt?" he demands, still looking skeptical. "How is she faring?"

"She and her horses were able to make it out, thank God. Thank you for asking." I sigh with relief, offering my best, teary smile. "I was so worried about her last night, but she evacuated in the nick of time."

His smile is tight. He may not feel emotions like other humans, but only a monster would disagree with me at this juncture, and he knows it. "Well. That's good."

I nod, looking up at him adoringly. "Thank you for being so understanding last night." I stroke his arm with my dirty hand. He wants to pull away, arm straining beneath my palm, but doesn't. "My aunt is the only family I have left, and she means everything to me. And she's so excited to know more about you, my mystery guy."

"You told her about me?" He sounds panicked. Blood-shot eyes dart back and forth between mine.

Why so serious, Brent? Afraid someone will know we were dating when you murder me?

"Of course!" I gush, pressing my advantage. "Even though I was seeing her for a stressful reason, I was so thrilled to tell her *all* about you, handsome."

"Delilah, you shouldn't have done that." He backs away a fraction, jaw tensing.

"Why not?" I ask, pretending ignorance.

"I thought we were going to keep things casual. You know. See where things go."

"But I thought . . ." I pout. "Don't we have a connection?"

"Yeah, but—"

"You know what? I had an *awful* night, and I only hurried back because I knew you'd be worried sick about me." I let the tears creep into my voice, warbling it. "But it sounds like I could've stayed and helped my aunt, for all you care." I shake my head. "I need to go inside and clean off. If you'll excuse me."

I drop the weeds with a dramatic huff.

"Delilah—"

I wrench open the sliding glass door to my kitchen and slam it closed, locking it, drawing the curtains.

Inside the safety of my home, I dust myself and kick off my retro sneakers. Brent knocks on the sliding glass door, but I tune him out. The high of getting away with evidence in my pocket is so sweet I can taste it, gulping it down like nectar.

I take out my phone, scrolling through the dozens of photos of his scattered paperwork. My wrist still throbs where he grabbed it minutes ago, small darts of pain lighting up my tendons, arcing down my thumb.

"Fuck you, you fucking prick," I whisper. "I'm going to end you."

I tuck my phone away and look up, stunned by the hard-eyed stare of the woman who bears my resemblance in the hallway mirror. Like all great actors, I've lost myself a little in the role.

Delilah the Liar may well be my favorite, though. My magnum opus.

I just have to stay in the fight.

My phone buzzes.

I don't see you on any of the cameras. PLEASE tell me you got out, Daniel says.

I did, thanks to you, I type back.

He doesn't reply, but he doesn't need to. I hear his distraught sigh in my mind anyway.

A few minutes later, he follows up. *I grew three gray hairs, Dylan. Can you not do that again?*

I grimace/laugh and type a hasty reply. *Your sacrifice wasn't for naught, sir. I may have found the key to ruining his life, but I won't know for sure until I get scientific eyes on this.*

I wait for more, but nothing comes. Apparently, he noticed my failure to promise I won't do it again. Daniel has always been too good at reading subtext.

Whatever. I have other things to worry about, and I'm not about to slow my hard-won momentum.

I call Dr. Chang on my way to the safe in my bedroom, where I've stored a reserve of cash. I'll give some to Diego to distribute to the crew in thanks for their trouble this morning.

"Lady Justice?" she asks, uncertain. "Is everything okay?"

"I think I found it, Doctor. The real data."

"What? Really?" She inhales, a sharp gasp. "You think so?"

"That's what it looks like based on the few papers I was able to scan, but I'm no expert." I chew my lip. "I could be wrong. It may turn out all the material is irrelevant and worthless, but I hope not. You'd know best, so I can meet you, or send it your way. Whatever is easiest for you."

The knocking on my sliding glass door continues, but I ignore it. Brent can knock all damn day. My jaw clicks and I massage it with my free hand, trying to loosen the clenched muscles.

"Send it my way. I'll take a look right now and let you know."

"Will do. Hang in there, Doctor."

"You too, Lady Justice."

I select the dozens of photos in my best attempt at chronological order and email them to her.

Then I text Rhys. *Still on board for the fellowship of fuckery?*

He answers a minute later. *Absolutely. Something come up?*

Maybe. I pop the knuckles on my free hand. *I'll let you know hopefully later today. Have you found anything? New sources?*

He calls me instead. Extroverts, bro.

I sigh and answer. "What's up?"

"I've found shit all. Everyone I've managed to track down has been too scared to speak up." He sighs, short and resentful. "Brent and his lawyers have done a number on these poor people."

The knocking on my door continues, rattling the entire downstairs. I wince.

"Jesus Christ. Are you near construction or something?" Rhys demands.

"Oh, you know. Just an unhinged abuser-in-the-making trying to beat down my door." *After I slipped through his grasp yet again.* I laugh, but it's not convincing. "I should add escape artist to my résumé."

There's a long pause. "Are you all right, Dylan? Do you need someone to come over?"

In the aftermath of the sky-high adrenaline rush, I'm hollowed out, burnt to a crisp, skin hot and stiff. To everything there is a cost. "I'm fine." My knife is warm on my calf. "And he's having me watched, so maybe ix-nay on the investigative journalist showing up, eh?"

"Listen, this guy is bad news. I was talking to a colleague who's already researched his background. There were sexual harassment and assault complaints against him all the way back in prep school on the East Coast, but the elder Wilder managed to have everything sealed up and sent the prodigal son out west for a fresh start. Of course, that was new hunting grounds. Several former Prometheus employees have quit over the years and settled out of court." He growls. "He's a predator, Dylan."

"I fucking know who he is," I snap. Why is it always such a shock to men to learn how deep the rot runs? Like they didn't believe us when we said with our full chest, *Me too.* "That doesn't change the fact I need to keep him on the hook as long as I can."

"You may want to rethink that strategy," Rhys says dryly. "Or at the very least, arm yourself."

"Not you too, Boy Scout." The sleepless night and the terror of being caught in Brent's office is catching up to me, shortening my fuse the longer I have to defend my methods to yet another guy. "Look, I appreciate the concern, but this isn't my first rodeo. I know what I'm doing." Mostly.

I end the call, fuming for reasons I can't pinpoint. Of course Daniel and Rhys are worried, but they don't understand the risk is necessary. It's going to take every dirty trick to take Brent down—and even that might not be enough.

Downstairs, it's quiet.

From my bedroom window, I watch Brent huff his way back across the low hedge between our properties and slam the door behind him. Gone for the time being, but not departed.

My phone rings, startling me. Brent, naturally.

I silence my phone, strip off my filthy clothes, and step to the bathroom to rinse the dirt and spider webs, and most of all, Brent, from my skin.

21

THE SKY IS hazy in sunset gold, and my nails are bit down to nubbins when I get a call back from Dr. Chang.

"I'll do it," she says.

My heart stops. Does she mean . . . ?

"You'll . . . ?" I need her to say the words.

"All of it. File a complaint with the SEC. Be a source for your reporter. Bring this information to his board somehow." Her voice is full of iron, her decision reached. After the freeze, my pulse beats faster and faster. Is this really happening? "I'll speak out against Brent."

"That's . . . I'm so glad. So glad!" I can't hide the joy in my voice. "Dr. Chang, I'm so thrilled. I'll take care of all the—"

"And I want to speak to a reporter today. Now, if possible." Her laugh is wry. "Before I come to my senses and change my mind."

"Okay, yep. That's great." It's a good thing we're having this conversation over the phone so she can't see my shocked face. "I'll contact him and set up a time this evening."

"Good. Let me know when the details are ironed out. Talk to you soon—"

"Wait. Hang on." I grip the white quartz counter in the master bathroom, looking through the window at Brent's palatial home. "Do you mind me asking what changed your mind?"

"The information you sent," she says, like that should be obvious. "The photos of the documents. I don't know how you managed to get a hold of the data, but it changes everything. Shows why he shouldn't be in business. Not a day longer." Her voice rises. "I am so damn *tired* of people who don't know anything thinking they can swagger their way through actual science. It's time to end this grifter's shameful career in health."

"Tell me how you really feel, Doc." I laugh.

She laughs too. "Tired, I said. With a capital *T*."

"Well, I couldn't have said it better myself. And I hope you know this, but you won't be the only one who speaks up. You're just the first. It'll be lonely for a little while, but—"

"I'm ready for it. I want my daughters . . ." Her voice breaks off, growing thick. "I want my daughters to know their mom stood up when it mattered."

I blink hard at my reflection, not expecting to be moved. It's the flip side of my strange business, watching people lift out of the ashes of their old lives and fly away. Fly to better things.

"They will." I wipe my nose. "They will. And I'll text you with the details, okay?"

We hang up, and I blow my nose before calling Rhys, pacing the hallway.

"My client wants to be a source for your article."

There's a solid five-second pause. "Really?" He, too, sounds wary. Like he's afraid to believe it's happening.

"Really, really. And my client wants to be interviewed tonight, if possible. I was thinking we could meet at my home in Sausalito. It's safer than trying to do it here, right under Brent's nose. I just have to lose anyone who's tailing me."

"I don't know how you managed it." There's a smile in his voice. "But yeah, I can do an interview tonight."

"It's my client's neck on the line, so you'd better make damn sure this interview is worth it."

"I will."

"Good. I'll send you my address. Let's say seven? And make sure you aren't followed. And your phone is turned off." I look at Brent's home again, worried he'll somehow sense my shift in mood. "I can't have this prick finding out where my home is."

"Will do, Lady Justice."

After I hang up, I text him and Dr. Chang my address and the meet time, with explicit instructions to take a convoluted route and turn their phones off so they can't be tracked. I have two hours to get there and sort my home out before I welcome them.

Still, I stare at my phone, as if hoping to summon a call, a text, anything from Daniel before going into battle. I hoped to hear from him after he talked to his parents about ending things with So Ah, but it's been quiet.

Of course it's quiet. Why would they want someone like me with their son when they could have someone like her?

My stomach growls. I've barely eaten all day, and I should have something before heading over, but unease sits heavy in my gut, blunting my appetite. Maybe after the interview is done, Dr. Chang and I can discuss the end game. What we'll need to do to bring this knowledge to the SEC.

From the master bedroom, I peer through the filmy curtains and check on Brent a final time. After he stopped banging on my door and stormed home, it's been suspiciously calm. My paranoia can't help but think there's more going on, but I don't have time to worry about it.

It's time to set up my checkmate.

* * *

Rhys is the first to arrive.

"I've always wanted to see one of these houseboats." He lifts the messenger bag off his chest and shrugs out of his field jacket. "This place is awesome. Wait, should I take off my shoes?" He glances at his black Converse high-tops and back at me.

"Yes, please, and thank you!" I take his jacket. "You're sworn to silence now you've seen the Fortress of Solitude, though." I smile through my nerves.

"Fair enough." He smirks over his shoulder and walks to the tall windows, taking in the view off the deck, the late-autumn light shining over the water. "I take it our source isn't here yet."

"Not yet." I don't want to panic until I have a good reason to. Evelyn wears a lot of hats, and anything under the sun could've delayed her—mom life, wife life. Her fears about stepping into the public eye, though she sounded resolute when we spoke on the phone.

Or the bastard's tracking her every move.

I push the thought away and move to the kitchen. "Can I get you anything to drink? Water, tea? Coffee? Stronger?"

"Stronger, if you have it." He rubs a hand through his messy, coppery waves until they stick straight up on end.

"I have a bottle of Pinot from a winery that burnt to a crisp last fall." I hold it up with a grim smile. "How's that sound?"

"Fitting for the times."

Consigned to wait until Dr. Chang shows, I pour each of us a glass, then bring them over to the low-slung sectional overlooking the deck.

Strange to think Daniel was here less than twenty-four hours ago. Marking me, claiming me. Owning me down to my last cell.

"That was a strange look." Rhys studies my face as I sit next to him, hazel irises flitting.

"Nervous." I clink my glass against his and take an eager sip. I'd like to appreciate the vino more, considering it's the last to come from this winery for the foreseeable future, but it just tastes like wine.

"Me too. I hope your client is all right. The radio silence is tough." He grimaces at the black mirror of his phone.

"I wouldn't have asked if I didn't think it was necessary. Brent's having people tailed, me included. If he gets the jump on what we're doing, it'll be . . ." I gulp more wine. "Bad. Not to mention he'll start a smear campaign against all of us."

"Or send us to swim with the fish." Rhys stares at the bowl of his glass resting in his lap.

I frown and reach to drag my laptop over. "Maybe there's an email?"

I didn't really think there'd be a message from Dr. Chang, but seeing an empty in-box makes my blood pressure rise a few more notches. The beginnings of another flattening headache throb over my temples, the sleepless night and lack of food catching up with me.

There's a knock on my door.

I leap to my feet, head whirling with relief. "That must be our guest."

But it's not Evelyn. Daniel stands at the threshold, hand lifted, caught midknock.

I drink him in. I hardly ever see him dressed down, but he makes anything look good, even jeans and a black

Henley. His hair is still mussed from the morning, wavier than usual with the high humidity. A tad too Byronic for my own good.

His easy smile disappears when he sees I'm not alone.

"Haas! What are you doing here?" My voice is strangled.

He gives me a puzzled look, maybe for my reverting to his last name, but old habits die hard. "Did you not get my messages?" He looks from me to Rhys, evaluating the situation in a matter of seconds and finding it wanting.

"No, I didn't. My phone's been off."

"Who is he?" He glances at Rhys, who has the sense not to contribute to the conversation.

"A journalist. A friend from school, like way back."

Daniel assesses my "journalist friend" from the entry, the way men have done for millennia. His gaze drifts to the opened bottle of wine on the kitchen counter. "What is he doing at your home?"

You'd never know he was angry by his passive expression. Nor by the calm tone of his voice. It's all in his eyes, blazing with questions and hurt.

"We're supposed to be meeting my client here." I pick at a hangnail, wincing when it doesn't tear off cleanly. "To be interviewed as a source for Rhys's article in the *Chronicle* about Brent."

"Lady Justice convinced her client to speak out," Rhys pipes up from the living room. "With that testimony, and hopefully others, we can expose his company's fraud."

I grimace, but it's too late. Daniel heard him use my alias. Comprehension makes his expression darken, like fog rolling in, absorbing all the light and color in the world, lending several degrees of chill to the air.

"When were you going to tell me about all of this?" he asks, teeth gritted.

Oh, man. That cast iron is still smoking. I cast an apologetic look at Rhys. "Excuse me for a minute."

"When was I going to tell you about this?" I usher Daniel outside onto my front porch gangplank and fold my arms against the cold. "Seriously? I wasn't aware I had to report to you."

Daniel looks away, jaw tightening. "And since when does a *journalist* know your real identity? Did *you* tell him?" He turns to me, gaze scorching. "How could you trust him with something so important?"

"No, I didn't tell him." I hug my midsection tighter. "Rhys put it together on his own. I offered to work with him to bring Brent down, so he'll keep quiet about Lady Justice's work."

"You have that in writing, I hope?"

Well, that stung. "I don't think I like your tone."

"And I don't like that not twelve hours after I was here, there's another guy at your home, drinking wine with you. Someone who knows your real identity. And all the while, you never thought to tell me about him?"

"You know, you're choosing a terrible time to go Cro-Magnon." I wave back to the door. "Despite the insulting picture you painted, I'm *working*. Trying to, anyway."

"Working. All right." Daniel rakes a hand through his hair, pulling hard, and shakes his head. "So I guess you won't be coming over to meet my parents."

Ice welds my feet to the deck. A frozen tide rolls up my legs and torso and throat. "Why would they want to meet me?"

He looks at me like I've grown another limb.

It's so disorienting, like we're speaking different languages, reverting to gestures and exaggerated facial expressions to communicate, when all we needed before was our unspoken vernacular. *What have we done?* Five years of friendship have disappeared; communion erased by our own ravenousness, replaced by something lesser.

"So I can introduce you?" he asks.

I blink. "To?"

"My parents."

"As?"

"As my girlfriend?"

"Oh, is that all?" I laugh, humorless. "For the record, a heads-up would've been nice. Any discussion with me about this would've been nice. I didn't think we were . . ."

I break off, not sure what I'm wandering into.

"Go ahead." His voice is strange and toneless. "Finish that sentence."

Of course. Daniel never backs away from the pale, nasty underbelly of life, not after he's caught a glimpse.

I meet his gaze, surprised to find tears swimming in mine, escaping when I blink. How infuriating, to cry when I want to kick and scream.

"I didn't think we were together-together," I manage to say. "And I don't know how you could think I'd ever be a suitable substitute for So Ah."

He's quiet so long, I don't think he'll answer. "If you thought I could go back to the way things were before, like nothing's happened . . . you don't know me at all."

There's a knock on the front door, from inside my house. I cringe, thinking of Rhys on the other side, over-hearing our conversation. There's TMI, and there's *TMI*.

He cracks the door and pokes a head through, look-ing uncomfortable. "It doesn't look like your client is show-ing up, so I'm going to head out." He casts a quick, furtive glance at Daniel, then back at me, eyes wide.

I glance at my phone, heart sinking. We're forty-five minutes past our meeting time. "Okay. I'm so sorry." I ges-ture to Daniel and me in a vain effort to corral our mess, spilling over into every area of my life. "I'll let you know if the situation changes."

Rhys nods, pulling the strap of his messenger bag over his head. "Keep me posted."

We step aside so Rhys can make his hasty escape. Daniel watches his large, retreating form for a long time. His face is like granite when he turns to me.

"We need to talk." He nods to my boat. "Inside?"

"Like I have any choice," I mutter.

22

DANIEL AND I enter my home, moving around each other in silence.

"I don't suppose you want some?" I wave to the wine bottle on the counter.

"No."

"Didn't think so."

Reluctantly, I turn on my phone. A dozen texts fill my screen, some from Daniel, some from Dr. Chang. I click on hers first.

I'm so sorry, but I'm having second thoughts. I'm still being followed and I'm not sure I can go through with this. Not when I'm the only person speaking up.

I'm so sorry for wasting everyone's time. I don't want to let you down, but I need more time to think.

"Goddammit. God-fucking-dammit." We were so close. So close to setting things in motion, finally. I grip my phone until my fingertips are white, then type a quick reply.

You didn't waste our time. We'll find another way, Evelyn. I promise. If it's not speaking to the reporter, we can do something anonymous.

I look up at the wooden beams crisscrossing my ceiling and type another message. *Just don't give up. Please.*

After, I update Rhys on the reason for the holdup with a terse message.

Then I silence my phone and turn my attention to a glowering Daniel, the slightly larger problem at hand. The more immediate one, at least.

He sits on the couch, arms folded, long legs sprawled. Gaze riveted to Rhys's empty wineglass perched on the tufted end table.

I pick up the glass and take it to the sink, feeling guilty for no good goddamn reason. Then I settle on the other end of the couch, studying his inscrutable profile.

"Well. You're pretty quiet for someone who seemed hellbent on forcing the moment into crisis. I assume you talked to your parents?"

He nods, frown deepening, if that's possible.

"How'd they take the news with So Ah?"

His gaze remains fixed on the water. "About as well as you'd think. They were furious with me for turning her loose." His mouth twists, like he's gotten a taste of something bitter. "And of fucking course I don't want to endanger Oma's health by creating more stress, but I had to tell them the truth. That I don't love So Ah. Maybe given enough time, I could again, but Dylan, I'm so . . ." He looks at me, eyes full of something I won't identify. "Not when I'm so in love with you."

Of course he'd name it. I blink, setting tears free.

"I'm sorry. For your mom especially." I edge closer to him. I can't help it. I still want to be near him. To comfort him somehow. I've gravitated to him too long to stop in the span of one night. Though the longer I study him, I fear the option may not be mine much longer.

"Why would you be sorry?"

"If I was out of the picture, things would be easier for you. *All* of you." I look at my hands, hating the way they shake. The way my world has blurred with all these dumb waterworks. "Maybe I've been selfish, keeping you as a friend, when you could have so much more without me."

Daniel holds up a hand, shaking his head. "Don't apologize."

"What do you want from me, then?"

"I want you to make a decision." He tips my head up with warm fingers on my chin. He too can't stay away. Can't keep his hands to himself. Not when we know what we can do to each other, making our dark magic. "I want us to be together, Dylan. I'm not asking for anything more than that now. But that's never been the question. The question is: What do you want?"

"Don't." I wipe my cheeks, trying to stanch the flow.

"Why not?" His hand drops.

"You won't like my answer." I borrow his words.

"Try me."

"I never wanted to be a wife, much less a mother. And I'll be damned if I give up on fighting these bastards who know no laws, legal or moral or otherwise."

He looks at me, closed-mouthed, forcing me to continue.

"Am I wrong in assuming that?" I demand. "That you want that kind of life?"

"Of course I want it," he murmurs.

Defensiveness would be better. Anything would be better than his quiet certainty.

The last of the day's light strikes his irises, making them shine lucent bronze. His smile is so sad, though. Flat and fake, as if he's been rendered two-dimensional.

"Of course I want my future to be yours. Of course I want to marry you. I want to watch you grow with life and I want our kids to take after you in every way. I want to start my days with you and end my days with you." He bites his lip and swallows. "I want to spend all the years I have left with my best friend. I've always wanted that."

I look away, scalded by his excruciating honesty. How could I have forgotten all the gold in the bottom of his river, waiting for someone to stir it up? Set it free?

"I know you don't necessarily want those things too, but I thought . . ." He breaks off. "I thought maybe I could convince you. I thought—hoped—maybe I'd be enough."

His admission burns, so hot it shears my nerves and leaves me numb. Somehow, I find my voice again. "You know we can't go down this road together, Daniel."

"Go down? I've walked it too long already." His voice is thick, filled with volcanic ash and regret. "I wouldn't know where to start to let you go. I don't know how to stop loving someone. Do you?"

He pauses, waiting. Waiting for me, as always, but I have no answer. None that will satisfy the demands of his very good heart.

The light fades, and his pupils expand. His eyes swim with tears, glassy black, riverine in the muted light. I have never seen him cry before. Like everything else about him, it wrecks me.

"If you don't feel the same way, you'd better tell me now. Tell me while I still have a chance of walking away with whatever I have left that doesn't already belong to you."

He may as well have hooked me with a fishing gaff, sliced it right through my abdomen. "Daniel . . ." I croak.

"Do you want any part of that too?" he demands, unyielding. "Do you want that life? Because anything less won't be enough for me. If you're going to suggest some bullshit friends-with-benefits thing, do me a favor and don't. Just don't."

Black and white. Binary code, a never-ending string of ones and zeros. He deals in the concrete, not in my morally gray comfort zone.

Worse, I never saw that future, the one he painted. I was too afraid to imagine that kind of happiness could be mine. Why should I get to partake in life's great joys when everyone I see has had their hearts broken, lives blown apart by the people they thought they could trust?

"I don't know."

He nods, like he expected such a tepid, worthless, gutless answer. Then he hardens, degree by degree, walling himself off.

"Maybe you should've considered that before you opened the door to me. Before you let me inside your home."

Inside you, he doesn't say, but the unspoken lingers in the air like mist.

He smiles again, but it looks all wrong, like an uncanny valley Daniel grinning back at me. "Obviously, I've studied this from every possible angle. You were not an impulse for me. I knew what I wanted before I ever touched you."

"You weren't an impulse," I say, but it's not convincing.

Can I do what he's asking? Fit myself into the narrow strictures he's offering? Give up on fighting the good fight?

"I don't know," I say again.

"Of course you don't." He sighs.

"You know what . . ." I trail off, bright spark of anger burning out as soon as it arrives. I've never had venom for him, and I can't start now, even when he hurts me.

"Why do you think I've never had a real relationship with anyone?" I demand. "In all the time you've known me. Why do you think that is?" I should still feel angry, but I'm just tired. "You know better than anyone my job does not leave room for attachment. It's a shit foundation for building anything more, and I resigned myself to that a long time ago." I shake my head. "I don't know what you want me to say."

"Do you mean it?" His eyes search mine, wide and probing. "You won't even try?"

I can't look away from him, but I can't keep latching on to him either. Holding him back from what he wants. And I have held him back. I took every bit of his generosity and kindness, soaked up his offerings like a sponge, and never considered what it cost him to give them in the first place. Gifts he gave so freely, gifts that made me better and smarter and wiser. Gifts that made my lonely life tolerable. Enough that it passed for fulfilling, more days than not. Without him, my days will look bleak indeed. My nights? Unbearable.

It doesn't matter. The only thing to do—the only right thing—is to cut him loose.

"I mean it." I force myself to look up. Force myself to say the words that will snap the wires of our suspension bridge. "You put your faith in the wrong person, Daniel."

The silence afterward takes me back to the worst days after Gabrielle tried to end her life, when all was hushed except for sirens keening in the night.

I hate this timeline, all right. I hate it so much.

All the while, I could've had him. Could've made something with my life, carved out a space for sunlight, instead of all the cruel and mercenary things filling my head, casting a perpetual cloud. Making my soul sick. A disgusted, crazed laugh threatens to bubble out of my throat. Me and my inappropriate humor, swooping in at the worst possible moment.

He stands as if sensing my unraveling, repulsed by it.

I look at him. The panicked laughter stops, but I can't breathe. Can't think for all the buzzing in my brain, filling it with static and terror.

"You don't know how it'd work in the end," I say. "What if I drive you insane? What if it falls apart?" I shake my head. "What if you tell everyone . . ."

His gaze sharpens. "Tell everyone what?"

My heart thunders, hard enough to break ribs. I make myself look up. Make myself unearth the deepest corner of my fear-warped soul. "What if you tell them who I am?"

He steps back, aghast, as if I've thrown acid at him. "You can't think I'd ever—fucking seriously, Dylan? If that's what you really think of me, no wonder you hold me at arm's length. Still." He blinks and tears run down his cheeks, trails of salt and irreversible hurt. "Still."

I know what it is to despise oneself now. He swims, blurred more with every passing second.

"I'm sorry—"

"Is this it?" He cuts to the chase, metal in his voice.

Three small words. How can they hold so much?

Beneath our feet, a series of waves roll in, pitching my boat. For the first time, the movement makes me nauseous.

"I'll always be your friend," I manage to say.

He shakes his head, looking at me like I'm a child. A disappointing naïf. "We won't ever be friends. I'll hate you." He must see something awful in my expression, because his softens immediately, eyes welling with tears again. "And I'll love you, until I can't stand it. But I won't ever be your friend." He shrugs, as if that explains it all. "I can't. I can't have only a little of you. And I can't be around for what you're going to do with Brent—"

"I told you why I have to—"

"Sure. But I can't watch you self-destruct, Dylan." He swallows, again and again. "I can't watch you choose to hurt yourself. That's what you're doing right now as Lady Justice, whether you realize it or not."

Ah, but there it is. The hard limit on *Anything for you*, at long last.

It's everything I can do to keep my despair bottled long enough to put on a brave face, but my eyes fill with tears, more misery escaping. I wipe my eyes, frustrated he's been reduced to a watercolor blur of gold and black again. If this is the last time I'll see his face, I want to remember, even though he'll haunt me.

Daniel looks to the door, then to me, jaw tight, breathing through his nose. One breath. Another.

Then he leans down, pressing a fierce kiss to my forehead. Hovering, lingering, lips warm on my skin. "Darling."

I lift into his touch like a stray, desperate to absorb whatever I can. Desperate to feel loved, feel worthy. Like I did whenever he turned soft eyes on me and said nothing, because he didn't need to. His wildfire love did all the talking, searing me. Ruining me for any other, even if I didn't know it then.

He frames my face with warm hands, fingers stretching into my hair. "If it's not me . . . let it be someone," he whispers. "Don't be lonely, Dylan." He brushes light kisses into my hair, my ear, so I have no choice but to hear him. "Don't give up."

"Daniel." I stop trying to be brave and cry, clutching his wrists. Filling the space between us with broken, ugly noise. As ever, he only sees the best or worst of me. "Daniel."

A choked sound leaves him, a hot burst across my skin.

Then he's gone, taking his warmth, his long legs carrying him away in strides.

The quiet snick of him closing the door cements the deal, final as the last handful of earth over a coffin.

For long minutes, I stare at nothing, stunned. Destruction happened so fast, the way it always does, nothing and nothing then violent abruption, breaking the earth. The way I fell in love with him, slowly, slowly, then all at once.

I slump onto my side, curling up like a wounded animal. I'd be forgiven for feeling battered. So far as I know, a Daniel-sized hole has cratered out my chest. Like all the love he ever gave me has been withdrawn, leached from my marrow.

I cry until my eyes are swollen near shut. Until the bile and wine travel up my throat and I lurch to the rail in the darkness, same as I did when I promised to pick up a sword for Gabrielle. Until I've thrown everything into the ocean, as though my body means to purge him. A last-ditch effort to prevent the inevitable free fall.

I grip the rail, trying to keep myself upright.

Yes. Love comes with such a high price sometimes.

CHAPTER

23

I STAGGER INSIDE, CRAWL upstairs, and climb into my bed,
lungs and throat aching.

Another mistake.

My pillow still smells like him, clean and lemony. Like
an addict, I press my face into the fabric and breathe deep,
filling my lungs to bursting. Again and again, until my tears
and snot wet the pillow and I can't smell him at all anymore.

The small taste is not enough, and still, it's too much.
How long will it take for every trace of him to disappear, for
me to have peace again?

I don't want to know. And I'm not going to stick around
to find out.

I lurch upright and yank a duffel bag from the hallway
closet. My hands are sure, even if my mind isn't, grabbing
whatever clothes look clean and shoving them inside.

It's quiet in the marina as I march out to my car. Everyone is tucked away at home, but not me. I can't stay there a
minute longer. It's too full of Daniel. I can't look anywhere
without finding another unwelcome reminder. Can't take
a clear breath in my own bed with his scent still on my
sheets.

I get into my car and point it north on 101. After making several stops and turns to ensure I haven't been followed out of the city, I drive into the darkness.

Somewhere north of Ukiah, I fuel up with terrible, burnt gas station coffee and keep going, headlights the only illumination on the empty road. I drive and drive and pull over to cry, then keep going.

The night grows several shades darker under the canopy of towering old-growth redwoods, blotting out the ocher hunter's moon, hanging low on the horizon. I grew up under these ancient boughs, running around massive trunks the size of living rooms. Made nests with Gabrielle in the fairy rings formed by young trees, curling up on the soft moss. Ran away and pretended to live off the land in the scorched snags of trees long since dead, their trunks hollowed out by fire, but still giving life and shelter to all creatures great and small.

Why have I stayed away? I should've gone home, shown my face to the people who watched me grow. Even if it would've meant coming clean about my odd career. Even if it meant sitting with their stifling sadness, steady and unrelenting as winter rain.

Seven years have passed, a hundred conflicts fought and won, but I'm still as alone as I was that day at the Changi Airport, the rest of the world moving right along without me. Instead of settling in my family's orbit, drawing comfort from their nearness, I jettisoned and pretended I wasn't adrift, floating aimlessly through space and time. My handful of visits in the intervening years have morphed into guilt so consuming, I don't know how I'm able to stand myself.

It could be different, Dylan. Everything could be different.

I wipe my eyes with the palm of my free hand, dismayed to hear Daniel's weighty, river-rock voice so clearly. How long will I have to wait for his exact inflection to dull in my brain?

The dense, alluvial redwood plains give way to the clearer vistas of the coast the closer I get to Eureka. Over my left shoulder in the gaps between trees, Humboldt Bay shines liquid black, reflecting the light of the full moon.

I look up Gabrielle's address, the house she bought several years ago. I wasn't there for the housewarming party, of course. I made my excuses and sent a gift, a large, gourmet espresso maker. Only now does my ostentatious gift strike me as tacky. Cruel, even. Like I could buy my way out of showing up.

She deserves so much better than me. Everyone does.

I can barely make out the home numbers on the dark, forested street, but I pull up in front of what I hope is her house, clammy palms slipping off the steering wheel. The time glows vivid blue on my dash: 12:03 AM.

"Whose brilliant idea was this? Fuck." I wipe my eyes.

There's nothing to do but show my face.

I get out and walk along the path of brick pavers, admiring the huge clusters of blue and green hydrangeas surrounding her home, glowing silver in the moonlight. The house itself is adorable, creamy yellow with teal shutters and a small white porch. Very cottagecore, very Gabrielle. A smile pulls at my lips, despite everything.

Before I can knock at the gorgeous Dutch door with stained glass, the light on the porch turns on and a young Black woman opens the door, wearing a pink, lacy robe.

She stares hard at me, slender arms folded, lips pursed. "Who the hell are you?"

Damn it all. I must've gotten the address wrong.

I back away, face flaming. I can't do anything right today. Not even when I try. "I'm so sorry to bother you—I think I must have the wrong house." A whimper interrupts my rambling. "So sorry."

"Dylan?" a voice from inside calls.

My sister appears in the doorway, leaning over her smaller counterpart. "*Dylan?* What are you doing here?"

She wraps her robe tighter and gently maneuvers around her friend, stepping into the light on the porch, red-brown hair gleaming carnelian. "What's going on? Are Mom and Dad okay? Are you okay?" She scrutinizes me from her place on the top of the porch. "And what happened to your hair?"

Panic roots me to the spot, but somehow I find my voice. "Ellie, I'm so sorry to show up unannounced. I didn't mean to interrupt . . ." I've used her old nickname without thinking, the one I used when I couldn't yet pronounce Gabrielle. I grimace and wave to her and the woman I assume is her partner. The enormity of what I've missed over the years is enough to steal my breath. Enough to make me collapse from the crushing weight of it, heavy as an ocean. "I just . . ." I swallow the chunk of coral in my throat. "I just missed you."

Gabrielle blinks, long lashes fluttering against her high cheekbones. I'm not sure how I could've forgotten her strong-featured, classical beauty. In the chiaroscuro lamplight, she could be the subject of a Titian painting. Even the scar running up her neck and cheek seems beautiful, an aged vein of white. No longer mean and raw, the way it was when I left.

She opens her arms.

It shouldn't surprise me, but the kind welcome is still the last thing I expect.

I climb the steps, slowly, afraid this all might dissolve, another nightmare building only to retreat into the creases of my brain when I open my eyes, leaving me uneasy without ever knowing why.

I step into her arms, wrapping my own around her slim waist. She smells the same, like jasmine, rounded out with something fresh and marine. The place she spends so much of her time. Our love of the water is the one thing we've always had in common, even when our lives took such different turns.

"I'm so glad you're here," she says, with gentleness I don't deserve. "God, I'm so glad to see you, Dilly."

The painful emotions of the night swell and the tears arrive without warning, leaving me shaky and weak. Right back to the breakers, tossed about in the churning, violent swirl.

She pulls away and studies my tearstained face. "Why don't you come inside and tell me what's got my tough little sister so worked up, huh?" A smile creases her freckled face. "Because it must be the end of the world."

* * *

Alicia, Gabrielle's partner, presses a steaming mug of chamomile tea into my hands.

"Thank you," I say.

She grunts by way of acknowledgment and returns the kettle to the stovetop before joining Gabrielle on the cute, floral-print love seat opposite of me. I should be put off by Alicia's grumpiness, but I can't help liking her—my tenderhearted sister needs someone hard-nosed looking after her. Also, I did show up in the middle of the night like a dumb, self-absorbed teen, interrupting their sleep. If I were her, I'd be pissed too.

Their three cats, having adjusted to my sudden appearance, have each taken a seat on our laps. Though coy initially, I've been graced by Mr. Darcy himself, a black, short-haired cat with an air of hauteur. Gabrielle has Mr. Bingley, an orange tabby who hasn't stopped meowing since I arrived, and Alicia has Miss Bennett, a fluffy Himalayan content to watch the proceedings with her fine eyes.

"So." Gabrielle leans forward on her elbows. "Tell me everything; omit nothing."

"Am I talking to licensed marriage and family thera-pist Gabrielle or big-sister Gabrielle?" I ask, wary. I stroke behind Mr. Darcy's pointy ears, rewarded with a loud, wheezing purr.

"Both." Her smile is mischievous.

It's so amazing to see, I can't help but sit in awe for too many beats. She's gone and become a whole new person when I wasn't looking, wasn't paying attention. I wonder how much else I missed when I was busy being a human pinball, ricocheting, never settling long enough to think too hard about what I was doing.

"Well . . . I guess it was easier to fix other people's prob-lems than to examine my own," I say after a while. "So that's what I did."

"How do you mean?"

"I mean, that's what I do for a living. I help people who've been wronged. Help them find revenge. Retribution. Justice, when I do my job well."

Gabrielle's delicate brows arch. She and Alicia exchange a speaking glance.

"How long?" Gabrielle asks, curiosity seeming to get the better of her.

"Seven years. Ever since I stopped being a nomad and moved back to California." I shake my head. "Can't believe it's already been that long."

"You must've been good at it, to make a living in the city."

"I am. It's a weird job, but it's fulfilling."

And lonely, as it turns out.

"It's aboveboard, right?" A bit of elder sister takes over. "You aren't like an enforcer or something?" She pets Mr. Bingley, gently shushing him.

"No." I laugh. "My methods can be . . . ethically dubi-ous, but usually not illegal. Not super, super illegal, anyway."

Alicia snorts and sips her tea, looking more and more incredulous and amused the longer I keep talking. "Taking gig economy to new heights."

"It sounds strange, but there are more than enough assholes out there to keep me in business."

"I don't doubt it," Gabrielle says. "And I wish I could say I find any of this surprising, but you've always been a fighter." The corner of her mouth hitches up.

There's just one person who managed to soften my flint edges. Watson to my high-functioning sociopath Sherlock, my tenuous link to normalcy and respectability.

Too bad my number-one sidekick's probably on the next flight to Seoul to propose to So Ah and show me the true depth of my idiocy.

"Still," she continues, looking pensive, "what did you mean earlier? About it being easier to fix other people's problems?"

"Could you pretend you didn't hear that?" I hide behind my mug of tea. "I know I should've gone to therapy instead."

She shakes her head, looking like she's trying not to laugh.

"I mean . . . it just felt like there was nothing I could do to help you, Ellie." The despair swamps me, fresh as the years I swam in it junior and senior year. Sharing our room again after she moved back home, her first semester at Cal abruptly cut short. Her anguish was everywhere, filling every space, seeping into the paint, the carpet, the furniture. Enough to suffocate on.

"I didn't know how to reach you," I go on, tears welling up. "Nothing I did seemed to help. And after a while . . . I couldn't stand it anymore."

Gabrielle's face crumples.

Alicia gives me a hard look and reaches over to hold her hand, twining her delicate fingers through my sister's larger ones.

"I'm so sorry. It's my fault for not being able to handle it. But I just . . ." I shake my head. "I wanted to help someone if it wasn't in my power to help you. Make *someone* pay for their sins if it couldn't be Brent."

"I never suspected." Her voice croaks. "I just thought you were tired of me."

"No. God, no." I can't let that misunderstanding last a minute longer. I reach across the gap between the love seat and my velvet slipper chair, offering my hand, palm up. "*No.* I was sick of waiting for karma to take its course. Sick of feeling so fucking helpless. So I left, and tried to believe in my own agency. And I've done it, Ellie." I squeeze her hand. "I have Brent in my sights."

She blinks, freeing more tears. "What?" She pulls her hand away.

Alicia shoots me another warning glance.

"I won't talk to you about it if you don't want, but I'm working to bring him down on behalf of another client, for something unrelated. Only . . ." I sigh, remembering the thwarted interview with Dr. Chang. Seems like it happened days ago already. "I don't know if I'll be able to do it the way I planned."

"I don't want you near him," Gabrielle spits. "Anywhere near that monster. How could you even think of—"

I hold up a hand. "I'm going to find a way."

Gabrielle and Alicia share another long look.

How I wish I had their easy intimacy. There's love and trust in their shared glance, visible in mere seconds.

I could've had that, too, I think. *But I let it all go.* Like a fool. I groan and press the heels of my palms to my tired, burning eyes.

"All right. But there's something else, isn't there?" Gabrielle asks gently. "What drove you all the way here in the middle of the night, in tears? It wasn't Brent, was it?" She bites her lip. "Was it?"

"No. It wasn't him." I sigh, resigned to ripping off the metaphorical Band-Aid. After all, I have only myself to blame for this sorry fucking predicament.

"I have—had—a friend who helped me with cases from time to time. Daniel Haas." I force his name out. "A digital PI, if you will." My smile feels brittle as a sand dollar shell. "He's the only person who knows me. My best friend, really. But we had a huge falling-out over this case. Among other things." I pick at the sleeve of my sweater, tearing a loose thread. "We want different things from life, and . . . I don't know if we're friends anymore. I don't think we're anything anymore."

"You love him," Gabrielle says, after a hefty pause.

"Is it that obvious?" I yank the thread, watching it run in my sweater. Mr. Darcy shifts but stays put, kneading my thighs, claws pressing through my jeans, purring loudly. He's sweet, really, now I've earned his trust. A bit too much like someone else I know.

"Afraid so, Dilly." She gives me a sad smile. "Your whole aura changed when you brought him up."

Only my sister could throw that word around and still be taken seriously. I meet Alicia's gaze, wondering if her thoughts tracked the same direction. Her small, knowing smile tells me they did indeed.

"Your sister's right, honey." Alicia strokes Miss Bennett, looking at me with sympathy for the first time since I showed up, brows furrowed over her deep-brown eyes. "You look like someone took your favorite puppy away."

"Well." I choke on a laugh, then slurp more tea, letting it burn my tongue, keeping me from airing more of my self-inflicted grievances. "Tell me something I don't know, I guess."

CHAPTER

24

I SPEND A RESTLESS night on the small, antique couch with three cats purring on my chest, watching the slow-rolling fire in the wood stove until nothing but embers are left.

When the sun rises, I give up on sleep and wander to the miniscule kitchen.

The espresso maker is nowhere to be found.

Fair. It'd occupy a large chunk of counter real estate, and probably look ridiculous amid the soft taupe-and-teal color scheme, like a time traveler's misplaced gadget. I open a few cupboards, searching for mugs and some tea, only to find the eyesore collecting dust in a corner of the cabinet.

Grunting, I lift it out and plug it in, then scavenge for beans. The least I can do is put my rusty barista skills to work after crashing here last night.

Gabrielle pads into the kitchen, hair a wild tangle, starting when she sees me.

"Good morning!" I wrap my hair in a knot. "How do you take your lava java?"

"I . . . I'm sorry. I actually have no idea how to use that monstrosity." She grimaces, trying to smooth the snarls in her hair. "I sound like an ingrate, but last time I tried, foamed milk went everywhere. It was this whole big thing."

I laugh and grind the beans. "Well, saddle up, sis. You're going to learn how to make yourself a fine latte."

She watches as I pull the shot and froth the milk, getting a nice sheen with the microfoam. Carefully, I add the milk to the mug, pouring from a good height. As the foam rises to the surface, I cut through the center of it with the final pour, creating a heart.

"All yours." I present my caffeine offerings with a flourish, sliding it toward her on the pretty tiled counter.

She takes the mug, expression soft when she sees the latte art. "Beautifully done." She looks up. "I guess you learned quite a bit while you were globe-trotting."

"I did pick up some obscure skills during my wandering days. Master of none, though, I'm afraid." I muster a wan smile for her. "I know just enough to be dangerous."

She laughs and takes a sip, eyes widening. "Dang. That's good stuff."

Then she lowers the mug, quiet for a long minute. "I've been thinking about what you said last night. How you need to find another way to target Brent, in addition to whatever you'd planned."

I freeze. The only sound is the hiss of the espresso shot hitting my cup. "And?"

"What if I came forward?" she asks. "Shared my story?"

"No." That's the last thing I want, to bring her into this.

"It's not your decision to make, Dilly." She takes another appreciative sip. "I know you're used to being the master of your universe, but if I want to come forward, you can't stop me."

"It's out of the question." Panic curls around my throat. "You already went to hell and back because of this sonofabitch. Don't put yourself in a vulnerable position to try and save my hide. I got myself into this mess." I heat and froth the milk for my cappuccino. "I'll get myself out of it."

"What does Daniel think?" She drums the countertop, the only sign of her annoyance.

I slosh milk over the rim of my mug, cursing. Gabrielle hands me a towel. I wipe the spill, buying myself time to answer.

"He's more of the heat-seeking missile sort," I manage to say. "Rather than messy, hand-to-hand combat. He offered to hack the company, Prometheus, to find whatever we needed to nail him."

Gabrielle leans a hip on the counter. "I have to say, this PI fella has a good head on his shoulders."

"He does. The jerk." I blink hard, looking at the small, framed picture of Gabrielle and Alicia above the breakfast nook. They're radiant with happiness in the candid shot by the ocean, photographer forgotten. "As opposed to my half-baked, occasionally brilliant schemes."

"Your words, not mine." Her eye-crinkling smile soothes the spiny edges of my defeat and humiliation. "Still, I have to think there are other people who've been hurt by Brent. We could build a damning case against him."

"There are," I acknowledge. "A reporter at the *Chronicle* I've been working with said there are complaints against him going all the way back to his prep school days on the East Coast, as well as more recent allegations from within his company. There are more, too—there's someone at a restaurant I could contact. Point her in the right direction." I'd be glad to see my BFF from the steak house again, learn what she knows, hear from the women Brent's harassed.

Gabrielle's expression is distant, amber-brown eyes gazing out the window, a thousand miles away. "Hardly surprising." She looks down at her cup, fingers pressed tight on the off-white stoneware. "Serial offenders don't stop at one, by definition."

"Fuck." I clank my mug on the counter and step into her space with a hug, determined to keep her from sinking back into the minefield of memory. "I'm so sorry, Ellie. I'm sorry I brought all of this up last night."

"Don't be sorry." Her warm hands pat my back. "The trauma will always be there, Dilly. But as time goes by, it defines me less and less." She pulls away, hands on my shoulders. "I'm not who I was when I was eighteen. And you're not who you were when you were sixteen." She brushes my cheek with the back of her hand, smiling. "You've become formidable."

My vision mists, tears at the ready. If only I knew how to shut them off. "That's what Daniel said."

How could I have forgotten his soft-spoken praise after we wrapped the case with the Philosopher/Provocateur/Wanker? The words were delivered easily enough, but I pretended not to see the heat and admiration flashing in his dark eyes. I've traveled everywhere, but I was still too afraid to wander that thorny, unpaved path with him. He was braver than me, every step of the way. Putting himself on the line again and again and again.

"He's right, Dilly." She squeezes my shoulder. "So, what are you going to do about it?"

Mr. Darcy joins us in the kitchen, brushing around my ankles. Looking up adoringly with his handsome face, fur rusting espresso brown in the morning sun.

"Would you really go on the record?" I ask, still looking at my new kitty bestie. My voice sounds small. "Even though you'd be breaking your NDA? You'd have to take a polygraph probably, sign an affidavit, have the journalists interview other people to corroborate your account—"

"Of course I would. I'm not afraid of him. He can't take anything away from me he hasn't already. And if it helps even *one* person not suffer at his hands the way I did, it'd be worth it."

I blink and Mr. Darcy's lank form blurs. Tears slide down my face, my neck, wetting my ratty T-shirt.

"What are you thinking?" she asks.

I wipe my eyes and swallow, getting rid of the tears and the tightness in my throat. Forcing steel back into my spine. In the light, the jagged edges of her scar are visible, glowing. Softened by time, in the way of all things.

"I think I could live to be a hundred and still not be as brave or as kind or as good as you. But I swear"—I take her hands—"I *swear* I'll make this worth your while. The journalist and I, we'll talk to everyone. All the women. It can't be 'he said, she said' when all of us will be saying the same goddamn thing, in the twenty-first fucking century. Everyone in the Bay Area, we'll find them and bring them to my place to make it happen. Bring everyone together under one banner. The people he's hurt, and the people he *will* hurt if he pushes his cure-all on the world."

Not one dark horse but many. Dozens. Enough to cover the horizon. A motherfucking Dothraki raid on an open field. After all, with a company named Prometheus, Brent's all but asking for a taste of Dracarys.

Even if Daniel isn't with me anymore for the fight, I can still do it. I can still help these women get what they're owed, and screw Brent on the clinical trial data too. A fight on all fronts, personal and professional. As if they could ever be separated.

"I have to go. Get back to San Francisco. Start organizing, putting things in motion." My head is full of bees—must be the rocket fuel—and I can't be still, foot drumming on the tile floor.

"I understand," she says.

"Do you think you can take time off soon? Drive down, stay at my place? You and Alicia?"

She smirks. "It's only fair, after you crashed here."

"My door's always open for you, Ellie." We still have ages of memories to catch up on, but I will never go back to the days of radio silence with her. Not ever again. No one, not Brent, not the shitstorm we'll weather when her story goes live, will take my sister away from me again. Not when a piece of my soul has been carefully restored, like a fragment of stained glass soldered into its rightful place.

"Well, then." Gabrielle lifts her mug in a toast, giving me a gimlet smile over the rim. "To overdue justice."

Her call to arms is poetic, as befits my high angel sister.

Mine? I grip my mug and clank it against hers. "Let's slump the bastard."

*   *   *

Gabrielle leaves for her first appointment of the day at her private practice, and Alicia heads out not long after with a latte to go, driving to the Mad River Fish Hatchery in her beat-up blue Subaru.

I have to charge both of my dead phones before I can start calling or driving. While I wait for them to reanimate, I shower in the claw-foot tub, pulling the shower curtain around it while Mr. Darcy sits on the toilet, licking his leg in a very un-Darcy-like manner. I scrub under the hot spray until I'm red as a lobster, a new person. Then I brew another shot of espresso and get to work while Mr. Darcy keeps my lap warm.

There are several missed texts from Rhys, another tiresome screed from Brent on the burner, and deafening silence from Daniel.

I brush the hurt aside and call Rhys.

"Tell me about the women you found on the East Coast who've been harmed by Brent. How many are there? Have you reached out to any of them?"

"Well." He clears his throat, sounding nervous. "No, I haven't yet—"

"Do it. Start right now. My older sister has offered to go on the record with Brent."

There's a long, freighted pause. "Your sister?"

"Her freshman year at Cal. With Brent. It was all sealed up, but she's willing to break her NDA, sign an affidavit, take a polygraph, whatever. The full monty. When can you interview her? And are you working with the other colleague of yours, Katie? The one who was ready to interview another employee from Prometheus?"

"Um—"

"Get yourself some coffee, sir, bring Katie into the loop, and *make it happen*." I hang up.

With that call out of the way, I move on to Dr. Chang, wondering how I can convince her to press forward with our own aims.

Before I can, Rhys answers with a text.

I don't work for you, you know.

I could put you on Dark Horse payroll if it makes you feel better, I reply.

Actually, I think the Chronicle should hire you. You've got the makings of an excellent journalist.

I blink at his text a few times, moved for reasons I can't articulate. Then I reply, *Trying to lure me away from the dark side?*

We have lots of coffee? And it's never boring.

I'll think about it, I say, before snark can get the better of me.

With a smile, I call Dr. Chang. She doesn't answer.

I won't go so far as to say it sounds ominous, but worry wraps around me like the vines of morning glory outside the window. I hope it's still her cold feet talking, rather than the men watching her every move.

Regardless, I leave a message, asking if she can call me back soon, because Gabrielle is right. Where there is one, there are bound to be many. This case was never only about Brent overselling his miracle drug to "end" depression. To focus on that narrow offense and exclude the rest of his wrongdoing was my first and biggest mistake. Anyone who sees half the population as subhuman should not be allowed to lead, period. Cruelty is not a prerequisite for greatness, nor will it ever be. All arguments to the contrary are noise.

My burner rings, startling me out of my caffeinated ruminating.

It's the Ken doll, of course. As if he could sense my fury from miles away.

I turn off the phone, calmly packing it back into my duffel bag.

And after I take care of Brent? The first order of business will be a long journey to parts unknown, where no one knows my name. Somewhere so far away I won't know Daniel's married to So Ah or anyone else until it's already happened and there's nothing left to be done. Somewhere I can perfect the fine art of forgetting. Somewhere I can do as he asks and try not to give up on humanity. Try not to give up on . . . love.

As if there could ever be another after him.

I scratch behind Mr. Darcy's soft ears. "Who am I kidding, huh?"

Maybe I'll find a new home by the ocean. Someplace I can watch the gray whales from my window as they migrate north and south, an everlasting loop. Somewhere to admire the dolphins and otters and sea lions and adopt my own cats and dogs and goats and chickens. I'll grow old with the only creatures who could love me as I am, petty and bloodthirsty, an admittedly terrible combination of traits. I'll be an old cat lady crone, wizened by the salt and sun and sea, ranting to all the young kids that I used to know the man who finally developed teleportation capabilities for Apple's latest release.

Like most things in my life, it'd be funny if it didn't break my heart.

CHAPTER

25

I'M STILL BUZZING with energy when I return to the city near lunchtime, even after the four-hour drive. My nerves have grown with every passing moment, wondering how Dr. Chang's doing. Finally, I'm near her apartment. I park a few streets over, grab a wig from my glove box—always be prepared—and slip my oversized shades on despite the drizzle.

An unmarked van is parked down the street. I don't know whether it's my security people or Brent's. Regardless, I angle my face away and knock on her door.

Dr. Chang answers, hair tied in a messy bun, eyes widening when she recognizes me. Toddler twins with round cheeks cling to each of her legs, looking at me with curiosity and a little fear. I'm terrible at guessing children's ages, but they look to be about two.

"Didn't realize you made house calls." She offers me a wan smile.

"When occasion warrants." I return her smile, relieved. "May I come in?"

She casts a hesitant look past my shoulder but nods.

Indoors, I kick off my shoes.

"I'm sorry about the mess," she says. "Trying to keep this place clean is like battling entropy."

"Don't apologize." I try to give her an encouraging smile. "It's not like you haven't had other things going on." The scent of sesame oil and simmering broth fills my nose.

"True." She laughs. "We were about to have lunch. Would you like some egg drop soup?"

"I'd love some, please."

The four of us sit at a small table, slurping. When I've finished eating, I sit back, mindful of our young audience in their high chairs. "I'm really glad you're okay."

"I am," she concedes. "Relatively speaking. And I'm so sorry about the other day."

As if sensing the tense undercurrents, one of her toddlers fusses in her seat. Evelyn lifts her and bounces her on her knee.

"Please, don't be sorry." I clear our bowls. "Everything about this is scary." *And shitty.*

When I'm seated again, I face her. "But! We have the evidence. The ball is in your court, Dr. Chang. Which is why I wanted to ask: If going to the press is out, would you consider the whistle-blower route? File a complaint with the SEC?"

She chews her lip, bouncing the young one on her knee, trying to get her to stop fussing. The other toddler picks up on the stress and joins in with a small shriek of displeasure. Dr. Chang tries to shush her, to no avail.

"Would you like me to hold her?" I ask.

"Would you mind?" Dr. Chang looks up with hope.

"Not a bit." I hoist the surprisingly heavy little one and settle her on my lap. "Hi, young miss. Nice to meet you." In new environs, she quiets, then gives me a sweet smile and reaches to yank on my red wig. A worthy sacrifice.

Before us, the table is scattered with legal notices from Prometheus and medical journals and cereal and play-dough. The mundane, juxtaposed mess brings a tiny smile to my face. Dr. Chang's earned her PhD, and she's raised two children. If anyone can walk through fire and emerge to the other side, it's a mom. I'd bet on her any day.

"You'd be protected from retribution. And there's the possibility of a monetary reward, though that could take a while to arrive. Still, there's a good chance you'd earn a substantial reward if you stepped forward." I jiggle twin number one on my knees. "Also, I plan to bring this information to his board. But only if you want me to take that last step—I can't guarantee your anonymity if we go forward from there."

Dr. Chang swirls her cup of tea, gaze glued to the pale-green liquid. A faint smile creases her face, fine lines bracketing her mouth and eyes, evidence of the strain she's endured over the past several months.

"Six months ago, if someone told me I'd be jobless, threatened with litigation from a huge, powerful corporation, and ready to get myself into even more trouble, I'd have laughed." She looks up, dark eyes twinkling with humor. "And recommended an antipsychotic."

I smirk.

"God knows I never planned on trying to slay a dragon. I have lived my life so carefully. Elder child, you know?"

I nod, and that's when it hits me. Her energy is so much like my sister's, it's breathtaking. No wonder I've taken her deep into my heart.

"And where has it gotten me?" She smooths twin number two's shiny black hair, tied in two neat pigtails, brushing away imaginary fuzzies. "In science, the process is sacrosanct. We follow the rules in the pursuit of truth because everything would fall apart without it. But it doesn't matter if I follow the rules if other people think the rules don't apply to them to begin with."

"'Snot fair," her daughter says.

Dr. Chang smiles, surprised, and boops her on her nose. "How right you are, my love." Her daughter giggles and smushes her own nose down.

I hold my breath. Waiting on the moment of truth.

Dr. Chang looks up, a fierce light in her eyes. "Just this once, I think I can bend the rules to set the world to rights. Let's file the complaint. And set Prometheus on fire."

"Yeah?" Hope spreads through my chest like a wave, filling my lungs.

"Yes. Write it in the sky, run down the street, and scream it at the top of your lungs." She laughs. "Whatever you have in mind, I'm on board, even if the whole world will discover my name."

"All right, Doctor." I'm so proud of her, I can hardly speak. "I'll do it."

*　*　*

After meeting Dr. Chang and filing the complaint together, I'm so pumped I won't be able to sleep unless I work off this stress. Ordinarily I'd kayak to settle myself, but it's raining again, a steady, cold drizzle. At home, I throw my duffel bag back in my closet, but my sneakers catch my eye.

Well, there's an easy choice. I can't stay in my house when my brain keeps dredging up Daniel with every small reminder, and I've been away from the Krav Maga studio too long anyway. Plus, I can't think of a better way to expend this adrenaline and get my head on straight. Kicking stuff always makes me feel better.

The drive across the Gate is quiet, and before I know it, I'm rolling up in the old neighborhood south of Golden Gate Park. I used to come here all the time before my business really took off. Daniel too sometimes, though our schedules hardly ever lined up, especially after he got promoted and spent more time in Cupertino. Still, I always loved sparring with him.

I park my car, letting the rain drum my windshield. The world would be gray and blurry anyway, but even this innocuous reminder of him has me crying again, a slow, continuous drip I can't shut off. Silent weeping is the new norm, apparently. It's unsettling after years of dry-eyed ferocity. Like all my cauterized feelings have returned, reappearing with the least bit of love. Wild flowers blooming in the desert after the rains.

Once I'm done with Brent, I'll never be able to set foot in San Francisco again. This place will always remind me of Daniel. Will always belong to him.

I sniff and wipe my eyes with my sleeve. "Tits up, Lady Justice." As much as I'm able in a stiff sports bra. I snort and run across the street, trying not to let too much rain soak through my workout clothes.

Kevin Levy, the owner of the studio, greets me with a hug and a crinkly smile. "It's been forever, Dylan. Good to see you. Almost didn't recognize you with the hair."

"Good to see you too, Mr. Levy. Still have an open gym on Sundays?" I pull my damp hair into a knot.

He nods. "Pretty quiet too. Just one other person in there."

Angry thuds echo from someone punching the heavy bag, one after another. Whoever they are, they sound like me. Pent-up and pissed.

"Perfect." I kick off my shoes and drop my bag in the cubby. "So long as they don't mind sharing the heavy bag." I give him a feral grin. "I've gotta take out some aggression too."

The thuds stop, and the silence afterward is freighted. They must've heard me.

I step into the mirrored room behind the front desk and pause at the threshold, heart pounding faster and faster though I'm frozen in place.

The gods have a cruel sense of humor, methinks.

"Dylan." Daniel's voice is hoarse.

He looks like a bronze statue under the bright lights, standing next to the heavy bag suspended from the ceiling. A statue that clearly hasn't slept, deep circles under his eyes and next-day stubble shadowing his jaw. A statue that sweats and breathes and looks at me with irises like black fire.

If Daniel's showing wear and tear, I can only imagine what I look like, tearstained and sleep deprived. Scary doesn't begin to cover it.

"What are you doing here?" My voice is hard and flat, even if my heart rate has spiked somewhere north of 150 beats per minute.

His expression changes, closing off after his initial surprise. "What does it look like?"

It's unreasonable to be so annoyed by his presence, but I came here to screw my head on straight. No chance of that now. I've forgotten everything with a hard reboot and lost the files that told me how to walk, how to breathe, how to act like I don't love him. How to pretend like seeing him doesn't cut me right open.

Nothing can ever be easy.

I take out the wrappings for my hands and wind them up.

"I can go, if you want," he says, right behind me.

I always forget how quiet he is, moving without even a rustle.

"I wouldn't have come if I'd known . . ." He audibly swallows. "If I'd known you were planning to be here too. This place has always been yours more than mine. I could go to another studio in the future if that's what you want—"

"No need for all that, Daniel." I turn around with a smile so forced, I'm surprised it doesn't crack a molar. "I don't plan on being here after I'm done with Brent. So come hit things whenever you want." I wave an arm in a broad arc. "The city is yours."

Daniel stills. Every part of him except for his eyes, searching mine. Trying to find purchase. "You're leaving?"

I nod and look away. I can't begin that slow, sinking descent into his dark irises, windows to the best soul I know.

"Where?"

"Don't know yet." I shrug. "I'll send you a postcard when I finally figure it out."

Whatever he sees in my face must convince him I'm serious. The realization passes over him like a cloud, darkening everything degree by degree.

"Well." After a long, tense second, he shakes it off and gives me a high-watt smile, bright as his white T-shirt, popping both dimples. "I guess this is your last chance to get a good punch in, then."

"You want to spar?"

I didn't bring any padding, having planned to keep to myself.

He's not wearing any either.

That feels right. He's the only one who could hurt me, because I gave him that power. Him and him alone. If anyone's going to wound me, it should be someone I respect.

"For old time's sake?" His voice is friendly, playful. Nevertheless, he lifts his arms, tucks his elbows, fists clenched, assuming his fighting stance. "Or are you too rusty?"

The fucker. He knows damn well I won't back down from a challenge.

"Says the old man." I roll my shoulders and neck. "You're on. But don't blame me when you wind up on the floor."

"We'll see."

He takes another step in my direction, leaving himself open, well within range of my feet.

I spin and kick, thwacking his side with the front of my foot. It's not full power, but any kick is going to hurt.

"Ow!" He grunts and clutches his oblique with a wounded expression. "Fuck." Then he laughs, shaky. "That wasn't very sportsmanlike."

"You of all people know I fight dirty." I shift weight from foot to foot, angling my body toward him.

"That I do." He sighs. "Why do I like it so much?"

In the half second it takes me to appreciate his comment, he sweeps my feet out from under me with a swift kick around my ankles. I fall on the padded floor, blinking up at the fluorescent lights.

If I wasn't ready to breathe fire before, I am now.

He leans over, upside-down face filling my whole world with black and gold and more concern than there should be, two deep lines etched between his brows.

"Dylan, you okay?"

"Yup." I sit up with a groan. "I'm fine." Just my pride wounded. I had it coming after my sneaky kick, though.

He offers a hand to help me stand.

I decline, jumping to my feet and backing up a few steps. Putting space between us, like I should've done the second I realized he was here. "You're a daunting adversary." My throat is tight again, warning. "But I think I like you better as a friend."

"Just not as a lover."

I hiss an exhale. "You couldn't be more wrong." My words are bitter as a burnt forest, charred by my own longing and regret. Then I laugh, shrill and grating, seconds away from dissolving into an ugly cry. "Daniel Haas, you can be remarkably dense for someone so smart."

He blinks, face slack with shock.

I spin on a foot and grab my things. I'm sure he overheard every word, but to his credit, Mr. Levy waves goodbye when I depart like a bat out of hell, escaping into the rain. I thank the weather gods as I run across the street back to my car—I couldn't ask for better camouflage, hiding the tears racing down my face.

I slam my door shut and slump over the steering wheel, letting it hold me up because I can't do it after seeing Daniel. My body is weighted with anguish, heavy and viscous.

I'd give anything to have him back. As a friend. As more. As anything at all. Failing that, I have to leave, but a small, bitter part of me knows I'll always be looking for him, no matter how far I run. Searching for his face in the nameless crowds. Ears tuned to the sound of his voice, deep and resonant, trying to pick him out of the babel.

Someone knocks on my window.

I shriek and jerk upright.

"Let me in," Daniel says.

I unlock my doors, pouting, and he slides into my passenger seat, bringing the rain with him. His shirt is soaked, stuck to his skin. He breathes hard, skin flushed. The scent of him is overwhelming in my small car, rain and sweat and cedar.

"What do you want, Daniel?" I stare straight ahead.

"What are you going to do with Brent?"

My skin crackles with annoyance, rolling over my skin in bristling waves. "If you're going to lecture me again, let's not and pretend you did—"

He lifts a large hand, slowing my acidic roll. "I'm not here to lecture, though I don't think I was doing that in the first place."

I fix him with my best resting bitch face.

"Maybe a little," he concedes. "Maybe a lot. But you understand it comes from a good place? Dylan . . ." He chokes my name. "You know . . . you *know* I'd rather die than see you hurt."

My lungs collapse in a rush, and the next breath saws in, a gasp of misery. I don't know how I can have tears left after the past forty-eight hours, but I do. I blink, setting loose a hot cascade. "Dammit. Please, don't. Don't make this worse than it already is."

"It's true," he says, no less determined for the softness. "And I won't pretend like it's not. So, please, tell me what you plan to do. And what I can do to help."

I search his face, his eyes, gauging him. Trying to navigate the aftermath, our treacherous minefield. One false step and I'll be blown to bits again, pieces irredeemably scattered. More than they are already.

"Even if"—he swallows—"even if there's nothing between us, I told you I'd help. I gave you my word."

The rain beats the car, louder and louder, so I have to speak up to be heard. "This is a bad idea."

"Probably." He laughs, a sudden rich sound over the roar of the rain, but it fades quickly. "But you've never been a bad influence, Dylan." He meets my gaze again. "You've always made me want to try harder. Made me want to be brave. Like you."

I love you, I almost say, words rushing up from the bottom of my being. He's dismantled my barricades, all right, scorching through layer after layer, finally exposing the naked, vulnerable heart of me.

It hurts. God, it hurts. But if I have to feel, I'll let this love raze me down to bone.

"Well." I clear my aching throat, stuffing the words back into a corner of my brain where they sit, glowing with heat. "First of all, I'm so sorry. I know you'd never betray me . . ." I grip the steering wheel with my right hand. "I don't know why I said what I said. Just terrified, I guess."

He gently pries my fingers from the steering wheel and gives them a quick squeeze before letting go. "It's all right, Dylan. I know that."

I wipe my nose. "Really?"

"Really."

Heartened, I sit straighter. "And second, well . . . I guess I'm trying to break space and time and be everywhere at once." I tick each scheme off on my fingers. "Dr. Chang and I filed a whistle-blower complaint and got that ball rolling. Then I'm going to alert the Prometheus board what Brent's been up to. Staying a private company has enabled him to skate by without checking in with investors on the regular, and I don't think they'll be pleased to know he's screwed them all over."

"How will you bring it to their attention?"

"If I can get into his contacts, I plan to email them the evidence."

Daniel's eyes widen. "You want me to hack?"

I shake my head. "Let me try my way first."

He frowns but nods for me continue.

"Then, when Rhys is finished investigating, we'll expose the data from the clinical trials. But!" I hold up a hand. "That's not all. He has a colleague who discovered women on the East Coast who were harassed by Brent in prep school. That colleague has also been in contact with someone from Prometheus who's been sexually harassed by Brent more recently, and I'm working with Dr. Chang to see if there are any more. And I'm planning to talk to another woman I met at a restaurant who said Brent's known for harassing the female waitstaff."

When I'm done, Daniel sits back, considering. "You're going to overwhelm him. The scientific front and the personal."

"In short, yes. We just have to convince everyone to speak up and add their names." I hold my sides. "Otherwise, the whole thing might fall apart. Boards can be reshuffled, but if we show the company is rotten through and through, it might be enough."

Daniel reaches out, long arm stretching across the center console. He hovers over my upper arm for a second before giving it a gentle squeeze, warmth seeping through my damp, long-sleeved shirt.

Even this small touch fortifies me. Grounds me. I take a deep breath. "My sister also offered to go on the record about Brent."

"You talked to your sister?" He lets go and leans over to study me, trying to find a way in.

"Last night. I went back to Eureka." I don't need to say more—of course he hears the subtext, lifting it out of the water like a handful of kelp.

"I'm sorry."

"Don't be." I muster a smile for him. "Thanks to you, I stopped being a coward and went home. First time in years. Met my sister's partner, Alicia. It was so nice to see Ellie. Gabrielle, I mean. She's . . ." I close my mouth. "I'm so happy for her. She's doing better than I ever thought she would." My hangnails haven't been picked at for a while, so I tear at one. "No thanks to me, of course."

Daniel remains quiet.

I look over, curious what's brewing in that head of his.

His expression is soft. "She's lucky to have a sister like you, Dylan. No matter what you say." A small smile folds the corner of his mouth. "Not many people would devote themselves to fighting on their sibling's behalf."

"Well, if anything happens to me, I hope you'll do the same and avenge me." I close my hand in a fist and smile. "Avenge me, Daniel!"

"All right, Roy Kent." He smirks. "But it won't ever come to that."

"No?"

"Not while I'm alive."

As if he's blown air over them, the three small words in the back of my brain glow brighter. Hotter.

They have to emerge before they burn me alive, but not yet. Not just yet.

"I don't want you involved in this, don't want you hacking," I tell him. "Not when you could go to jail for it."

"Don't put the programmer on the pedestal," he says, with another smirk.

I smother a startled laugh with the back of my hand.

"I know you want to protect me, but my help doesn't have to be illegal. Dylan . . . I just . . ." He sighs. "I want to be there for you."

I crack my knuckles and sigh, too tired and charmed to fight. "I must be going soft," I mutter.

He lifts a dark brow, waiting in that infuriatingly patient way of his.

"How 'bout that home security system in the houseboat, then?" I hate, hate asking for help, hate admitting weakness, the damsel in proverbial distress, but it's a wise precaution knowing who's approaching my home. And it's Daniel, after all. If I have to lean on someone, it should be him. "The newfangled one you offered to install this summer, with fourteen cameras and the duress alarm and all that? I mean, don't get me wrong, it's overkill, but maybe—"

"It doesn't have fourteen cameras, and I'd be happy to." He gives me a zillion-dollar smile. "Was that so hard?"

"Yeah." I grunt. "It was."

He smooths his smile away. "I'll get it set up tomorrow before work. Shouldn't take me more than an hour."

Though he's coming to my home for a prosaic reason, I can't deny my outlook has brightened like sunlight streaming through broken clouds.

So fucked. Still.

The price I pay for ignoring the words in the back of my skull.

"It's a date," I manage to say.

26

Ꭲʀᴜᴇ ᴛᴏ ʜɪꜱ word, Daniel shows up bright and early the following morning, several large boxes tucked under his arm. He toes off his shoes.

"I come bearing gifts." He deposits everything onto my kitchen counter and rolls back the sleeves on his tailored, soft-gray dress shirt.

I press a plate of homemade cinnamon rolls into his hands. "Looks like you're going to need this."

He sets the confection of cinnamon sugar on the counter without a glance. "I got a few add-ons. Motion detectors, range extender. The duress alarm. That's why it looks like a lot."

"Well, thank you." I hide my sad puppy face in my urn of a mug, downing the rest of my now-cold coffee. "I appreciate it."

"Wait. Is this what I think it is?" He finally looks at his breakfast/dessert, eyes wide.

I nod. As if I could forget his favorite pastry, the one he never makes for himself because he never has time. Also because he values not being on a first-name basis with his dentist.

"And you don't even have a mixer." He looks at the mixing bowls and measuring cups filling the sink. "Dylan . . ."

"Don't *Dylan* me." I find a fork and slide it his way. So what if I woke up at four AM to make it? "Just eat it."

He does, groaning with unfiltered delight. "Why is it so good?"

"The three cups of sugar probably have something to do with it."

"Three?" He chokes on a bite. "I can never eat this again, can I?"

"Maybe on your birthday?"

His smile changes, wavering, weighted by an emotion I can't pinpoint. "Well, send me the recipe, so I can still make it even if you've gone walkabout."

Damn. Reality hurts like a punch to the solar plexus. "I will."

After finishing his plate of goodies, he works for the next hour, muted and focused.

Then he asks for my phone. "I'll need it for command central. You'll be able to monitor everything from the app."

"Music to my control-freak ears." I hand it over, unthinking.

The lock-screen photo shines, the one I changed the night I was in and out of sleep in Eureka. It's a snap of him from the speakeasy, taken earlier in the night—before the Scotch—when I still had my wits about me, but only just. In the photo, he's in half profile, backlit by the pink-and-orange neon tiger, a phosphorescent halo.

Smile, Haas, I'd told him.

He did, just for me, wide and real. So devastating I could hardly stand it, scorched by my yearning. The knowledge that I wanted him in every way. The knowledge, too, that I didn't know how to ask, how to invite something so fine and precious into my nasty, venal life, except in the most superficial of ways. In the end, what could I do with such a gift except ruin it?

I should've deleted the photo ages ago. I tried more than once, thumb hovering over the proxy garbage can that'd absolve me of this lacerating reminder, but I never did.

I kept it instead. Cutting myself with the burden of knowledge, the way I always do. Elevating him front and center when I knew it was over, so I'd never forget he deserved better than a queenpin like me.

Putting the programmer on the pedestal, apparently, if I'm to borrow his words.

I'd laugh, except terror has clamped around my throat like a huge, crushing hand.

Daniel looks at the screen, then back at me, expression inscrutable.

"Sorry! Duh, you need my pass code." I pretend like I didn't reveal an ace-high flush. "Or my face, as it is." I snatch my phone from his hands and let facial recognition do the job of removing the telltale photo, relegating it to the background.

"Thank you." Daniel takes my phone and wordlessly installs the app.

I pour myself more coffee, though what I need is a month at a Buddhist monastery to help my thudding heart and runaway pulse. While I fix my mug with heavy cream and enough sugar to ensure cavities—solidarity!—I steal a few furtive glances at him as he connects all the cameras and sensors to the mother ship.

He still hasn't said anything.

He doesn't need to. A small, pleased smile tugs at the corner of his mouth, pulling his cheek taut, revealing the hint of a dimple.

"Twenty dollars for your thoughts?" I venture. "I'm prepared to go higher."

"You'd need more than that." He tucks his smile away and returns my phone. "All done."

I take it, careful not to brush his fingers, sliding the incriminating device into the pocket of my robe. "Well. Thank you again." I blow on my coffee.

"You'll want to update your profile with emergency contacts. People the system will alert if you're in trouble, aside from the police."

"Sure thing."

"Don't wait to do it." He slides his leather messenger bag across his chest. "Take care of it today, okay? Please?"

"Are you calling me out on my procrastinating ways?" I lean on the counter, amused despite myself.

"Yes," he says, without apology. Daring me to be mad.

As if I could when he smiles at me like that, backlit by the morning sun. "All right." I burn my mouth with a too-hot slurp. "Anything for you, Daniel."

He inhales, big rib cage expanding.

So far as I can tell, no breath comes out.

A moment later, he gives himself a shake, rue filling his expression. "I have to get to work."

"Giddyup, then." I wave him on. "Skynet won't create itself."

He laughs, shakes his head, and closes the door.

As soon as he's gone, I slump against the wall.

Everything hurts. My head, my heart, even my finger-tips, clenched around my mug.

"It's not forever," I tell myself. I have to endure this painful balancing act with Daniel only a little longer. Long enough to finish what I started with Brent and watch him be brought to account.

I unlock my phone and admire the impressive assemblage of video streams Daniel's put together on the app. I'll see every Tom, Dick, and pelican approaching my home, that's for sure. Good to know in case this whole operation goes tits up and Brent's out for blood.

Under my profile, in a remarkable feat of cognitive dissonance, I type Daniel's name and phone number as my emergency contact and hit save.

* * *

That evening when I return to the townhouse, I send a mea culpa text to Brent, setting my plan in motion. My hands are sweaty, and I wipe them on my skintight jeans before I type.

Hi, babe! Been thinking about the other day and hoping I can make it up to you with dinner. My place, let's say seven. Hoping to see you. 😚😚

As I hoped, he replies immediately. *Sure. I can be there.*

Trap set, I ready my temporary home, preparing food. Lighting candles. Grinding more antihistamines.

Brent knocks early—again—perhaps hoping to catch me off guard, but I'm ready. Hair dried and curled, a low-cut silk cami underneath a prim angora cardigan, buttons popped. In the soft light, my reflection in the mirror glows angelic. A lesser angel, maybe. Ready to sully my hands among the humans and do the Lord's dirty work.

His eyes widen when he sees me, then the candlelit kitchen and dining room. He lifts an inquiring brow.

"Like I said." I take his hand with a smile and pull him across the threshold. "I wanted to make it up to you."

I feed the monster my mother's own decadent pasta specialty, penne alla vodka with a generous serving of chopped pancetta.

All the while, the monster drinks his Chianti full of antihistamines. I will him to pour every last bit of comeuppance down his throat.

"You didn't answer my calls earlier." He twirls the stem of the wineglass, looking at me with thinly veiled hunger but recrimination as well. Irises like hard blue marbles, exuding no warmth at all.

I knew he'd bring it up. He can't help but list my faults and missteps, trying to tear me down and prove my unworthiness. My fickleness and faithlessness, and by extension, that of all women. Proof we deserve mistreatment.

"Well, I was pissed after we talked." I let truth seep into my voice, granting it a layer of authenticity. "My family means everything to me. If we're going to be together, you'll need to understand that." Little does he know how true my words are.

He nods like he cares, finishes his wine, and crosses the table to meet me, kneeling at my feet. "Of course, babe."

I look into the monster's eyes, touch his hateful face, and don't look away.

He blinks, looking dazed. His skin is flushed, perhaps from the wine. Maybe from the substantial dose of diphenhydramine.

"Are you feeling okay, babe?" I fix my expression into one of concern. "You're looking a little feverish." I touch his forehead with the back of my hand. "Do you want to lie down?"

"I am feeling . . . off . . ." He shakes his head, confusion slackening his features. Confusion and anger. As if weakness is an affront to his very masculinity.

"Come on, then." I stand and support his ungainly body. "Let's get you comfortable."

He lists, a heavy weight sagging against me, footsteps uneven. I drag him over to the couch. "Can I get you some water, maybe?"

"No. I don't want . . ." He shakes his head, agitated, eyes slipping closed before he snaps them back open. "Don't know why . . . just had a glass . . ."

I sit by his side holding his hand, a regular Florence Nightingale, and lean over to drip Nurse Ratched poison in his ear. "Well, you have been drinking a lot lately, *babe*." I pat his chest with my free hand. "Is it any wonder you black out from time to time?"

His eyes remain closed. His breathing has slowed, a sluggish rattle.

I disentwine my hand and step away to clean the kitchen, waiting for him to reach a level of stupor and dissociation he can't rouse from.

When the kitchen has been restored to unoccupied order, I pack my belongings into the suitcase, bag the trash and leftover groceries and deliver it to my car, removing every trace of my existence. I smile, imagining Brent's confusion when he comes to.

Only then do I approach the slumbering monster.

I snap by his ears.

Nothing.

I lift his hand.

It drops like a dead weight.

"Well, look at you, you stupid fuck." I shift him to the side with a grunt and retrieve his phone. His background photo is a picture of himself, naturally. Getting ready to blast himself into space on a giant rocket phallus. The phone unlocks when I lift his eyelids with one hand and hold the screen up to his sagging face with the other. "Thanks."

I was prepared to venture next door if facial recognition let me down, find his contacts in his office, but his failure to disable this setting makes my life considerably easier. Within minutes, I have access to his photos, including more than a dozen anonymous women in various states of undress, all of them unconscious. Horror spreads through my insides like oil, a film I won't ever be able to wash off.

I don't have time to sift through them all, so I send the trophy album to my burner, evidence for Katie. I'll do an image search after I've disappeared, see what the almighty Google pulls up. Maybe Daniel can help me find these women too. He has ways more powerful than mine.

Then I scrub the evidence of the sent message and delete myself from Brent's contacts. I won't have my burner's SIM card up and operational, but every blockade I can put in his path will make it that much harder for him to find me.

I tamp the fury down and cross-reference his contacts with the Prometheus board members, a dozen men who look just like him. Prior research revealed no one has a background in science and they were all chosen for their ties to Brent above all else. A group of enablers if ever I've seen one.

"Frat party's over." Sipping wine, I open my laptop and ensure my VPN is running. Then I email the board one by one from an anonymous, encrypted account, delivering the evidence of fraud right to their in-boxes. Half an hour later, all my missives have been sent. If anyone deletes the email, it will only make them look more culpable, especially when the SEC begins an investigation, even if that's months from now. Lady Justice plays a long game.

Brent snores and stirs, like he knows a cataclysmic shift has rumbled the ground beneath him while he was dead to the world.

I snap my laptop shut, replace his phone in his back pocket, and give him a final look.

I could stab him right here. No one would know until I was out of the country, and I know how to disappear. For too long, I fight the urge to end it here.

The only thing that holds me back is Daniel's voice, luring me away from the abyss.

Instead of consigning myself to fugitive status, I lean over and spit on Brent's Ken doll face.

He doesn't even flinch.

"Happy trails, babe." I stand and take my handbag. "Don't choke on your own vomit."

CHAPTER

27

LATER THAT NIGHT, back at my houseboat, I begin the search for the women. Pearls in the ocean, if I can hold my breath long enough to pick them up from the seafloor. Daniel works on his own set, and no doubt he'll make more progress on the technological front, but between the two of us, I hope we'll make a dent. There's no time to lose if this one-two punch to Brent is going to be successful.

A reverse Google image search reveals fragments of identities, shards of people and their shifting selves as years pass and hair colors change, and jobs and friends and even families come and go. Finally, after sifting through pages of images, I find a name to go with the first face.

"Hi, Deidre."

She lives in the Bay Area, if her Instagram feed is any indication, though it's been a while since she posted. Cats and coffee, wine tasting with friends. Someone handsome is in some of the photos, with kind green eyes, winking in and out of existence before settling like so much sediment, something that could be sturdy given time.

I push away from my desk and steeple my fingers. Hesitating.

How do I ask someone to exhume memories better forgotten? How dare I assume this is the path anyone would want to take?

All I can do is ask. And hope enough will say, "Yes, I have something to say. Yes, I have someone to name. This is what happened to me, and it matters because I matter."

I open the page and type Deidre a message, choosing my words deliberately. With more care than I've ever given anything. I wish I had the bona fides of *Journalist* attached to my name, but all I have is myself, and a promise that if she wants to speak, others—myself, Katie, Rhys—will be her foghorn, blasting her message into every ear.

I hit send, offering it up to the universe.

Then I search for the next. And the next, and the next, and a dozen more, and my cups of coffee grow cold, but I still identify too few of the women in the photos. Only three out of the ten, in addition to the other eight with Daniel. Some women have just disappeared, all traces seemingly erased from the crawling, seeking tendrils of search engines. Removed themselves from invasive social media platforms, the parasites mining our personal lives for the highest bidder.

Whether the disappearing act is intentional or not, I can't say. I chew a hangnail. My real identity wouldn't show up online, either—I've taken care to make sure it doesn't. How could I blame others for doing the same? Starting clean. Protecting themselves because no one else will.

In the witching hour, wearing down the wood planks of my floor, I text Daniel.

There aren't enough. I can't find enough. Please, please tell me you've made more progress.

Well, naturally 😊, he replies. *Why else would you keep me around?*

I cackle, startling the quiet of my boat. Oh, let me count the ways, Daniel. I'd be here past sunrise, composing my ode.

Don't lose heart, tiger, he adds a minute later. *We'll find them.*

I blink, screen going blurry. Pixels distorted by tears.

I love you, I type, fingers flying over the keys. *I love you so much I'm sick with it.*

Slowly, I delete the string of letters. Delete the truth.

When I say it, I want to see his face. Life comes with so few true surprises, after all. I could give him that and watch the fog lift, watch him burst into brighter color. Turn his volume all the way up.

Thank you, I say instead. *Quite literally, I couldn't do this without you.*

I know.

It doesn't feel cheeky. Just a quiet statement of fact. He and I could both spend our time differently, but here we are, doing the work. Like we always have.

I kiss my phone, then turn back to the computer.

I'm getting back to work, I say, so he knows I haven't ghosted, per my usual.

Get some rest, he says. *The sun will be up soon.*

I laugh, punch-drunk after being up all night. Everything has lost meaning and shape, except for the words he's spoken to me all along.

Get some rest.

Be sure to eat something.

Your safety isn't nonsense.

I gave you my word.

Anything for you.

I love you, he told me, in every shade and permutation. Reaching a hand over the edge of an unfinished bridge, nothing but open ocean below his feet.

The least I can do is throw him my lifeline.

* * *

I wake with a gasp. Wipe drool from my chin and sponge it off my keyboard with the sleeve of my robe. Jesus. Guess I didn't make it to the bed.

I refresh my page and lo, a reply to my message. Deidre.

A low, static charge builds in my chest, hums in my fingers. I sit up, all tiredness gone.

Will she join? Or will she rightfully keep her wounds to herself?

I bite my lip so hard it stings, hovering over the message with my mouse before I summon enough nerve to hear a no.

I'm so sorry for what happened to your sister. I don't know how you found me, but I've wanted to speak up for a long time now, especially if others are going to. I just didn't know if I could do it on my own. Looking forward to meeting you and the Chronicle journalists.

Tears stream down my face. Salvation.

Is this what hope tastes like? Sweet as spun sugar, and just as fragile.

I crack my knuckles and send Deidre the tentative place and time. The summit at my humble houseboat. The place where we can shift the tide, Gaia willing, and pray that more can come.

* * *

"I can't believe this is happening."

I wipe my palms against my jeans and look around my tidied-up houseboat, making sure all the candles are lit and boxes of tissues are available. Weeks have passed since Daniel installed my security system, time filled with frantic phone calls and travel coordination, trying to line up the schedules of a dozen women total, as well as the journalists. I hope it's enough. Dr. Chang's going to be here, too, after I assured her she'd be in very good company. Her topic of conversation might be different with Rhys, but we're all on the same mission.

Now the day has come. In half an hour, my guests from across the country are due to arrive for this unusual gathering.

Becca, the blond, tatted server from the steak house, gives me a thumbs-up from the kitchen. "Sweet little place here. Think you'll rent it out when you skip town?"

"Probably. I can't imagine selling it." I turn to her with a smile. "Thank you for helping me get ready. This food looks amazing!" I had her help with catering from the restaurant, and I'm even more glad she's staying to give her account of Brent to Katie from the *Chronicle*, along with several of her coworkers.

"Do you think it'll work?" she asks quietly. "Do you think there'll be enough of us?"

"It has to work." Maybe if I say it, I'll believe it. How sad it should take a dozen-plus women speaking their truth to be taken seriously. I crack my knuckles. "Wine?"

"Please." Becca tucks the long, flopped-over ends of her hair behind an ear. "And I hope you're right."

"Just because we're the first doesn't mean we'll be the last." I fill a wineglass of sweet Shiraz for her, then pour for myself. "If other women he's harmed see us stepping forward, they might feel safe doing so too."

"Like a wave," she says, green eyes turned toward the large windows. "More and more, until we reach critical mass."

"Exactly."

A knock at the door has me running to open it.

It's my sister, followed closely by Alicia, suitcases in tow for their extended visit.

I hug them, tense mood lifting, hope expanding in my chest. "I'm so glad you're both here."

"As far as house parties go, this one's going to be pretty strange." Gabrielle smiles. "But I'm glad I'm here too."

"Come in, come in." I bring them inside. "Get something to eat."

Rhys and Katie arrive not long after, loaded with laptops and notebooks and coffee, even though it's six PM.

The latter introduces herself with the brisk air of a woman who never slows down. She's in her fifties, short and svelte. When I compliment the lovely soft-gray shade of her bobbed hair, she grins.

"Yeah, I finally had enough with dyeing it. Looked like a cartoon villain for a while there, but we're not going to talk about that."

"Well, it looks great now." I shake her hand, amused, liking my first impression.

"Rhys tells me you've got an eye for investigative journalism," she says.

"Generous on his part," I hedge, "especially considering I have no formal training. But sometimes my work does require getting into the weeds."

She hands me a business card and smiles, gray eyes sparkling. "Well, if you're ever contemplating a career change, I'm always eager to take a protégé under my wing."

I stare at the embossed card with the *Chronicle*'s font a few beats too long. "Thank you," I say. "You'll be the first to know."

I thought Rhys might be flummoxed by all the estrogen in the room, but to his credit, he seems right at home, sandwiched between my sister and a young Latinx pharmacologist who worked at Prometheus. I smile. The kids are all right.

More and more women show, and each arrival feels like a miracle. I hug anyone who'll let me, feeling more like my mother than I'd care to admit. After hugs, I make introduction after introduction, so everyone in the group knows everyone else. In an hour, the full group has filled my home with chatter and the peculiar vernacular only survivors know.

Dr. Chang elbows up to me, joining me at the periphery. Aside from my sister, I'm gladder to see her than almost anyone else.

"Hey you." I lift onto my toes to wrap an arm around her shoulder and squeeze. "How was the interview with Rhys?"

"Hard. But I'm glad to have everything out in the open at long last."

"And your job interview?" I ask, sotto voce. "Did you like Dr. Sanchez?"

She rocks back and forth on her heels. "I think the interview went well. And I liked her very much. There's no guarantee she'll be able to secure more funds for Series B financing, but her home-delivery model for diagnostics is stellar." Her smile is equal parts relieved and elated. "I'm going back for a second-round interview next week."

I nod and cross my fingers. "Sounds promising."

"Thanks to you."

"All in a day's work."

She smiles again and sips her wine. "This is amazing," she whispers, looking to the assembled group. "Look at all of us."

It's a motley crew, all right. Young and old, some binary, some not, and every skin tone and sexual orientation imaginable. Every different socioeconomic background too—lawyers, doctors, servers and writers and personal assistants.

None of them were spared Brent's predation. And still, we're here.

"It *is* amazing." I'd never guess no one had met before, gauging the easy flow of conversation. It's as if everyone knows we're meant to meet for this evanescent moment, like a group of monarch butterflies resting together for the night before continuing a long migration.

"You made this happen, you know." Dr. Chang nudges me. "I never would've known other women from Prometheus had been harassed if you hadn't suggested it. No one was allowed to talk to each other."

"Hardly your fault," I say. "It was just another way for him to exert control."

A text makes my phone buzz in my pocket. I fish it out, breath leaving in a whoosh when Daniel's name flashes on the screen.

It's been quiet with him after he helped me find and contact the other women Brent's harmed. I've typed and deleted a hundred messages before consigning myself to the quiet. It's a soul-crushing, joy-sucking silence, but that's the price I agreed to pay so he can live his life. Rebuild it with someone else. Someone who is not me.

Good luck tonight, Lady Justice. Wishing you (and all) courage.

My lips pull into a smile without permission. *Thank you, Daniel,* I reply.

Dr. Chang eyes me with a speculative gleam. "Let me guess. A certain tall, dark, and disastrously handsome someone?"

Daniel was right—the auntie network is formidable.

"By the name of Daniel Haas, yes." I shove my phone into my back pocket, willing myself not to read too much into his brief message.

"Well, you wouldn't be the first to find lots to like there."

"I think that was meant to make me feel better, but I don't know if it did." I laugh.

"But I have it on good authority from my friend—his cousin—you're the only one he's ever mentioned to his parents. Well, aside from the heiress."

"Really?" I can't help but ask. My skin feels tight all the sudden, hot and prickling.

She nods knowingly.

"Is he . . ." I bite my lip. "Did his cousin happen to say how he's doing?"

Dr. Chang shakes her head. "But I could find out, if you're interested?" She whips out her phone, dark eyes sparkling.

"No, no." I smile, feeling transparent as a moon jelly. "That's okay. I just wondered."

Her answering smile is kind. "Tell him."

I blink. "Tell him what?"

"That you're a goner, Lady Justice."

I feel dizzy, like I've fallen from one of the Golden Gate's towers. "I wish." I sip my wine, letting it sit in my mouth for a while before answering, tannins desiccating my tongue. "But it's more complicated than that."

"Is it?" she asks. "You of all people don't strike me as a coward."

"Shoot, Dr. Chang." I bark a laugh and wipe my lips with the back of my hand. "Drag me, why don't you?"

She shrugs and adjusts her delicate, rimless glasses on her nose, the picture of innocence. "Tell him, you ninny. God knows we all need good news after this shit show with Brent."

"Aside from him losing his job?" I lift a brow. News on the Prometheus front has been quiet still, but not for much longer, if I must guess. Once the allegations are public knowledge, all hell's going to break loose.

"Justice is important," she says. "But it's not the only thing worth living for. Maybe not even the most important thing."

It could be different, Dylan. Everything could be different.

I lift my glass in a gallows-humor toast. "Well. You got me there."

"THIS IS . . ." I read the first article on my tablet, flitting over the three thousand damning words as quickly as I can. Rhys left no stone unturned in his exposé for Brent's falsified clinical trials data.

I move to the next article, written by Katie, detailing Brent's long history of sexual harassment and assault. It's all a variation on a theme: Brent harasses, Brent's daddy pays off, at least until Brent had the funds to do so himself, buying his way out of any problem. His personal assistant gave some of the most incriminating testimony, including the history of settlements—at least six over the years.

I look up. "Rhys, these are gobsmacking."

He leans over the small café table, hands on his mug, brows furrowed. Only a week has passed since the meeting at my houseboat, and it looks like he hasn't slept in the interim, dark circles of fatigue framing his eyes. "Do you think so?"

"I do, yes." Tears well in the back of my throat, hot pressure behind my sinuses. Fitting for this drizzly, foggy day, world passing by in a gouache haze, holed up at the same coffee shop where we met earlier. "You and Katie have done an incredible job."

"The women were gobsmacking," he says. "Everyone from Dr. Chang onward. We just tried to convey their accounts as accurately as possible." He sips his black coffee and rubs his overlong hair until the red waves stick up. "We still have to let legal go over this with a fine-tooth comb and make sure everything is airtight."

"How long will that take?"

"Katie says they should be wrapping up right now. Then we'll present Mr. Wilder with our findings. We'll give him the weekend to respond and post on Monday." A grimace. "Least-favorite part of this whole process."

"I know you have an obligation to show Brent your articles, but is there any way to shorten the time frame?" I press. "He could try to pressure the women to recant. I wouldn't put *anything* past him, especially considering he's already having people followed."

"You included?"

"I think so. Still." Noah, after much complaining, dyed my hair back to its usual dark-brown shade. I've been wearing a hat and sunglasses whenever I've had to go out and about. So far, these changes seem like they've been enough to stall the dickbags charged with tailing me, but who knows how long that'll last.

"Katie and I and our editors will talk to them, let everyone know what to expect. You can do that too. Make sure they record any intimidation, any threats." He taps the table. "All of that should go into the article."

"I will. I'll make sure everyone knows." My knees jiggle under the table. "And I have a backup plan, if need be, but I really wish I could scoop everyone up and seal them with Bubble Wrap until all this is over."

Rhys smiles, soft. "But not yourself?"

"No." I reach into my wellies and lift the hem on my stretchy leggings, revealing my knife. "As you can see, I'm good."

His eyes widen, losing a little of their exhausted glaze. "Jesus Christ. Who are you, Dylan?"

I rock my shoulders left and right. "I like big blades and I cannot lie."

He covers his laugh with a freckled fist, then looks up again. "Still. Be careful, okay? If Brent finds out you were the one to put all of this in motion, that you tricked him—"

"He'll kill me." I down the rest of my coffee, more than just jittery. Every sound in my houseboat has made me edgy and anxious, waking me from fitful sleep. I'd hire my own security, except I can't foot the bill when I'm already doing that for Dr. Chang and her family. Still, if my sister can expose the darkest corner of her soul to the entire world, I can deal with fear. "Believe me, I know."

"Call me if you need anything. Day or night. I'm awake most of both, so don't worry about interrupting my sleep." He offers a self-deprecating smile, stands, and shoulders his dark-green rain jacket back on. "I mean that, okay?"

Even though it hurts my pride, I swallow it and answer, "I will. Thanks."

I stand too, and for a few awkward seconds, we look at each other, neither sure what to do. The fellowship of fuckery should've decided on a cool handshake by now, but we've got nothing.

"Hug?" he asks, looking sheepish. "Of the strictly platonic, consensual variety?"

I smile. "Sure. I could do with a hug."

He steps into my space and wraps long arms around my shoulders. "Your sister has done an amazing thing. I promise, we won't let Brent wriggle his way out of it this time."

"I hope not. Otherwise, I'll be coming after you with Dark Sister."

"Dark Sister?" He lets go.

"My big-ass knife," I clarify.

He laughs. "Fair."

Then we fist bump and part ways.

I slip into my raincoat and walk back to my houseboat, content to splash through the rain, letting the cold seep through my jacket. It gives me time to think. Time to sort out my thoughts before I go home to Gabrielle and Alicia, tell them we're about to go live. That we'll soon know whether the truth will be enough.

Only, the lovebirds are gone when I return, out for a movie and dinner, according to the note on my kitchen counter, complete with hearts and smiley faces. I sigh. They're so adorable, it's sickening.

"I don't mean that," I say to my succulents on the windowsill. I only want happiness for Ellie and Alicia, forever and ever and ever.

As for myself, I haven't been able to forget what Dr. Chang said about Daniel. That he told his parents about me. I assume the news that he cares for a questionable sort like me didn't go over well, as I haven't heard a word from him. Can't say I blame his parents. He could do better. So much better. Someone tall and wealthy and educated and connected and fit for polite society. Someone like *him*. More importantly, someone who *wants* to be a wife.

The rain has let up, and I eye my kayak on the deck. Maybe a turn on the water will lift this gloom. After all, it might be one of my last chances to go for a long ride before it gets too stormy over winter.

I store my knife, change into my wetsuit and life jacket, and set out on the water, pushing away in strong strokes.

Instead of taking my usual route in the protected waters of Richardson Bay, I veer south, toward the Golden Gate and the open ocean near the Point Bonita Lighthouse. It's too quiet in my home without other people there, and I'm in no hurry to return to silence, the emptiness. Every second of this future without Daniel hollows out my chest, opening it further and further, misery scouring my insides clean.

It's darker out than I expected, though, another front of clouds moving in. Combined with the sun setting earlier each day, my daylight will be short. I'll have to keep my trip brief, no matter what.

Soon into my journey, it dawns on me I've made a colossal mistake. The winds are ferocious on the west side of the peninsula, and I struggle against the enormous swells, arms and shoulders fatiguing way sooner than normal, even with my streamlined ocean kayak.

"All right, Mama Nature. I take your point."

With a grunt, I make a sweep stroke and turn back for home, tail between my legs. The incoming tide should help—but not if it pushes me too close to the coast. I paddle furiously away from the exposed rocks, trying to avoid getting pinned. I'm not wearing my helmet, but even if I were, I'm no match for that power. My body would be crushed, dashed to pieces like so many ships before me.

That's when the rain arrives, a cold slap in the face, turning the surface into a misty, slate-gray churn. I'm covered in neoprene, but it's a thin layer, only .5mm. Rain pours into my foot well and ices my legs, then my feet, even with booties.

"Shit," I hiss. I didn't bother with gloves, and my hands are cold and stiff from the rain and frigid spray kicking up from the whitecaps, making my grip on the paddle tenuous. I grit my teeth and press every bit of strength into my fingertips. I'll be lucky if I make it back before getting hypothermic.

It's so hard to see in the rain, erasing the border between ocean and sky. The cloud deck is so low, it blots out even the massive Gate. I could be heading further out to sea for all I know.

Daniel.

My brain summons him with vivid clarity. His deep, riverine voice, his warm hands in my hair. I've wandered too far this time. Dropped off the horizon.

I should've told him where I was going. Should've told Ellie and Alicia too, but I didn't. As if I wanted to be mislaid.

I thought that was my job. Worrying about my wayward friend.

He'll be furious if he ever finds out. Can't say I blame him. How could I chance it? How could I take the risk, with no thought to the people who care for me?

"Goddammit!" I shout. "What am I doing with my life?"

Through a swell of self-pitying tears and rain, I look up at the steep headlands, rising like dark knuckles out of the ocean. The bright flash of the Bonita lighthouse sends a ray of gold in the pewter dark.

"Oh, thank fuck." I aim my kayak in the right direction and pull myself back from the brink, stroke after stroke. Powered by not just the strength in my limbs but the fierce hold on my heart.

I have to tell Daniel the truth—today. That I've loved him longer than he knows. Longer than I could admit to myself. Maybe it won't matter, a meaningless, voiceless shout from the bottom of the ocean, but I still have to do it. If I don't, I'll wonder the rest of my life.

Carried on the tide of resolve, I fight my way around the point, into the safety of protected harbor waters.

The waves ease and I gulp air, folding over, letting the panic ebb away.

My hands are white and bloodless, my lungs ache with every breath, but I paddle the rest of the way home without stopping.

By the time I return, I'm shivering so hard, I can barely hold my paddle, despite the exertion. My legs and arms feel like strands of kelp, liable to fold, but I lash my kayak to the deck with two good knots and climb the ladder, back onto solid ground.

It's not solid, though. Everything sways and heaves beneath me, undulating. I stumble back inside my home, teeth chattering, soaked to the marrow. Colder than I've been in my whole life.

"Warm up," I say. "Warm up."

Shivering, shaking, I shrug out of my life jacket and let it fall. The zipper on my neoprene suit is next, but that's when I see him.

I didn't think I could be colder, but my blood turns to slush, freezing me with it.

"Hello, Dylan." Brent flicks on my salt lamp and smiles from my armchair. "Look what the waves rolled in."

CHAPTER

29

IT TAKES ME too long to process Brent's presence in my
home. My brain is cold, slow. Too full of Daniel and fool-
ish hope. Adrenaline saturates my blood, a fiery rush, but
not quickly enough. By the time I lunge for the end table,
ready to grab my knife, he's already on his feet.

"Looking for this?" He palms Dark Sister, watching the
flash of metal in the dim light. He lifts his gaze to me, a
small smile playing on his mouth.

"Or maybe this?" He fishes my phone out of his pocket
with his free hand, studying the background photo of Daniel for two, three beats before throwing it at the floor with
all his might. The glass cracks and splinters, scattering like
so many diamonds.

Fuck. There goes plan A.

How did he figure it out? That I'm not Delilah, yes. But
my real identity too?

Then I see the photograph of Gabrielle and me on her
graduation day, resting on the coffee table like a scarlet let-
ter. Only it's not my framed photo. This one is crumpled
and marred with age.

"I *knew* I'd seen your face before," he says. "Sneaky fucking bitch. It just took me too long to remember I had it with me all these years." He touches the corner of the photograph, almost reverent, then flips it over.

My handwritten message is still visible, though the ink has faded.

Go forth and kick ass, Gabrielle! Berkeley isn't ready for you but give 'em hell anyway!

Love always,

Dylan

I want to swat his hand away. Lop it off at the wrist. "You stole it from her. After you . . ."

"Before the age of smartphones, I'm afraid." He gives me a faintly apologetic smile, as if it just couldn't be helped. "I took my own photos later on. I do love my souvenirs."

"I'll kill you." Red starbursts cloud my vision.

"Quite a blade you have here," he continues, as if he hadn't heard me. "I suppose you thought you'd use it on me."

"It crossed my mind." I smile, trying not to let my teeth chatter too much.

A strange, manic energy pulses under my skin, lightening my steps, loosening my joints. There's power in not pretending. Power in letting artifice fall away.

At last, he'll know me. Not Delilah, not Lady Justice, but Dylan.

Daughter. Sister. Lover, to approximately one Daniel.

Fighter. I learned the steps to this dance ages ago. Recalling them is only a matter of instinct, shifting my weight to account for his movements.

Nevertheless, backup would be nice. I swing in a wide arc around him, past the glass, trying to get closer to the kitchen. To the duress alarm under the counter.

He blocks my path with a single step. "You've been causing a lot of trouble for me."

"You made that trouble yourself." I dodge and keep working my way to the kitchen. "It was always going to catch up to you. I just helped it along."

I don't need Dark Sister to maim. This fucker invading my home is going to meet the pointy end of a knife, any knife. He may be larger and stronger, but he doesn't have my speed.

He seems to realize it, brows furrowed, focusing on me with new intensity.

"You must've thought I was stupid," he says. "That I wouldn't figure it out."

"Still do." I let my smile grow. "Something about your face, I guess."

The face in question contorts, mouth hitching in a sneer. Losing the cordial demeanor. The monster writhes, close to the surface.

"So. Did you get a call from the *Chronicle*?" I back up another step. Keeping him distracted. "They have lots of fun things to discuss with you."

Blue eyes narrow. "I did."

"Figured you'd be holed up with your army of lawyers, if that's the case."

"It's all bullshit." His voice raises a few decibels. "You think anyone's going to believe a scientist I fired for incompetence? Believe a bunch of whores whining about bad dates and hurt feelings? Shit that happened twenty years ago?" He scoffs. "As for *you*, you're going to jail—"

"You still haven't done your homework, have you?" I back away. "You worthless, legacy admission douche. We have the documents, we have settlement records, *and* the disgusting trophy photos. Proof you've harassed, proof you've paid blood money. Proof you lied, over and over." I shrug and offer a syrupy smile. "It's over, neighbor."

Doubt passes over his face. A small wisp of fear, a ripple of reality entering his warped mind.

Instead of humbling him, it enrages.

"Fuck you and your fucking cunt of a sister. All it'll take to end this is one libel suit, then I'll own that fucking paper too."

I laugh. "Whatever you say. But I don't think it'll be that easy."

He scowls and follows me. Into the kitchen, where women belong. With sharp objects, of course. Sharp objects and a duress alarm.

I square off, sensing his rising rage. It burns dark and hot, making his skin look red in the lamplight. Like a demon.

"When I'm done clearing my name, I'll deal with you," he says. "I'll fuck you like I did your sister, while you cry for me to stop."

I dive for the silent panic button, sending my plea out into the dark.

Brent smiles, sick and leering. Smug, beneath it all. Always so goddamned smug.

"Your security system was pretty nice." He points to the ripped wires on my counter. "But I can't have anyone witnessing our lovers' quarrel. Hope you understand."

Only then do I feel fear again, flooding me. My vision wanes, contracting for precious beats before the fog clears.

If I'm the last one standing against this man, so be it. I'm not going to run. I'm not leaving California, not leaving the city, not leaving this goddamn boat. I've waited sixteen years for this moment. This is *my* home, and I will stay and fight.

"Fine by me." I reach for my santoku with its exquisite Damascus steel, a beautiful, prescient gift from Daniel years ago, ripping it from the magnet holder. My grip is upright, thumb on the spine. I vault over the counter, back into the living room. Giving myself more room to maneuver.

Brent shadows, knife in hand. Holding it blade down, with an ice-pick grip. Either he knows what he's doing, or he's clueless. I'll find out soon enough.

I circle Brent, blood flowing like lava, muscle memory taking over. Always moving. Prowling. Always keeping my eyes on him.

"Do you know what I like about knives?" I ask.

He lunges in answer, telegraphing his move without realizing, lifting the knife high over his head.

Amateur.

I slice his outstretched arm with four snap cuts, cutting through cloth and skin with ease, then dart away. "Knives hurt."

He howls and rears back, clutching his forearm with an expression of disbelief.

"Bitch." He spits the word out, full of impotent venom.

"Feels personal, doesn't it?" I feint when he gets too close. If he wants to hurt me, he'll have to catch me.

There's still time for him to wise up. If he has any sense, he'll cut his losses, but anger makes him stupid. Makes him think he has a chance. For all he knows, it might work. He's powerful. Used to his size and strength being enough to subdue. If he managed to sink that knife into my chest, it'd kill me, no doubt.

He'll never get that far.

He swings and I skirt him, slashing his knuckles, his wrist. Sharp, swift bites of metal, tearing skin and ligament. Seconds later, blood drips from his arm onto my floor, pooling like spilled wine. His first two fingers hang by threads, and he drops the blade.

I kick it away.

I nod to his mangled fingers. "Leave. Get stitched up."

Every time he sees his hand, though, he'll remember me. Remember Gabrielle.

He assumes a fighting stance, bloody hand and opposite fist raised.

"Rising to the occasion?" I take aim. "First time in your miserable fucking life."

He jabs and I slash his other hand as I flank him, gouging fingers and knuckles with as many cuts as possible. Carving him like steak.

"My sister deserved better," I hiss. All my ice has disappeared. I feel hot as a star, light as air. Invincible. "She deserved better than to meet a monster like you."

He roars and swings a bloody fist.

I duck and slice up his face, then his side, in the soft places where ribs don't cover. Three quick stabs, turning him into a human pincushion.

Before he can turn, I leap out of range, opening space between us.

He staggers to face me. Blood pours into his eyes, gushes down his face. He pants and tries to clear the red cascade.

Whenever he sees his reflection, he'll think of me too. Assuming he lives. The gash is an improvement, I daresay. Now his outside matches.

"But Gabrielle forgives you, because that's who she is." I bare my teeth in a smile. "Not like me."

While he's blinded, I strike again, cutting up and down his arm and shoulder as I sweep past.

He backs up a few steps, limping. Breathing hard, a wet, gurgling noise.

I think he understands. The game is over. His time is up.

"I'll kill you," he gasps. "I'll fucking kill you."

Or not.

I raise my blade, ready to lift more flesh off him. "Need another taste?"

Still, he tries. Desperate.

"Dylan!" a hoarse voice shouts. Daniel stands in the doorway, wide-eyed with horror.

"Daniel? What—"

"Watch out!" he shouts.

Brent's fist lands on my jaw like an asteroid, snapping my head to the side.

I cry out, stumbling and falling to the floor, dropping my knife. My ears ring and I blink, trying to clear my head. Clear it before he traps me on the ground, before another blow—

A kick shunts the air from my lungs and cracks a rib with an audible crunch. I need to get up. I can't take another kick like that. I curl inward, lifting my knees to my chest.

Instead, Brent straddles me, bloody hands clamping around my throat. He squeezes and squeezes, letting the weight of his upper body do the work of cutting off my air.

"Fucking die," he roars. "Die!"

With all my might, I lift my hips, destabilizing him, and break his choke hold. He rolls and I knee the side I stabbed, again and again.

Then his weight is gone.

I lurch to my feet, still dizzy from the punch, try to find my knife. Try to find Brent. Determined to end this once and for all.

There's no need.

Daniel has him pinned facedown, pressing Brent's bloodied face into the floor.

"What do you want me to do?" he asks over his shoulder. Dark eyes search mine.

Long moments pass with the fate of three lives in the balance.

If I asked, he'd help me bury Brent. It's in his eyes, full of fury. Reflecting my own bloodlust back to me.

If anyone else were here with me, I'd thrust my knife into Brent's neck and leave it.

Salvation comes in the form of Daniel's micro expressions. The painful swallow, the knitted brows. I've never seen someone say so much without speaking a word. I've become a cartographer, etched his topography on my heart.

All of it summons the better parts of me to the foreground. The part that tries to make him laugh. Tries to shield him, and everyone, from cruelty. Tries to care for him, in my own ferocious, imperfect way. The share of my soul I'm most proud of.

Justice is important, but it's not the only thing worth living for. Maybe not even the most important thing.

I could ask this terrible thing of him, of myself, but I won't. This is no way to start a life. Not by ending another. Even when every cell in my body wants to, wants to erase this cancer from the world, it's not my call to make.

I have to let go.

I have to travel to the other side of this dark mirror, where the light might still shine. If I'm very lucky.

"Call 911," I finally say, choking every word out. I grab my knife and crouch over Brent, blade pointed into his neck to ensure he doesn't move a muscle in the interim. "Before I change my mind."

30

LATER, MUCH LATER, after the paramedics, police, and neighbors have left, after Gabrielle and Alicia have gone to a hotel, after I make a grudging trip to the hospital with Daniel, I whimper as we leave, leaning against a pillar. I feel a thousand years old, joints aching, freezing, muscles stiff and glued together.

Daniel's at my side in an instant. Then again, he hasn't left to begin with. "Dylan. What do you need?"

I roll my head to him. My rib hurts with every breath, and my jaw has swollen to the point of grotesque. "I need to go home. Take a shower. But . . . I'm afraid to move."

"Then let's go." He stands. "I have a bag packed for you. You can shower at my place."

I blink up at him. "Say what?"

"If you thought I'd leave you at your home, alone, after you've been attacked, suffering with a broken rib and nearly broken jaw, you're mistaken." He smiles, all sweetness.

I heave an enormously put-upon sigh, then wince. "Okay. Let's head to Casa Daniel."

I feel ridiculous walking through the lobby of his apartment in my neoprene, but honestly, it's the last of my worries. My jaw throbs with every step, as does my rib. I'm grateful Daniel forced me to get over myself. I wouldn't be able to remove this wetsuit on my own.

I'm desperate to soak under a hot spray, but Daniel insists I eat first so I can take my pain medication. While I sit on the leather couch, curled up under a blanket, he heats a bit of that homemade gomtang soup. Then, despite my protest, he feeds me spoonful by spoonful.

Sure enough, the salty, umami broth warms me from the inside out, lifting my misery to manageable by the time I've finished.

Still, I shiver.

"Could I convince you to make a fire?" I ask, a little timid. All my heat has burned out. "It's freezing in here."

"It's not." His voice is kind. "But I will."

He lights the gas fireplace and tucks another wool blanket around my shoulders.

"Thank you," I croak.

"Of course." He kneels next to me, well within my space, still looking unsure. Like he wants to touch but doesn't know whether he should.

Wordless, I reach out, offering my hand, palm up.

After a second's hesitation, he takes it, cradling my fingers within both hands. Carefully, reverently, though he's seen a side of me I never want to unbridle again. How could I ever be worthy of this man?

How could I let him slip through my fingers?

"Thank you for staying with me tonight." My voice sounds ground up, and it hurts to talk, but he needs to know how much his steady presence has meant. How he kept me from falling apart in the aftermath. "For talking to everyone. And for getting in contact with the lawyer. For taking me to the hospital. For soup. For the fire . . . just, thank you."

His worried expression softens into a familiar half smile, revealing a dimple. Familiar and beloved. "Anything for you, Dylan."

I try to sit up. "How did you know what was happening, anyway? How did you know to come to my house?"

"I didn't." He strokes my open hand with a light fingertip. Erasing the memory of a knife in my palm with each gentle pass, tracing the lines spelling my secrets. Beyond him, the tall, floor-to ceiling windows are glazed with rain, sealing us in with the firelight. "When I saw your cameras were offline, I had a bad feeling. Especially when you didn't answer your phone." He finally looks up. "Broke the sound barrier on my way."

I swallow, gulping down the raw memories. "Thank Christ you did. I don't want to know what I would've done . . ." My throat tightens, voice so thick with shame it chokes off my words.

"You would've done whatever you needed to," he says, with such certainty I have to believe him. "Without hesitation. And no one would blame you." He lifts my chin. "Brent would've done the same to you. The same or worse. He *meant* to, Dylan, never forget. Only, you flipped the script on him."

"I know, but—"

"But nothing. You defended yourself against an armed assailant. And if I hadn't distracted you, you would've done it without incurring a single scratch." His face falls into a severe frown. "I'm so sorry for that."

Gradually, deliberately, his hand travels from my chin, glides along my jaw. So soft, the added pressure doesn't even hurt.

"Don't be." I lean into his palm, ignoring the ache it spurs. I was lucky to not lose any teeth, but the bones are bruised. Will be for some time.

His eyes travel over my face, my body, examining for the nth time.

It's unbearable being seen, but I don't have to fight anymore. I don't have to build walls. Compared with Homicidal Dylan, I can only rise in his estimation.

So the fragile theory goes, anyway.

As if he can hear my thoughts, he strokes behind my ear. "The world needs fighters too, Dylan. Like it needs watchers, teachers, lovers. The world needs people like you too."

Finally, I look up. Crying but absolved, finally, by the one person whose opinion I value more than any other.

He continues his gentle exploration, touching the neoprene, fingertips rubbing over the thick material by my neck. "You were on the water this afternoon, obviously?" His tone is mild, though I can tell he'd like to scold.

"Yep. I've used two of my kitty lives today." I shake my head before remembering not to. "I thought it'd help to get out, but the weather was shit, and I just about drowned by Point Bonita." The stormy sea already seems like ages ago. After the downpour, the rain has dwindled to a patter, nature's easy percussion on the windows in the late hour keeping us company. "I only managed to fight my way back because I was afraid I'd die before finding the courage to tell you something."

He stills. Not a breath, not a blink.

"Daniel . . . I love you." My voice is strong and calm, speaking the words from the brightest corner of my soul. "I have for as long as I can remember. And it scared the shit out of me." I hold my laugh in. "I didn't know what to do with any of that, but I was sure I'd find a way to ruin it. So . . . I put the programmer on the pedestal."

A tiny smile lifts the edge of his mouth, but he looks like he wants to protest.

I shush him with fingers over his lips. He's warm, so deliciously warm against my icy fingertips. I let my hand fall before I can chase my fingers with a kiss, drink him in, let his warmth heat me from the inside out.

"But I think I had it all wrong. I've made . . . *a lot* of questionable decisions in my life, but loving you isn't one of them." I pick at the loose thread on the seam of my neoprene sleeve. "You're so good, Daniel. Kind, even to people who don't deserve it. How could I not admire that? How could I not love you for that?" I look up, watery. Weak with the force of this love, dissolving my cowardice in a single wave. "You kept me from straying too far into the dark. Made me want to try harder. Do better."

"Dylan . . ."

"It doesn't have to change anything, if you don't want it to," I say. "I'm not trying to ask anything of you—"

"Aren't you?"

"I just want you to know"—I smile with the memory of Dr. Chang's claim—"that I'm a goner."

For a few seconds, Daniel looks at me. Dark eyes enormous pools. Thinking. Gears turning at light speed behind the composed facade.

He reaches into his back pocket and retrieves his phone.

The pixels glow in the dark, revealing a photo I never knew he took.

"My lock screen three years running." The smile spreads. "That's what was on my mind the morning I installed your security system."

Hands trembling, I take his phone.

It's a photo of *me* at the speakeasy. Wearing that ivory, cowl-neck silk dress, the one I bought just for that night and spent way too much money on because #priorities. I have no idea when he took the photo, but in it I'm laughing so hard my eyes have squeezed shut, dark hair flowing down my back and fanning around my face in soft waves, thanks to Noah.

I look . . . incandescent with happiness.

And beautiful.

I've never seen myself that way, too used to cataloging my deficits, character and otherwise.

Through Daniel's lens, I see it. He made me feel that way, after all. He's always seen me, even when self-imposed loneliness threatened to render me invisible.

How I wish I'd been kinder to myself all these long years. Given myself the same credit and trust I give to my clientele. Believed I deserved nice things too.

"Well!" I laugh, a shade too bright. "Wasn't I a dish?" The trembling has moved into my body. I shake with the riot of emotions the photo has brought back, spinning through the memories from that singular night like a wild, roiling galaxy. "Shouldn't I Venmo you at least forty dollars for your thoughts? Like I promised?" I return his phone, trying to sound cavalier.

"I couldn't put a price on it." He tucks his phone into his slacks and moves to face me, parting my legs. Arms running up the length of my thighs, hands settling by my hips. Filling my whole view with him and him alone.

"Wish we were there, 'stead of here. I swear to God, Daniel." I huff out a bitter laugh. "You only see the best or worst of me." I wipe at the water leaking from my eyes.

His eyes narrow. Heating with anger, of all the things, filling his irises with his own embers. Even so, his voice is gentle. "Do you think I only love you when you're smiling? When the sun is shining?" He shakes his head. "I've never been prouder of you than I am right now. Also"—he gives me a wary glance, tongue in cheek—"a little frightened."

I laugh, even though it hurts.

"I love every part of you, Dylan. How you try. The way you never give up. *And* your anger. Your grief. The parts you're so sure I don't already see." He pauses, as if weighted by his own words, and squeezes my hands. "All of it. Whatever you throw my way, I can take it."

Of course, the magnifying glass works both ways. Just as I've mapped his fine topography, committed his every expression to memory, he's taken me within himself too. Absorbed my callousness, my spite, but also my love, my grit.

I only want to give him good things from here on out. As much as I can, for as long as I'm alive. Will he let me?

Tears spill over and track down my face. "I heard through the vino vine you discussed me in depth with your parents."

He nods, faint traces of amusement around his eyes, not bothering to ask who spilled.

"And?"

"They were surprised, I think, but not because of you and your nonstandard career." He slides a smile my way. "More because I hadn't told them how much you mean to me for so long. For that, they were hurt. And I don't blame them. I should've been honest from the get-go. Given them more credit."

I pop my knuckles out of habit, before forgetting my rib is having none of that. "You don't think . . . it won't make your mom's illness even worse, right?"

He grips my face, hard. "Absolutely not." He enunciates every syllable. "It wasn't even about me getting married, not really. It's just . . . the timeline can be hard. You and I both know that, but no one knows it better than her. She just wanted to know that I had someone in my corner. That I'll be okay, you know . . . when she dies," he croaks, letting his hands drop.

I squeeze his hands, dangerous close to an ugly cry. "You know you do, right?"

A nod. "So, when I told her I had a small tiger of a woman with very sharp claws looking after me, you should've heard her laugh. You wouldn't know to see her now, but she's always been a spitfire too. Keeping Dad and me in line." A dimple appears. "She said she'd never seen me happier, talking about you . . . us. And that was the thing that mattered to her above all."

I'd say something else, but my heart is too full of rainbows to make sense of it.

"May I meet them?" I ask quietly. "If I promise to hide my inner sailor?"

"If you're ready to be smothered with love." He lifts a brow in friendly challenge.

I trace his fingers and wrist, marveling at the long bones and intricate blend of muscle and tendon. I look up, unable to match his teasing tone. "I'd be honored to meet the people who brought you into the world."

"The same applies for me," he says. "I want to meet your parents. And your sister."

I nod, imagining the scene. My mom will fuss, and force-feed him decadent pasta dishes because he's too thin. My aging beatnik dad will ask whether he likes guitars and vinyl and Bob Dylan, by any chance. Gabrielle will lead him down other esoteric intellectual paths, but Daniel will follow along and surprise her, because that's what still waters do. "They're going to love you."

He says nothing but links his fingers through mine, like we did not so long ago when I learned who my target was. Pieces were in motion between us then, had been in play for a while, even if I didn't yet realize it. How lucky I am to emerge from the end of my long odyssey with this very good man still by my side.

I wait, expecting him to follow with something else. Anything else.

He doesn't, the devil. He'll just drop all the variables in my lap and let me do what I will. Rewarding me for my own long-overdue candor, but insisting, in his own quiet way, that I make a choice.

Information is a gift, I tell my clients.

So it is with the most important person in my world. A gift by way of a photo and bracing honesty, cold and clean and pure, my love language indeed. Information he lays at my feet, waiting for me to pick it up. Add it to the treasures I've collected from all corners of the earth.

"Will you be mine, Daniel? Be my person?" I send the words out into the misty night, casting my line into the unknown. "Will you make an honest woman out of me? Because I don't want to live one more day without you."

His eyes widen, his mouth falls open. In the dim lamplight, his pulse throbs above the collar of his shirt.

I wait. And wait.

"Yes, Dylan." His smile splits the dark open, an opaline lighthouse showing the way forward. "I'll be your person."

The world spins, glowing with firelight.

Then he takes out his phone.

I wait a few beats, trying not to be miffed.

That lasts all of two seconds. "What are you looking up, right now?"

"'Fractured . . . rib . . . healing . . . time,'" he says as he types. Then he looks up, trying not to smile. "Twelve weeks."

"What?" I can't help sounding horrified. "*Twelve* weeks?"

He smothers his laughter in my neck.

"This is bullshit," I say, so the world knows.

He pulls away, still looking amused, and cradles my face.

I don't think I've ever seen him so light. As if he feels buoyant too, floating a few inches above the ground, defying gravity itself.

"Do you have any idea how happy you make me?" he asks.

"I might." A smile draws at my lips. Slowly, slowly, I lean in.

He closes the last divide, pressing his lips to mine. Achingly familiar, tantalizingly new. The sweet rush is more than I can stand while motionless, a closed circuit.

"Daniel," I murmur.

"Hmm?" He pulls back, but only a fraction.

"Maybe if we're really careful?" I kiss the corner of his mouth. His jaw, his throat, then back to his lips, because I can't stay away, can't stop breathing him in. "Like, I don't move, and you just barely move, and then . . ." I sigh. "We totally could."

"The painkillers must be talking." His lips pull taut beneath mine, parting in a smile. "I'm going to have to keep running to keep up with you, aren't I?" he whispers.

"Afraid so."

"Figured as much." His laughter fills my ear, and his hands deftly unzip my wetsuit. "Anything for you, Dylan."

EPILOGUE

Six months later

To celebrate the coincidence of Daniel's half birth-day and my first official byline in the *Chronicle*, there's only one place for us to go: the speakeasy.

That's my plan, anyway. Trying to make it a surprise affair for Daniel has proven my toughest assignment yet. His BS detector is even more finely honed than mine, proof I've chosen unbelievably well for myself.

I even had to rope Gabrielle into my efforts. Suppos-edly, the two of us are meeting Gabrielle and Alicia for a double date tonight. I text her before hitting the road in a rideshare, handsome cargo in the back seat with me.

Good luck, Dilly, and congratulations on your article! I can't wait to read it. Hope you and Daniel have the best night! Gabrielle replies.

Ellie, thank you! I add a long string of emojis, finishing with about twenty hearts.

Daniel fidgets in his seat, adjusting his onyx cuff links. "So. What's the name of this restaurant again?"

"It's a new place. I forget what it's called. Some improbable combination of nouns with crossing arrows. Fox and Fennel. Pig and Pepper." I smile at him. "You get the idea."

"Glad I'm not on the receiving end of that wit." His eyes crinkle with amusement. "The Food section could hire you as a critic, though."

"Please." I reach across to take his hand. "As if you'd ever be at the end of my rapier, good sir." I press a kiss to his warm knuckles.

Daniel's expression changes when we pull up in front of the restaurant/upstairs bar, almost four years later to the day. We hop out into the rain and dash inside the restaurant, ascending a familiar set of stairs.

"Remember this place?" I ask.

"How could I forget." He looks me over when we reach the landing, as if he can divine what's beneath my black trench coat, a tentative smile on his face. "We're not meeting Ellie and Alicia, are we?"

"Nope!" I cackle. "Not tonight, anyway."

"I knew it."

I sigh, all my fantasies about stealth punctured. I don't have any secrets with this man, and that's just as well. "Humor me and pretend like you didn't see this first-date re-creation coming light years away?"

He nods, eyes soft, and links his fingers through mine.

Inside, the speakeasy hasn't changed a bit. The walls are glossy gold and black, like the stunner by my side. We sit at our own table and the jazz is low and still somehow loud, resonating in the chest the way only live music can. The first sip of my drink tingles over my tongue, tart and bracing, and the rain still drenches the windows looking out over the city.

Just as we never step in the same river twice, however, all else has changed.

Daniel's hands are in my hair, around my waist, glued to my hip, heat pressing through the red silk of my dress. His gaze never turns from mine, searing me the longer I look. The way we might've done for ages had I permitted myself. Sometimes the perception of time wasted steals my breath, but I let the thought go like a moth, releasing it into the night.

After all, taking the long, circuitous road only makes this ephemeral slice of life all the sweeter.

Daniel lifts his cinnamon-spiked old fashioned in a toast and smiles. "To scum being scraped off the earth and sent to jail. A new benchmark, hmm?"

"A group effort." I clink my glass of bubbly. "But I'll be glad when it's over."

The months since Rhys and Katie's article dropped and I pressed charges against Brent have been a blur of stressful legal proceedings, including time spent at trial. It's a good thing I'm not on social media anyway, because I'm sure the trolls and incels are having a field day dissecting me, the man-eater. Daniel shields me as much as he can, setting up filters on our internet, auto-forwarding threats to my attorney and the police officer on my case. He doesn't like me being the tip of the spear yet again. Nor do his parents, or my parents, but some things must be done, even if it means serving as a lightning rod for a while, attracting the best and worst of humanity at once. If anyone can do it, I can.

Besides, the ugly misogyny bothers him more than it does me. Most of the time, anyway.

"Let them howl from their parents' basements." Daniel bites off each word like chips of glass. "With your case and the rest of the women, and the judge, Brent's going to wear orange a long time." He reaches out to take my hand.

I link my fingers with his, swallowing back my tears. He always seems to know when I'm losing faith. Simply put, I wouldn't have survived the last six months had I been alone.

One more reason to thank my lucky stars I have my best friend with me, holding my hand as we walk this rocky path.

"I know, right?" I sip my bubbles. "Judge Sforza isn't messing around." The next part of the trial will be for everyone to read their victim statements, a move she insisted on despite protests from Brent's camp. The frantic reshuffling on Prometheus's board after losing their CEO gives me hope too.

"Did I tell you Prometheus lost their three largest investors?" I ask.

"I hadn't heard." He snickers. "People are getting nervous, aren't they?"

"Only a matter of time before they have to shut down for good. I would've written the article myself, but alas, a mild conflict of interest." I smile, wicked. "Also, happy half birthday, love! I swear I didn't bring you here to discuss Fucker McFuckFace."

"Half birthday?" He laughs at my non sequitur and lifts a brow.

"You don't celebrate half birthdays?" I *tsk*. "Well, you do now."

"Do I get presents on these occasions?" he asks, too quick by half. He leans over for my answer, but not before I catch the wolfish gleam in his eyes. "I remember being promised a gift for my actual birthday."

"I'm wearing it," I announce.

He gives my dress and fine-gauge fishnet stockings a thorough once-over, as though hoping to ascertain what's beneath. A smile tucks the corner of his mouth. "I'm not sure if this present is for you or me."

"For you," I say primly. "But hope you don't mind if I cut myself in."

"How generous of you." He leans over and presses a kiss to my neck, teeth dragging against my skin, laughter in his voice.

"Mercenary habits die hard, sir."

"I don't suppose you'd like to leave now?" He lifts a brow.

I shake my head, holding in a laugh.

"Worth asking. Lucky for you, I'm willing to be patient." Then he reaches into his suit pocket and retrieves a small velveteen box. "At least on some fronts." His voice drops an octave.

My heart rate skitters, doubles.

A dazzling red gemstone large enough to sink my houseboat sits in the center of the ring, anchored by tiny silver tiger-claw prongs, surrounded by a double halo of diamonds. At first glance, the ring looks modern, but the tiny milgrain details and scrollwork beneath the stone are distinctly vintage. As Daniel moves, the stone changes color, flickering blues and greens emerging before switching back to violet and red.

I have never seen something so lovely in all my years.

"What kind of gem is that?" I sound breathless.

"Alexandrite. A type of chrysoberyl." He holds it to the light, and it becomes blue green again, absorbing different wavelengths.

"It looks like the ocean now," I whisper, awed.

"I thought so too." He gives me a sly smile. "What better stone for someone also always changing."

I bite my lip, hard, staring at the ring. "Should've known you'd have a few tricks up your sleeve." I look up, meeting Daniel's expectant face through my tears, reaching for his suit coat. "Anything else I need to know about hiding in here? Jesus Christ." My laughter is shaky, wheezing.

"I learned from the best, and no." He grunts and laughs, evading my acquisitive hands with ease. The alexandrite and diamonds shine even in the dim light of the bar, but his smile is brighter. "No more bombshells. I promise." He studies the ring. "Do you like it? I know it's unusual—"

"But so am I."

"*Exceptional* was the word I was going for." He looks at me, a smile in his eyes. "Little chameleon."

He takes my left hand, gingerly holding my small fingers in his own.

"If you want to keep going as Lady Justice, I'll support you. If you don't want to have children, I don't want to either. Whatever you like, Dylan." He looks up again, eyes welling. "So long as I'm by your side, I'll be the happiest person alive."

I reach to touch his face, wiping his tears. Then I fan my fingers across the curve of his cheekbone.

He kisses my wrist. The palm of my hand. Oaths, though he hasn't spoken.

Then he looks to me, pupils blown out in the dark. A whole world glows within if I look hard enough. "Will you marry me, Dylan?"

"Yes." Joy fizzes in my bloodstream like so much champagne.

He slides the gilt offering onto my ring finger.

I used to think happy endings were fairy tales. Stories we told ourselves when life became too bleak to endure.

Now I know the way love brings out the best in everyone, a seam of gold in their bedrock. Light in a dark room when all other sources have been snuffed out. The very thing that makes them hold on when there's every reason to let go.

As if on cue, the band on the stage opens with the first chords of "Misty."

Daniel casts a speculative look toward the floor crowding with couples, then back at me. "Would you like to dance? The ballroom classes of my youth have to have been good for something."

"Follow me." I beam and take his hand—so warm after a few sips of whiskey, opening blood vessels—and lead him into the fray.

We dance in the dark, pressed length to length, floating over the floor. The way we should've all along. At least until he lowers me into a dip I didn't see coming and feasts on my throat. "Whoa," I breathe.

He looks smug. As well he should.

"Thanks for being my person, Daniel." I can't help but laugh. "Objectively, you're really killing it."

He laughs, rich and full. The laugh I want to hear the rest of my life.

I plan to. I'll be the first to admit my goals look a bit different these days, but I wouldn't change a thing. I won't waste my second chance.

After all, this timeline has potential.

ACKNOWLEDGMENTS

Writing a story often feels like navigating a dark room, and I'd be remiss if I didn't thank the many people who helped me shine a light and give the dim world of an unpolished manuscript some shape, color, and clarity. Thank you to my lovely editor, Jess Verdi, for understanding this story and for being a warm ray of sunshine in human form. Thank you also to my agent, Eva Scalzo, for your wisdom and always believing there'd be a home for my writing somewhere. I'm so glad to have you in my corner.

Thank you to Rachel Keith for your keen eye and the kind notes in my margins that brought a huge smile to my face. Thank you, Heather VenHuizen, for designing a cover that perfectly encapsulates Dylan. Thank you to everybody on the Crooked Lane team Dulce Botello, Hannah Pierdolla, Madeline Rathle, Rebecca Nelson, and everyone else who laid hands and eyes on my book. I couldn't do this without your time and expertise.

Thank you to Erica Covey, my very first, very kind critique partner way back when I was young and decidedly clueless. Thank you to the South Texas Authors of Romance group for being such a supportive place for this itinerant writer to land, particularly Willa Blair, Kit Hawthorne, Laya Brusi, Gail Hart, Janalyn Knight, Cai Smith, and all others who came to critique group and shared their time, critiques, and commiseration. I miss you all.

Thank you to members of my Golden Heart group, the Persisters. In Denver, I thought you were all such talented, funny, wonderful human beings and creators, and I still do. Thank you to my dear friend, Amy Russo, the first person in "real life" to learn that I wrote, for being so kind and sharing my excitement when publishing a book felt within the realm of possibility.

I send my deepest thanks to all the early readers of *Close Enough to Hurt*, including Allison Ashley, Ambriel McIntyre, Carrie Lomax, Claudia Ambrose, Despina Karras, Kathryn Ferrer, Jessica Joyce, Megan McGee, Michelle McCraw, Nikki Hodum, and Sarah T. Dubb. Your collective insights and enthusiasm (and friendship) helped me polish this story into something that gleams. I'm so lucky to know all of you.

Thank you to my family near and far for your endless patience, love, and support, especially my mom, dad, and brother. You never lost faith that this day would come, even when I did, and I'm so glad to say you were all right. Never give up, never surrender!

Not quite last and certainly not least, thank you to my husband—my alarmingly competent hero in an astronaut suit. If I know what a love story looks like, it's because you've walked by my side all these many years, across continents and oceans. Home is where you are. I love you.

And to the Fay Queen, my raison d'être: you've been my champion since you were old enough to understand that me tapping away at a keyboard—cackling and crying by turns—meant I was writing. Thank you for always believing my stories would see the light of day. I hope I've written a book worthy of your fierce, loving heart.